Praise for Rodrigo Fresán

"A kaleidoscopic, open-hearted, shamelessly polymathic storyteller, the kind who brings a blast of oxygen into the room."—Jonathan Lethem

"I've read few novels this exciting in recent years. *Mantra* is the novel I've laughed with the most, the one that has seemed the most virtuosic and at the same time the most disruptive."—Roberto Bolaño

"Rodrigo Fresán is a marvelous writer, a direct descendant of Adolfo Bioy Casares and Jorge Luis Borges, but with his own voice and of his own time, with a fertile imagination, daring and gifted with a vision as entertaining as it is profound."—John Banville

"A splendid though demanding entertainment, playful and pensive at once and beautifully written throughout."—*Kirkus*, starred review

"Fresán's paragraphs can be mere single lines, his lines phrasal, his phrases elliptical, his ellipses infuriating and provocative, but in the end his prose bristles with energy. He never lets the reader feel totally comfortable or linger in the groove. He withholds resolution until the reader just about wants to give up—but then he delivers."

—*Los Angeles Review of Books*

Other Books by Rodrigo Fresán in English Translation

Melville

Rodrigo Fresán

Translated from the Spanish

by Will Vanderhyden

OPEN LETTER
LITERARY TRANSLATIONS FROM THE UNIVERSITY OF ROCHESTER

Originally published as *Melvill* by Literatura Random House, 2022

Copyright © Rodrigo Fresán, 2024

Translation copyright © Will Vanderhyden, 2024

First edition, 2024

Library of Congress Cataloging-in-Publication data: Available.

ISBN (pb): 978-1-960385-16-1

ISBN (ebook): 978-1-960385-23-9

This project is supported in part by an award from the New York State Council on the Arts with the support of the governor of New York and the New York State Legislature

Printed on acid-free paper in the United States of America

Cover design by Daniel Benneworth-Gray

Cover concept by Daniel Fresán

Open Letter is the University of Rochester's nonprofit, literary translation press.

Morey Hall 303, Box 270451, Rochester, NY 14607

www.openletterbooks.org

In the name of Ana and of Daniel,

this other name,

with all the letters of my name.

TABLE OF CONTENTS

Who rides so late in the night and the wind?
It is the writer's grief. It is the wild
March wind. It is the father with his child.
VLADIMIR NABOKOV
Pale Fire

Allan Melvill lived in Herman's memory not as an American merchant or a hired
clerk. Instead, the father in Herman's memory was a cosmopolitan gentleman
in whose veins coursed the blood of the earl of Melville House and the blood
of remoter noble and even royal ancestors—that queen of Hungary, those kings
(and surely queens) of Norway. Allan had been one of the great travelers of the
world, for Herman [. . .]. With his amazing stories of adventures on sea and
land Allan Melvill had made himself heroic in Herman's eyes. More than that,
whenever a Frenchman came into his store, he had transformed himself into a
man of deepest mystery, for the familiar loving "Pa" suddenly spoke a tongue as
incomprehensible to the boy as the language that God spoke.
HERSHEL PARKER
Herman Melville: A Biography,
Volume 1, 1819-1851

I write precisely as I please. God keep me from ever completing anything.
HERMAN MELVILLE
Pierre; Or, The Ambiguities and *Moby-Dick; Or, The Whale*

That's my story, but not where it ends.
BOB DYLAN
"Key West (Philosopher Pirate)"

Fathers are teachers of the true and not-true, and no father ever knowingly teaches
what is not true. In a cloud of unknowing, then, the father proceeds with his
instruction for the son. They began to read the book.
DONALD BARTHELME
The Dead Father

I

THE FATHER OF THE SON

All of life is a foreign country.

JACK KEROUAC

Selected Letters: 1940-1956

(June 24th, 1949, letter to John Clellon Holmes)

Now he knows he's surrounded by everyone and everything, but he feels more alone than ever. Here, the perfect solitude of one outside but with no way out. Freezing but soon to burn, the fire of a fever already rising inside him. Speaking in smoldering, scorching tongues: sparking words that flame and name, far away and foreign to any warmth of home, to that home he's dying—and where he'll die—to return to.

Ready to be one more among so many memories. Wanting to be remembered like this. Epic in defeat. Broken but stronger than ever because there's nothing left to break inside of him. Nothing to hide, all's been revealed. All of him to everyone. Exposed to all and after all.

His name pronounced (mispronounced, emphasis on the ultimate syllable, foreignizing, Frenchifying it, making it more removed and, perhaps in that way, worthier of greater rejection) with a combination of shame and condemnation.

His name before a jury that would never dare find for him and, prejudging, would reach a unanimous verdict: "Young Wastrel of a Patrician Family," and that's the way—all-caps when written and italics when spoken—people write about him in letters and speak about him at balls and banquets and masses.

Thus, his sentence to be served posthaste with no possibility of appeal or pardon. But here he is, still begging for someone to at least testify on his behalf and to write his story and to put him into words and, in a way, if not justify him then at least give him a modicum of redemption, a modicum of significance and purpose and reason to exist.

To be written.*

To be a being written (him being someone who more than once wished and dreamed he could write it all down and is already ready to transfer the acquittal of such a sentence) on empty and frozen pages like the waters he's walking across now, barely keeping warm with the breathless breathing of dead supplications and unheard prayers. Messianic and miraculous, yes; but not like the Omnipotent and triumphant Creator on high but like a deity plummeting from higher still, in free fall, prisoner and fallen in his disgrace. His once divine voice no longer commanding, deafening, proof of love and respect but, trembling and weak, dwindling until it becomes a silent and flashing sacrifice he makes to himself. And, meanwhile, as he prepares his own execution ceremony, asking himself, without an

---

* But no, not yet. It will be years before that happens: the sad masquerade of my father (there's no need for me to wait for the revelations of a future yet-to-be-revealed science that will be dedicated to the interpretation of dreams and daydreams) rewritten wearing different masks like that of a riverway conman or that of a delusional captain or that of an incestuous decadent or that of a by-product of the Revolution or that of a more confusing than confused pale-gray colored scrivener, among many others. And it will be even longer before I comment on it from here: from the marine and oceanic depths of these pages en route to the last and final shore. Me holding and losing my breath; because nothing is more exhausting than swimming upstream, taking in air, in pursuit of the always forgetful founts of memory.

answer, why (wasn't this a distinctive trait of mortals? that almost last and willful gift of your whole life summarized in seconds and in reverse so you could understand it better or not bother? wasn't that the explanation of the mystery of why so many people died with a *Momma, Mommy, Ma* on their lips?) all the people and things of this world that he loves or that don't love him, the whole history of his story, now seemed to converge in this white darkness. Darkness he advances through, previously opaque and obscure and so late, suddenly without time and as if untethered from time, forever and ever, implacable and clean and transparent.

Record and file it, even if you prefer not to:
It's the night of Saturday, December 10th, 1831, and Allan Melvill walks across the frozen waters of the Hudson River.

Α nd, oh, when you walk on ice, on water in suspended animation, moods shift and thoughts are thought differently, Allan Melvill
thinks. He thinks about how thoughts are thought with the most
burning coolness. He thinks about how you think of anything other
than that which, once deemed unthinkable, is, as such, impossible
not to think about: about how that ice could break and about how,
then, sinking to never again rise back up to that surface of superfici-
alities to be ignored or attended to, you would cease to think forever.
He thinks about the cold that freezes into crystals that bind together
and break apart to separate and rise into the sky to then fall on the
living and the dead in always different shapes.* With that cold that

---

* Imagine a book always at high sea. A book adrift and drifting in swirling digressions
and dodging not icebergs of small tips and massive bottoms but compact glaciers that
have as much to show as to hide. A book that is nothing but a perpetual draft, because
every book is never-ending. A book that is the draft of a sketch; because the smallest
constructions can be completed by their original architects; while the largest, the truest,
always leave the conclusion on the tallest rooftops to fix and secure there the posterity of
whoever reads them beyond the one who wrote it.
My case, without looking any further.

forces you to close your eyes to discover that, like certain lizards, you can see through your eyelids: his now almost sliced off by the freezing blade of the wild wind that whips his hair into disarray.

The same thing would happen (Allan Melvill thinks now, like he's never thought before, thinking about what would be thought about or about what one would never dare to think about again but that, in the act refusing, one thinks about, thinking about how he once thought, afloat in a damning floating city of the damned) when we find a way to remain aloft, airborne and truly and joyfully displaced. When man can fly aboard marvelous machines (not just aerostatic balloons) whose sound will be like that of thousands of men clearing their throats after the morning's first pipe. And with and in those machines, battles will be waged among the stars, and they'll even make it to that fleeting moon, which, at this very moment, the clouds cover and uncover only to cover it again, and hurl down almost merciful white flakes of snow on Allan Melvill, as if they were soldiers laying siege to that defeated and humiliated deserter of the crucifying crusade of his own life.

But we've got a long way to go before that. Now, beneath his feet, that ice is the only solid thing left to hold him up, while around him and above him everything is thin ice in suspense, and the important thing is not to fly but to keep from falling or sinking or drowning.

Thus, in the dark, Allan Melvill remembers first; but then it's as if he were dreaming, as if he were dreaming himself, or seeing himself from above. And he'd read somewhere that people who lived and wandered through landscapes of endless ices often felt that someone, their doppelgänger, was walking beside them (like that vanquished and enslaved *memento-mori* walking beside a triumphant Caesar or other victorious generals) and whispering in their ear the more than fifty names snow can be given, but not the names for each and every one of the infinite and always-different flakes that make up that snow and that, first, give the shape of snow to whatever they happen to come to rest upon and, then, to all the shapes they take after giving shape to the snow.

Then, suddenly, to the surprise and wonder of Allan Melvill, his whole life (his life as a father) is lived and relived, it melts away only to resolidify, like an invention invented by the boy who, though he would never theretofore have imagined it, has turned out to be the most inventive and imaginative of his children.*

---

* His light casts my shadow. The one is the eclipse of the other. I, at his feet, will tell what he, lying there, tells me. He is bound and I'm bound to him; and I trust that all the information that I'll offer has, moreover, some literary and dramatic value, beyond the tragedy and sorrow of the events that keep that man prostrate here. Thus, I shall send my indefinable imagination (truly the most exact of sciences) off to hunt and track and catch the facts. And then, flay and eviscerate them, as once upon a time I did whales. To those whales that, as the years pass, seem to me more and more the product of youth's liquid dream. Always taking care to keep their stomach gasses from bursting and covering me with guts and blood and excrement. And to keep from spilling that illuminating sperm of the truth that, once processed, will be irreconcilable as something that happened but, at the same time, will be read (will be read by the light of candles and oil derived from that same whale sperm) as something even truer than it ever was. Reality only becomes really real after crossing the stormy sea of art and arriving safe and sound to the other shore. Not while we live it or write it, but later, when we read it; and only then does everything become logical and inevitable and we ask ourselves how we failed to see it or see it coming.

Thus, everything that one invents ends up (or starts out) being true and, taking place, ends up having taken place to thereby begin to take place.

And that boy doesn't know it yet, that boy doesn't know himself *like this*. His is an age (twelve years) not yet concerned with exact dates and precise locations. His is an age at which there's not yet any need to invent anything, because the whole of reality is like an invention that never stops expanding and becoming more complex with each passing day. His is an age at which one still lets oneself get carried away, and so his comings and goings are still ruled not by his own time but by the tempo that marks the time of his elders. Little space to imagine there, in that world that was already formed and functioning long before one's arrival to it and that isn't yet anything but the continuation of the pursuits of others: instructions and orders, rewards and punishments, sleeping and waking and rising and shining. Then and until then, one only knows (there's no need to know more) that it's day or night. Or that more of the week transpires at school than at home. Or that it's Sunday: because the church bells toll, calling everyone to mass, to ask forgiveness and to give thanks and (a strange discordance) to honor the Father who on that day rests and the Son who on that day is resurrected and to sing hymns read in little books.

Books that fit in the palm of the hand and where the lines (of harmonious sound but often enigmatic meaning as only a proclamation of faith in something invisible can be) are commented upon and explained in footnotes of shrunken script marked by a diminutive symbol.*

---

* A script like this that, yes, sorry (not sorry), will present certain difficulty for the reader, interrupting actions or rupturing moods with information that, if only complementary, I deem indispensable and as necessary as the underwater keel that stabilizes and holds up a ship, the sunken thing that keeps the not-sunken thing from sinking. But I would like to think that any of my very few readers would already know and understand the shadowy reaches they're headed for and with whom they're embarking. And the truth is that at this point I can't help thinking as if I were reading and, at the same time, commenting on what I'm reading. In bigger letters, everything that I think that I have no problem at all discussing aloud with acquaintances and strangers alike; and everything that I think about what I think: in smaller letters, what I only dare explain to that increasingly difficult to recognize stranger that is me. What I wrote in my books, in my books that were written and read in both letters at the same time. In all those books that subsequently sold little and not at all and that burned (like a first and so symbolic funeral, a Viking funeral while alive) in a fire at the warehouses of the publisher Harper & Brothers, in 1853. (Did the only manuscript copy of my *The Isle of the Cross*—narrating the woes of a woman abandoned by the sailor whom she saved from drowning—also burn there? Where could it be? Can I not find it? Or is it maybe that I wrote it *after* the fire? Or that I never wrote it? Or was it really about something very different and didn't take place in Nantucket but in Venice? Who knows . . . Dates here are like arrows that never really hit the mark.) And I confess: sometimes I was inspired by real events that I turned into impossible fictions. Yes: I wrote everything rewriting something so later I could read it and only then understand it. And what I read in the books of others and what I in a way finished, writing notes in their margins and underlining their lines (like in my oft-consulted copy of Thomas Beale's *The Natural History of the Sperm Whale*), I also carefully erased to leave no trace of my having been there and, also, to amuse myself thinking about the researchers of the future. All of them analyzing the legacy of what they'll call my "ejaculatory prose" and recognizing its genes in the traits of my descendants and acolytes. All of them looking at these pages, holding them up against the light, looking for the impressions of my pencil, like banknotes whose authenticity and value had to be certified before they were put into circulation. Looking at them in the same way that, one morning not long ago, in the bookshop of John Anderson, on Nassau St., I opened wide a copy of Robert Burton's *Anatomy of Melancholy*. And among all those quotations of and references to others (on the blank page before that of the title and author, in the upper righthand corner, I discovered in pencil, almost invisible, an *A. Melvill*. Yes: there

And that is enough, I hope.

And, confronted with doubt, praying as if kneeling down to pray on the bottom of the sea.

And that from there, before long, rises into the heavens an Our Father, Who art in River . . . Hallowed be Thy Name . . . Thy Kingdom Come . . .

But not yet.

Not yet.

And so, the boy doesn't know that it's Saturday, October 9th, 1830, but he does understand that he's somewhere in the lowlands of Manhattan. In an empty house that will soon no longer be his and where now he helps his father (these are his words) "to break camp" and "abandon ship" * and other things that the boy doesn't

---

the sudden materialization of the signature of my father, who must have sold that book when we left New York, so many years ago now. How strange! And stranger still is, now that I think of it, the paradoxical mystery that reading is an act that comes after writing. Because as rudimentary as it is to put it in these terms, the first writer had to precede the first reader; though, how and where and with *what* was it that *that* first writer learned to read? With what primary and primitive text in which all possible permutations of a story already existed? Should it not be the task/genesis and challenge/apocalypse of all writers to write/read that first/last book? One thing is certain: for centuries, the incommensurable disproportion between the number of writers and readers allowed people to think that the natural thing, the common thing, was to read. And that, for that reason, writing was just the exception entrusted to beings who had to know they were exceptional before picking up the pen. But something (my natural and floating pessimism) makes me think that in a not-too-distant future the (bad) writers will outnumber the (good) readers. Good readers will be like whales hunted to the point of extinction and, for that reason, they won't be able to mate and give birth to good writers. And the most luminous darkness will fall across a world which and in which almost nobody will concern themselves with discovering in writing; because they'll all be too concerned with discovering and, *also*, describing themselves in writing: in writing not dazzling for its talent but blinding for its stupidity. And all of it will fall into the most deafening stillness and the elegant silence of the most eloquent spell ever cast will be broken: the silence in which you read and write and (and if there is any luck in this wretched world) you read what you wrote for and to yourself in the same way you wrote for someone else.

* I'm sure he said the first one; but I'm not sure regarding the second. In any case, in my memory he *did* say it to me, I tell myself when I remember it nine years later, in 1839, already enlisted as a *boy* or *green hand* (which is equivalent to "inexperienced youth getting experience" on an initiating and formative baptismal voyage). Me hanging upside down from the masts of the merchant vessel *St. Lawrence*, doing the New York-Liverpool route, going and taking notes for what, though I didn't know it yet, would be inverted in

understand but that involve many numbers, figures longer and taller than he is, written in sinful red ink, in defaulted IOUs with names of brands that are also places and surnames.

Both of them, father and son, walk through rooms where nothing remains but the memory of what had once been: the ghosts of furnishings positioned here and there, seeming to flicker in their absence in the spots they once sat. Rooms that now (with neither curtains nor tapestries nor paintings) are like skeletons of what they once were. Their naked walls like bones, so white. A few books on the floor, in the center of rooms, as if waiting for someone to set them on fire. It pains the boy to leave them (a new kind of pain), but his father tells him that if he's already read them there's no point in having them weigh him down. "Books are carried in your memory," he explains with a smile that's hard to take seriously.*

"Quickly, my son, put those papers in that bag . . . They're important," his father now insists.

His father rocking back on his heels with true mechanical ingenuity, hands rummaging in pockets, as if burying and searching for treasure at the same time. And there's something in his father's

---

one of my future books, seeing it all in reverse, but, justly, taking a spin around the world that I'll soon set a 'spinning.

* It's true that that abandoned bookcase (my father has decided to take the empty piece of furniture and not its "organs," as if preserving the carcass for an exhibition and discarding everything that Allan Melvill considers perishable) was never home to a collection of great works. There, always, little more than commercial catalogues and romance novels and serialized melodramas with smugglers and killers and pirates and evil dukes. The family Bible already departed for Albany (my mother, Maria Gansevoort, clings to it like a life preserver). But it's also true that I will miss my habit (a habit that I will regain with the passing years and the cultivation of my own library) of standing in front of its shelves, hands behind my back, to read the titles and connect the ones with the others to form sentences and, sometimes, even using them to compose the seeds of brief plotlines that might one day germinate into long stories. Me, there, as if bewitched and possessed by all those dead voices reincarnated in immortal letters.

Know this: ghosts live in books. No house can consider itself really and truly possessed and haunted if it doesn't have a respectable library to respect and, on occasion, to terrorize the people who live there with the fact that the horror of everything they'll never read will always surpass the joy of the great deal they have read.

face that bears no resemblance to the happy face captured in his portrait painted decades before.* In that small watercolor (the size of a carte d'identité; not of who he is but of who he was, of someone who has gone and will never come back, never come back into being) surrounded by snow-white passe-partout. A wide band of white embroidery and inside an oversized frame. His face lunar, as if stealing pale fire from the sun; half smiling, sitting in a careless yet elegant way, his hair carefully disheveled.† His gloves and hat sitting on a table where Allan Melvill appears to want to lean an elbow that doesn't quite reach and is left hanging, awkward and frustrated, in the air, just as so many other parts and things of his will be left hanging, in suspension, so many ambitions and undertakings.

And Allan Melvill once told his son that he remembers that the painter (who, he said, had about him something of a caricature-esque melodrama villain or first-rate secondary Shakespeare character, a little Puck and a little Caliban) asked him over and over, almost despairing, to, please, hold still. But how could he obey such an order, Allan Melvill thought then, in times when time was running out and you couldn't help but feel obligated to chase time to keep from losing time? Time was gold, yes, but all that glitters is not gold; and that's why you had to choose the best days and opportunities as if they were elements to be combined in miraculous

---

* Your favorite.

† The audacity of a disheveled portrait, I think. A curl of hair there (could there be a science that allows personality to be defined or even the future to be predicted based on the capillary behavior and mood of a particular person?) that seems to raise its tentacular tail to intertwine it with another curl. And in that way making a circle that is like a tunnel whose entrance is visible, but not yet its exit. Or, better yet, like some kind of giant wave (one of those bellicose waves of the Pacific) whose crest I'll ride bareback a few years from now: whinnying with foam, crashing down on itself, breaking near the shore, to later retreat to the bottom of the sea and, rearing back, rising up again, over and over, until the end of time . . . And there, meanwhile, me counting waves the way others count days, hours, minutes, hellos and goodbyes. And thinking about how while others remember eyes or noses or mouths or voices or ways of standing and walking, I remember a curl of hair.

and enriching alchemical formulas (and what was that thing about the ancient Romans and the colored stones with which they defined their days . . . ?).

Thus, thence, it is a portrait of a man who can't hold still for more than a minute.* There, between his fingers a ticking pocket watch whose hour doesn't matter, because he's still master of all the time in the world or, at least, that's what he believes.†

No more, no longer, never again.

There, Allan Melvill not long ago, not so long ago; but at the same time as if it were a distant and impossible to recover era. That version of him that resembled one of those recently written gallant characters of Jane Austin. Though now (his son recalling him so many years later) closer to the then not-yet-written, but already gestating, fierce and diabolical brutes of the Brontë sisters than to those desperate wretches of Charles Dickens who, in truth, he recalls more and better.

---

* Painted in 1810 by the Englishman John Rubens Smith, the son of the engraver John Raphael Smith (notice the quite pathetic artistic detail/stigma of the middle name of both, attempting to compensate for the banality of their last name, condemning them to be what they are and to be, also, eternal apprentices in memoriam of their masters and, oh, the horror of certain supposed vocations that are nothing but ancestral mandates impossible to contest or disobey). His initials and the date in a small patch of the ochre background delimited by arm and gloves and hat.

My father would pose for another portrait, signed by Ezra Ames, a very popular artist among Albany society who would also sign the companion portrait of my mother, Maria Gansevoort Melvill. A far more conventional portrait than the first and with better combed hair and thus, in a way, already more preoccupied and trying to appear more respectable, in 1820, when his luck began to abandon him and his bad fortune to impoverish him, and the fiction of the stately portrait was no longer of any use to someone who'd lost all estate.

† I'm not sure either if what my father was holding then and will hold forever in that portrait was a pocket watch. Now that I think of it (and I think of it so I can put it in writing much later, dedicating a whole chapter to it in an ambiguous and cursed novel; in another cursed novel that nobody will like and, over which, I'll even be accused by a literary critic of having gone mad, recommending my immediate reclusion to thereby protect the impressionable minds of sane readers), it could also have been a bunch of keys that don't open any doors; or an ear trumpet so he could pretend not to hear what he no longer wanted to hear; or the seal with the supposed family coat of arms to invoke the good old days; or the tooth of . . .

Now it's as if a terrible wind had corrected those features, tearing them away. Thus, his father looks a little like a possessed preacher high up on a holy dais (standing atop the condemnations of a sulphureous sermon that condemns him, clinging to the masts of his faith, its sails are swollen with everyone's rejection) and a little like the ecstatic demon possessing that preacher.* And you no longer know where the one begins and the other ends,[†] the boy thinks of his father and of the lightning and sparks that flash across his father's face. And he doesn't think but senses that this is one of the many kinds of things you think about when you don't want to think about anything. And, frightened at seeing his father like this, the boy also thinks that there's nothing more frightening than a frightened person.[‡] Thence and thenceforth the boy focuses on the solid and certain things he knows about his father to keep at bay the dizziness and nausea that racks him now and feels nothing like the nausea that, not long ago, he felt when he snuck an entire tart. This nausea has a bitter aftertaste and not a sweet one, he thinks; and he tells himself that maybe it'll pass if he repeats the few certainties he could swear to without fear of being punished (like when, again, he devoured that apple and rhubarb tart and then on the heels of the nausea came nightmares); but this time with a punishment whose limits are far more diffuse, albeit permanent for the punished.

---

* Father Maple. Once a sailor of a true harpoon. Now, proclaimer of sermons like hooks and nets from a stairless pulpit in the form of a prow, replacing it with a ladder like the ones used to ascend to the heavens of a ship from the purgatory of a boat at sea. And, from there on high, already as if it were terra firma above the waters, the best of both worlds, looking down on sin or catching a glimpse of salvation.

† And this is only the beginning of the possession of the dispossessed man. Warning to sailors: this is when my father's true White Delirium begins.

‡ And who was it who said, says, will say this? It happens to me more and more: the feeling of capturing thoughts and ideas of others past or present. Of being like a kind of magnet or mouth and throat of a Maelström that pulls toward it everything it needs from other people, and uses it, and once it's chewed up and digested, sends it back up to the surface completely transformed and, hopefully, transformative.

Let's see, he says to himself, challenges himself, imposing a re-demptive test: again and again, to overcome the malaise, revisiting the things that can't be changed and that offer some modicum of security. A true but not entirely secure security, like that of fur-nishings on ships: bolted to the floor to keep them from shifting during storms.

Like this:

His father's name is Allan Melvill. And on his ID cards it specifies, with dubious heraldry, that he devotes himself, perhaps with excess enthusiasm and lack of caution, to the importation of fabrics and French lingerie and perfumes of various scents and other exceedingly diverse luxury dry goods. To be consumed by the ever-voracious wives of slave traders and patriots and patriot slave traders.*

His father is forty-eight (or forty-nine, he's not entirely sure) years old and . . .

And (yes, right away the reliability of his narration is destabilized like a ship losing ballast and what *should* have happened is imposed over what *did* happen) he has heard behind closed doors

---

* I learn to read by reading those catalogues in the form of folded pages with illustrations (some of them of unsettling and sensual female torsos with heads or arms or legs), connecting drawings with words: "Fancy Hdkfs, and Scarfs . . . Elastic and Silk Garters, Artificial Flowers, Cravat Stiffeners & c. Also in store . . . rich stain stripped and figured blk Silk Vestings, Gros de Naples Hdkfs, Balt and Watch Ribbons, 7-16 & 7-22 Silk Hose . . . Horse Skin Gloves . . . Cologne and Lavender Waters, & c."

and in whispers that his father is already three months in arrears on rent for the house that they must leave today, posthaste, at nightfall. Cast off moorings and get away ahead of the anticipated visit of a prowling band of loan sharks smelling blood in the water, not from miles away but from a nearby street where concentric creditors seduce and circle.

Yesterday, Friday, his mother, Maria Gansevoort Melvill, and his older brother, Gansevoort Melvill,* departed in a carriage with all the furniture and silver and China that it could fit.† That carriage like a lifeboat. Women and children first (all the young Melvills but him; and the small boy wonders if he should feel proud at having been left behind with his captain or feel sad at maybe being considered the most dispensable of the brood). The first thing his father loaded into the cart was the first of his portraits, wrapped in a blanket (he wasn't as worried about protecting the other one). He did it as if it made him feel that that version of him, at the best and increasingly distant moment of his professional career (the moment when he wasn't yet spinning out of control and still had everything in front of him), was going with them: like a not-yet-very-holy but

---

* The favorite child, the best of all of us, the one who would end up a stand-out academic and orator and Democratic Party politician and foreign diplomat and, oh, dying young in London and having his body shipped home with honors and interred in Albany: Gansevoort (with the dignifying surname of the family of Maria Gansevoort) as the one of us called to do great things and attain a bright future at Harvard and who (in the pages of the same journal in which my father dismissed my talents and abilities and criticized my crude posture and unrefined manners) was described as someone "of tenacious memory and brilliant excellence." Poor Gansevoort who would soon find himself head of the family and obliged to take over the "hats and furs" business whose shop (where I worked as clerk after a brief stint as an employee at the New York State Bank, all those banknotes of others passing through my hands, their fresh ink leaving prints on my fingerprints) would burn down in 1835. And, later, the financial crisis of 1837. And all of them sinking again, holding hands, because (as I'll write so long thereafter, in the novel that'll end up ruining and precipitating the fall of my literary career) "in our cities families rise and burst like bubbles in a vat."

† That rolltop desk, that grandfather clock, too many mirrors, a piano, another clock, assorted relics (including camping mats) from the battles for Independence in which my patriotic and heroic grandfathers fought.

definitely repentant effigy, protecting his own and at the same time watching over the remains of the shipwreck of his business.* Then they were loaded into the storerooms of the *Ontario Tow Boat*,† and his mother and one older brother embarked for Albany, where brothers and daughters and sons and sisters already awaited them.‡

They don't flee, this time, like so many times they escaped up-river to take refuge during the annual visits of cholera and typhoid fever and, in 1822, of the even more feared and "pestilent yellow fever": mouths and noses and even eyes covered by goggles like

---

* Again: women and children first, yes.

† The names of the boats (my father, always more interested in coats of arms and family trees, he never specified the names of the boats that he boarded and, I suppose, that's one of the many things that distinguished and differentiated us) are for me as important and defining as those of people. Aboard boats, everything shifts, everything is free or tied down, everything tilts and tumbles. That's why it's best to state their names firmly (names that should never be changed, it brings bad luck to do so, and it is as suspicious and unnerving a thing as changing your own surname), to maintain all the order that can be maintained. So that, like people (and the always poorly secured ideas of people), they don't sink or split in two or run aground on the rocks, so close yet at the same time so far from shore.

‡ At the time, I know that yesterday was Friday (a different Friday, a particular Friday, a Friday that would turn all future Fridays into the day of the week I most dreaded) because I'd had an oratory exam I did not perform especially well on. And because it was the Friday of the departure of my mother and my brother. Forerunners in the return to the family enclave where Helen Maria Melvill, Gansevoort Melvill, Augusta Melvill (who will edit my first texts and correct the proofs of my first books), Allan Melvill, Jr., Catherine Gansevoort Melvill, Priscilla Frances Melvill, and Thomas Melvill already waited. Warning: none of them will appear in this story, not because I wasn't my father's or my mother's favorite (I swear, I swear that's not it), but because they are of no dramatic use to me. Likewise, come the moment to describe all my own progeny, I will devote my almost exclusive attention to only two (Malcolm and Stanwix, because the fuel of their deaths will be vital to the somber drift of my final days) of my four sons and daughters (Bessie, who lived forever ill and who, when she dies, will bequeath my unpublished manuscripts inside a breadbox to Fannie, who over the years will come to forbid my cursed name from being mentioned in front of her, they don't deserve to be manipulated and recreated for the benefit of my imagination). My granddaughters won't get a single mention (though I think they loved me and enjoyed when I took them on walks through the old Manhattan and invented stories for them about who had lived in this or that building) because I don't consider them entirely of my authorship. I believe (it's taken me a while to understand this) that I create (as Jehovah created according to the ancient Kabbalistic texts) through elimination and contraction of what is mine to thereby make more space for the rest of the universe, including that dag gadol (דג גדול), that great prophet-swallowing fish.

Or maybe I just need or want to make people believe that I create like that . . .

those worn by blacksmiths and masks of silk and linen cut and sewn from rolls of cloth that Allan Melvill has imported from the great warehouses of Paris.

Allan Melvill remembers seeing the sick:* wandering as if having just emerged from a deadly party, faces varnished with a sweat that never entirely dried, smiling like sleepwalkers through a Manhattan that, at the time, is just south Manhattan and, farther on, a grid of streets traced across an empty space and, farther still, the virgin forest that at some point will be violated and summarily submitted to the new map of Central Park.† And Allan Melvill watched them, the sick; and now, still with his health (maybe the only thing that his lenders can't take away from him), he envies all of them a little: because to fall ill would be, perhaps, the cure for all that ails him, he thinks. The solution not to the red blotches on his skin but to the columns of red numbers in his accounting books.

---

* I remember little of all that. Back then, I was at that age where everything is unforgettable and, at the same time, impossible to remember later on. That age when you were young and you shone like the sun and you were menaced by the shadows in the night to be exposed to the light the next morning. Thus, the early childhood of all people has the consistency of a dream wherein you pass more time asleep than awake, but with eyes so wide and almost lidless. Thus, too, in truth, childhood (not a period but a region) never really ends; and part of it is prolonged and expands with time and with the passing of the successive ages of a man (like his nose and ears) right up until the last day of his life.

† And the light of the city then (I can see it as I remember it, illuminating my childhood) is a childish light, like from a fairytale: it's the light of the kerosene lamps and candles lit using the spermaceti squeezed from the heads of whales (as if lighting up a lightbulb inside of them, as if they had a fixed idea) that someday I will hunt aboard floating slaughterhouses, sweating gallons of blood, streaming down its sides until the color of the sea changes. Before, that light marking the streets that are more roads than streets for some hundred thousand inhabitants of the city who, just seventy years later (when I think, when using childish notes I write it in order to read it, all of this, already as if ancient), will already number more than three million. Uncontainable multitudes crossing colossal bridges (and no doubt there will already be a bridge in Albany from which to contemplate the frozen Hudson down below), illuminated by electricity and their voices and messages running through wires atop posts and not masts. And there I will be, knowing myself to be of another age; ignored in my present, but sensing, perhaps, that my place will be a future where I will no longer exist, but where everything I made—and, as such, everything that I was—will live on.

And it's in this way, now, that Allan Melvill doesn't flee the mysterious forces of nature but escapes his own unenigmatic shortcomings: there's nothing to resolve there and, at the same time, everything to resolve with no resolution in sight.

Now, he and his father don't walk. His father and he run (it surprises him first and then worries him to discover that he runs faster than his father now, that he bests him in speed and stamina and agility) and there they go, in the moonlight, far faster than the moon moves above them.*

And the boy quickly reads the names of the houses they're passing by; and all those houses have names, because all the houses look the same, and a number isn't enough to distinguish one from another. And they turn (like the closing of that knife of Catalan steel his father is always playing with) at the corner of Pearl St., where the son was born.

And they head to the dock at 82 Cortland St. †

And they embark last minute on the *Swiftsure*.

---

* "Moonlight is sculpture; sunlight is painting," my admired Nat H. (Nathaniel Hawthorne for all of you) once said to me. Nat H. who won't hesitate to distance himself from my person, discomfited, perhaps, by my adoration that never wished to go any further than that or hoped for anything in return from him. And then I thought: "Don't forget that. Don't ever forget it . . . Thinking like that . . . Seeing like that is what lets you go from being just somebody who writes to being somebody who can call himself a writer."
† Many years later, I retrace the trajectory of that journey, but walking not running, through the same Manhattan that's no longer what it was. Over and over again. Prisoner of a private Purgatory or the Bardo or rocky Scythia of a circular trance. Walking as if sailing, flanked by tall buildings where once there were small houses and, suddenly, great and tall constructions that until not long ago had seemed impossible, and the perturbing realization that almost everyone is younger than you. And aware that you've turned into a sort of lost piece in search of a museum that, every so often, someone pauses to appreciate, even though they don't really understand it and, much less, do they wish to touch it when the guards aren't paying attention or are looking at other more popular and tempting works.

I make note of this, not in the actual chamber of my study but vibrating in this reverent replica that my equally spurned and long-suffering wife worked to create, I don't know if to preserve my memory or thinking that maybe in that way she would frighten away my revisitation. I know the time, but on more than one occasion I struggle to pin down what year it is.

Low sky, high tide.

Suddenly, as if gnashing at his heels, baring its lightning fangs and howls of thunder, the island of Manhattan is like another ship shaken by a biblical storm.*

And Allan Melvill looks to the heavens and crosses himself and makes all the promises he'll never be able to keep. Allan Melvill promises to keep promising.

And a ship officer informs the father and the son that, due to the bad weather, the ship won't be able to embark until the morning. The ship officer says *ship* first and then, to be more precise, *Swiftsure*; but the boy hears it and feels something new and something special upon hearing it; and he understands that that name is like that of a person, like that of a living being, like the first of many to say and to know and to accompany and to sail and to live.

"We left New York in the *Swiftsure*,"† Allan Melvill briefly notes without going into detail in his journal; though such a sentence seems sufficiently ominous and explicit for anyone who wants to read not between its lines but between its letters. In plural. Without names. Together. A team of two. Inseparable. And he adds: "Detained all night at Cortland St. dock by a severe storm."

And there's no need to add anything else. It's all there: the return to the point of departure, the direct route traveled by hapless men whose luck has bent until it breaks. He writes that and, without waiting for the ink to dry, Allan Melvill closes his journal once overflowing with grand descriptions and great distances and landscapes far happier though no less unsettling; and now, on the other hand, reporting in a shaky hand disoriented by thunder and lightning and waves and aware that one reports on the weather

---

* Storms are biblical when they seem to renounce their simply meteorological and scientific condition to thereby recover their immemorial condition of divine punishment.
† I am the one who adds the name of the ship here. I can't help myself.

when there's nothing left to say or to add or one prefers not to and to remain in the clouds.

There, Allan Melvill below deck with his son. This is the last time the two of them will travel alone together (not counting the very near in time but far in space mental adventures with which the father will infect his son by inviting him to come along). And now the father embraces his son, but really he clings to him. He embraces and holds and clutches his son (exhausted and finally asleep, his mouth open, like those sleeping children who look both dead and more alive than ever), who dreams a dream of a fleeing king. And that dream leaps from his head to the head of his father, who falls asleep too. The same dream, then. And the fear that that dream will suddenly turn into a nightmare. And that that king (moving with difficulty due to the weight of his cape made from the hide of a bear from the Urals and of his crown inlaid with the lost and sharpened teeth of a swordfish of the Caribbean,* arriving to a beach buried in snow and, there, waiting for a ship to take him to a safe land where he can plan his righteous and triumphant return) will be caught and captured by the conspirators who have followed him from his palace now in flames, the blaze of that fire like an aurora borealis on the horizon. This dreamed king without a throne who (there's no need, again, to wait for someone to postulate a dream science for decoding dreams) is the father in the son's dream and the father in the father's dream, in that two-headed dream.

And, yes, in the ship's hold, surrounded by rats, the son discovers (suddenly awake, as if someone yanked the threads that cause his legs and arms to cramp) that *this* is what fear is and was and will be. Here, the discovery of fear: the initial fear with which, inevitably

---

* All those faraway places that I already explored with the help of an atlas and globe in the library at my Gansevoort grandparents' house.

and automatically, the son will compare all fear yet to come and yet to arrive, even with the fear that he'll feel for his own children.

Above, on deck, a group of cabin boys kiss and grope each other's button flies. And they sing lascivious sea shanties and sad ballads about drowned or hung mates. And they pass around strands of the rigging from which the most beautiful sailor in the world was hung with the same reverence that others devote to the supposed nails of that unrustable Nazarene. And they compete over who has the biggest tattoo (anchors, sirens, dates, Mommy, crosses of different religions, Lolita, the tatters of a map, an I Would Prefer Not To in the font of a legal document), and there's even one of them with his face completely covered in indelible ink, making it almost impossible to read tears or laughter on it.* And they all roar like sea lions and howl like lobos del mar. And they mock one (who has dressed up as a woman and sways his hips with a keen smile and blows kisses to both port and starboard) who has committed the stupidity of learning to swim. Because it's science that the best sailors don't know how to swim; because in a shipwreck, knowing how to swim won't accomplish anything but postpone certain death; because what sense could there be in knowing how to swim in the middle of the ocean, amid implacable waves that repeat like the prayers that out there nobody will hear, mouth full of saltwater and no land in sight. It's far better to sink quickly and full of energy and wearing a smile capable of seducing the most slippery-skinned nymphs.

Allan Melvill knows how to swim and always did so elegantly, barely disturbing the waters, the way some regal-plumed birds swim; a skill he showed off at seaside resorts in Italy and France. But there's

---

* Queequeg, the son of a king, who leaves his small kingdom on land (Rokovoko, a faraway island located in the South Pacific. It doesn't appear on any map: true places never do; the same thing happens with the truest passions and never-entirely-faithful love letters) to be an imperious servant on limitless waters where he dreams of letting himself die like someone falling asleep.

nothing (the feeling right now is that he's swimming backward toward a waterfall) any of that can do to keep his sinking business afloat.

Here and now (no longer on terra firma but on shifting wood; the ship suddenly shudders like a giant animal waking up at dawn and yawning an *Aaaahlbany* . . . as it starts to move) beside his only real and unquestionable belonging. There and then, the only thing that's truly his is the son who accompanies him. The son who (on another page of his journal,* where he now adds but doesn't accept more impossible-to-please numbers instead of pleasant and precise phrases) not long ago, he diagnosed as "delayed in expressing himself & somehow slow in comprehension," master of "awful orthography," and yet with "a gift for understanding men & things in a solid & profound way at the same time, & with a docile and friendly disposition."†

---

* Or was it maybe in a letter where he presents me as an associate of his and a "pioneer" in the "special care and patronage" of my uncle Peter Gansevoort, so that I can start working at such a young age, describing me additionally as "A Knickerbocker of strong roots and honest heart with the authentic stamp of Albany"?

† But, even still and though you won't live to see it and to hear me, Pa, entering and exiting schools whose matriculation and installments we can no longer pay; excelling in competitions and debates and even starring as Shylock in a performance of *Merchant of Venice*; being awarded a teaching position and studying engineering before deciding that my thing would be the sea and not the land. Letters and not numbers. Returning to water but (I've read the new theories of the immemorial Charles Darwin, a sailor in his own right) for the sake of evolution not involution. Not a Second Coming but a Second Going.

The son's name is Herman.*

---

* Call me Herman. Or, forgive me, better to dismiss the supposed humor of this self-referential suggestion out of hand. It's beneath me. It's a bit banal and cheap. The kind of nonsense that occurs to me after one too many bottles and one too many sleepless nights. I'm sorry, truly, I mean it. You can call me whatever you want to call me. Or better yet: don't call me anything. Sign a truce and let this sailor disarmed in the armada of seas and letters rest in peace.

*A*lbany is a name that's pronounced as if it were being sung, as if it were the ritornello in the aria. Albany is what you shout from the kitchen to someone in the living room or from the already warm and sudsy bathtub demanding more clean and hot water. Albany is like a family play (and Allan Melvill never liked the theater;* he always found it suspect, the thing of people repeating lines over and over again from memory; it always sounded so hypocritical to him,† like all those actors who are his relatives: all of them pronouncing commonplaces to which they return again and again, reciting them at gatherings where all they do is lovingly despise each other and get updated on the value of the different surnames in that provincial city putting on metropolis airs). Albany is the first shore, the first of many shores.‡ Albany is

---

* Me neither.
† To me too.
‡ And, sure, I was born in New York City, on August 1st, 1819, at 11:30 P.M., at number 6 Pearl St.; but New York is an island and, as such, its shores are not really shores—they are borders. I note here the day and time of my birth, so many years later, on the same day and time; and I do so with the same exactitude with which I once interrupted the

the trees of Albany, by the river, upriver, on the western bank of the Hudson.* Albany, original colony founded in 1614, incorporated in 1686, and made the capital of New York in 1797, once the union of states became the United States.

And Albany is not Boston, much less Manhattan, just as the Yucatan Peninsula is not the Iberian Peninsula. And, yes, a time will come (it is and will be true) when the whole world will be equal. A single place without borders: all the buildings and stores with the same names. And, later, even a single religion with an omnipresent God and, as such and only for that reason, believable and to be believed in. And a single language that everyone can understand.† And all skin colors blending into a single shade resembling that of black tea into which you pour a stream of heavy and warm and freshly ordered milk. But it'll still be a while before all of that. To travel is still to *depart*, to go *somewhere else*. And everything seems to change completely in a matter of miles and, sometimes, even from one street to the next. And, from one city to the next, sometimes, it's as if you were moving through a planet still under construction: vast empty surfaces no different from the barren deserts

---

* Before my father ever did, the Hudson River was explored by the Portuguese Estêvão Gomes, by the Englishman Henry Hudson, and by the Italian Giovanni de Verrazzano; but long before any of them showed up, it was known as Ca-ho-ha-ta-te-a ("The River") to the Iroquois and as Muh-he-kun-ne-tuk ("River that Flows In Two Directions" or "Never-Still Waters") to the Mohawks. My father referred to it as "That Damn River that Always Makes Me Go Backward"; and it was the Hudson in which he invested, in a patent of dubious utility, a sizable sum in the production and deployment of a "Great Hydrostatic Apparatus" based on, he told me, "plans stolen from Cosmo the Magnificent II" for the dredging of swamps and marshlands along the river to turn them back into fertile fields. Or maybe it wasn't totally like that, and I've done nothing but judge as true one of his many deliriums, there, in his bed, like a raft never motionless yet no longer floating up- and down-river but caught in the circles of an eddy, a whirlpool. And all of it liberated first by me and then dragged by the currents of my supposed wit until (I confess my flaw without guilt) it ended up coming to shore in one of those brief and supposedly funny pieces that some journal had the pity, perhaps, to pay me for and to publish without including my name in the byline.

† Signs? Symbols? Ever fewer words to try to say things with? Will it really come to the uninspired nadir of just drawing a whale to describe or signify nothing more and nothing less than a whale?

of the moon or the voluptuous forests of Venus and there, every so often, catching sight of some local denizen, of indeterminate sex and wrapped in different animal skins making it hard to distinguish where the human ends and the beast begins. Beings that rather than speak seem to roar.

There, to Albany, from Boston, came Allan Melvill.

Direct descendent of fierce Scottish warriors* running across the moors of the eighteenth century: their swords and shields and maces brandished in the name of savage monarchs whose castles were just giant stones. Ones atop others, aligned in astrological and megalithic configurations and awaiting astral conjunctions, following instructions that nobody could apply to anything now and, nevertheless, motionless, and united by the moss of millennia.

Allan Melvill, born Sunday, April 7th, 1782, son of Thomas Melvill and Priscilla Scollay. Named in honor of his merchant-sailor grandfather. One of eleven siblings† in one of Boston's most traditional families. But it's been a long time since Boston was his

---

* Pa's voice regaling me with the exploits of *excercitus Scoticanus* instead of fairy and witch tales to conjure "sweet dreams" and achieving the opposite effect: all of that blood running down from the Highlands like a waterfall, all those battle cries preventing me from falling asleep, all those men in kilts the colors of their clans, and, there below, their cocks in the air and erect like sabers.

† Thomas Melvill, Jr., Mary D'Wolf Melvill, Nancy Wroe Melvill, Priscilla Melvill, Robert Melvill, Jean Wright Melvill, John Scollay Melvill, Lucy Melvill, and Helen Souther Melvill. And I'm missing a few, I don't remember all of them, I'm not sure I've met all my uncles and aunts. And sometimes some of them melt into others and they blend together, they were all the same and said the same things: not at all useful as characters.

home. Allan Melvill leaves Boston in 1801, when he is nineteen, to go on the traditional Grand Tour of Europe.* To educate and train himself for the future on the stage of the past. Something, according to his father, who liked to think himself modern and practical, far more beneficial and instructive than sitting back in college classrooms. His older brother, Thomas Jr., makes the trip first. And a few months later, Allan Melvill in England and Scotland and in the revolutionary and revolutionized France and even in a Spain that still appeared bound to the jousts and tournaments of the Middle Ages.

Allan Melvill buying prints and postcards of palaces and landscapes first and then sending himself to visit them.†

Allan Melvill among the immortal columns and ruins named for forgotten gods and the bell towers of San Pedro‡ and Westminster§ and Notre-Dame,** with the world at his feet. Allan Mel-

---

* Enumerating and moving on, if possible, his comings and goings and his highs and lows and lower lows as if they were part of an academic report: the "official part" of his Grand Tour with a structure and clarity (with logic and reasoning to be obliterated by the other version, by the White Delirium of that same journey) that I, infected, could never count on when accounting for my own existence.

† The postcards and prints that my father would show to me years later. Bound with colorful silk ribbons. One by one, like cards telling the fortune of a past, prophesizing that those increasingly distant times in the increasingly distant past would never come again.

‡ I will never understand (could someone explain to me the driving impulse?) the idea that an important and almost essential part of that pagan and almost invasive activity that is tourism runs through and passes in and out of visiting slews of churches and temples. Is the unconscious thought that God is some kind of big tour guide and Earth a particular museum where we're nothing more than the slippery and wasted bacteria to be corrected with correctives, every so often, in successive and interminable and cataclysmic restorations? And this is undoubtedly true: without ever fully wiping us out because, I suppose, what the gods like best is that we erect shrines in their names. And that, please, we never stop visiting them there and leaving cash gifts more material than spiritual, visibly moved, proffering "oohs" and "aaahs" of admiration at what their invisible grandeur inspires us to do in their names. Names that should not be taken in vain, but yes (when it comes to the most arrogant architecture) with enough vanity to make their creators feel borderline divine in divining the divine.

§ Religion is simultaneously the most exotic and most familiar of lands whose final destination you'll never make it to.

** Books written by others are portable shrines that travel with one as one travels with them. Books of one's own aspire to be grateful offerings, but more often than not and vill very quickly learning to speak and write French perfectly and (why? to what end?) even more quickly traversing the Pyrenees on horseback.

Allan Melvill hand-in-hand with princesses and princes of oxidated blue blood who invite him to salons where poets mingle with politicians and publishers and philosophers and statesmen and famous captains and merchants and even pale-skinned and red-lipped creatures who appear to have come from the past or the future, from underground or beyond the sun.

And, of course, Allan Melvill can only stand out among them by playing the card of the shiny and new noble savage.

And Allan Melvill tells tales of new names on barely drawn maps and invents encounters with first Mohicans and free-roaming trappers and florid aristocrats from Florida. All with firearms always ablazing.

And they return the favor with recommendations regarding trendy products and propitious commercial routes.

Allan Melvill has received a privileged upbringing, which was why the provincial novice from what until very recently were colonies traveled to the Old World. Not like someone returning to a Promised Land but like a promising youth come to receive the revelation of a great idea that would allow him to, once back home, make a fortune on that continent where everything is yet to be made.

And, finally, Albany is thus the point of departure that, upon his return, turns into a goal to arrive at victorious. Albany is for Allan Melvill another place to conquer, another kind of ancestry, more new palaces imitating those old palaces: the traditional customs and dance steps adopted and executed by him with a discipline and grace that border on fanaticism on the floors of those salons that he slid across the way he'll one day slide across the frozen Hudson River.

working in reverse (like wine into water), they are transmuted into the spilled blood of more or less unforgivable sins.

And, oh, the desperate need of that new governing class to be monarchs of a territory to be tamed. It's not the same, it's something else: in America, the loftiness of noble titles is conferred for the printing and impressive valuation of rustling and freshly minted banknotes and not for the number of turrets of a European castle almost crumbling into cold and hard rubble.

And, sure, there's no history, but there is an abundance of possibilities for making history.

And the absence of past is compensated for by the omnipresence of future.

And Allan Melvill thinks that there's no product with greater and more immediate presence today than tomorrow.

And it's in Albany that the young Allan Melvill unfurls the sails of his lineage, hoping to catch the soft and sweet and gentle breeze of a young woman of good name and better dowry.

Allan Melvill is propelled by the favorable wind that blows from his familial past. His father, Major Thomas Melvill, is the son of a wealthy immigrant from the Scottish Highlands: an orphan who, nevertheless, managed to get accepted at Princeton with his sights set on becoming a minister, but (after a prolonged illness and recovery on the family farm) he had a vision and discovered that he preferred a flock of submissive sheep to a flock of ever-restless parishioners. And so, Thomas Melvill settles in Boston and becomes a merchant and (dressed up as a native) participates in the Tea Party uprisings of 1773 alongside the Sons of Liberty. And, later, he fights for the continental cause after the Declaration of Independence and is appointed Inspector of Customs by George Washington himself (a post he was reappointed to in the subsequent administrations of John Adams, Thomas Jefferson, and

James Madison) to later be named Naval Officer of the District of Boston and Charlestown by Madison (a position he is reconfirmed to by James Monroe and John Quincy Adams as well).

That's where Allan Melvill comes from; and nothing seems to augur a perilous voyage or a lack of innumerable safe harbors in which to dock and be welcomed with reverence.

Before long, Allan Melville sets his eyes on the beautiful Maria Gansevoort, of an even more distinguished extraction than his own: prized descendant of Dutch emigrants who came to Albany in the middle of the seventeenth century, when the city was known as Fort Orange and was still part of New Amsterdam. A strategic location: a hilltop settlement along a stretch of the Hudson River with more than sufficient depth (even during droughts) for the largest and most heavily laden oceangoing vessels to dock. The Gansevoorts prosper as master brewers and soon ferment matrimonially with the best imported Dutch names (the Douses, the Ten Eycks, the Van Schaicks, the Van Vechtens, the Killianens)* and so it is that Maria's father, Peter Gansevoort, graduate of Princeton and hero of the revolution, attains Olympic heights. Almost a giant. As tall as Washington (some claim even taller, but, when walking beside said Founding Father, Gansevoort hunches his shoulders and bends his knees with respect and veneration to thereby avoid diminishing the stature of the Great General and Father of the Nation).

Peter Gansevoort as the founder and trainer of a company of grenadiers admired for its courage and discipline. His men (all selected by Peter Gansevoort himself; having an above average stature was an obligatory condition to serve under his command) worship him like a god. And his company's actions end up being decisive

---

* I've said it before, it's been known since Homer: names (and numbers and origins) of men and women are as important and defining for me as the names of ships; like those of all the symbolic ships that will pass through the symbolic ship of my novel: *Albatross, Jungfrau, Jeroboam, Rosebud, Samuel Enderby, Bachelor, Delight, Rachel* . . . The names are, always, what tells the story.

both during the Invasion of Quebec in 1775 and in 1777 when the English attempted to disrupt the supply chains of the New England colonies by taking control of the great river. Then Peter Gansevoort becomes the "Hero of the Defense of Fort Stanwix" (where a statue of him will be erected so his memory will never fall) by preventing, along with the seven hundred and fifty men under his command, Albany from being taken and razed by the one thousand seven hundred combined forces of Tories and Iroquois. Thenceforth and until his death in 1812, every Fourth of July the residents of Albany and Fort Stanwix (that with time and the growth of the city would be rechristened with the imperial name, Rome)* gather under his balcony to huzzah the man who continues ascending in rank and importance: Sherriff of Albany County, Lumber Baron of Northumberland (part of the area is renamed Gansevoort, because Peter Gansevoort is the founder of that place where the screeching of the saws is heard until well past midnight), commissioner for fortifying the northern and western frontiers, elegant yet firm diplomat when it came to making treaties with indigenous tribes as Commissioner of Indian Affairs, military agent of the Northern Department (with a signature from the fist and pen of Thomas Jefferson among his credentials), Brigadier General of the United States Army (with the signature of James Madison), and he was called to preside over the

---

* Stanwix, which will be, also, the name of one of my own sons, one of my dead sons. First Malcolm and then, almost twenty years later, poor Stan. Stan dying alone in a San Francisco hotel room. Stan shivering in another bed, far from all of us, but unable to distance himself from the failures he carried in his fevered blood: wholesaler, miner, sheep breeder, metallurgical impresario, dentist. Frustrated attempts that, nevertheless, never ceased throughout his uninterrupted effort to follow in my nomadic footsteps until at last, just like Malcolm, Stanwix triumphed as a precocious dead man. The one and the other, my dead sons. The other and the one whom I cast into something that began like a poem and ended up my inconclusive return to prose after so many years just to say goodbye: not with few words but with just the right words. So far from the florid and torrential excursions of my youth and, I would like to think, with the wise circumspection of old age. Recreating them I created the innocent and angelic and beautiful yet condemned to die and summarily executed Billy Budd.
May all three rest in peace.

court-martial trial of General James Wilkinson for his "treasonous machinations" in Virginia.

Upon returning from that trial, Peter Gansevoort falls ill and (regretting missing out on participating in the new war with England) he suffers a fall* and dies in 1812.†

Thus, based on the quality of their respective pedigrees, it was impossible for the Gansevoorts and the Melvills not to end up uniting forces, and for Maria and Allan, the one and the other and the other and one, not to notice each other. Both descendants of patriotic and revolutionary legends and both part of high colonial society. Both had grandfathers born as New-World Brits and transformed by their own violent wills into New Men. The smelting and forging of their surnames is viewed as inevitable and they are repeated, together, like a mantra that (if used incorrectly and inelegantly) could devolve into the worst of karmas.‡

But soon, something unexpected happens (and it is there and then that the differences between the clans that over time will prove irreconcilable are put into evidence); and what happens is that, without warning, everything seems to happen more quickly. The New World imposes a New Time. A recurrence in sudden theretofore unknown accelerations and ellipses. A new way of recounting the years, which suddenly seem to have the duration of months and, even, of only weeks or hours. Everything seems

---

* Death enters through his hip. I've seen the best crewmen of my generation destroyed by a maddening pain (those who threw their bodies face first into black hurricanes and white squalls) after, nothing epic about it, slipping and falling on a poorly rinsed deck, still soapy from washing away whale blood. Then the dry sound of snapping bone and, before long, that of the liquid tolling of death as it finds out that now is the time, its time.

† I never met my grandfather but did meet my grandmother: always surrounded by his war trophies, recounting his feats with a voice like that of an oracle of yesteryear.

‡ Because it tends to be forgotten that Sesame is not a magic word but, merely, the name (or surname) of a bottomless cave concealing the temptation of sinful treasures; and that just as it obeys so it can disobey. Its name being one (and that, as such, should not be invoked, as is erroneously done, to open extraordinary portals) that might be derived from the Cabbalistic-Talmudic šem-šamáįm ("shem-shamayim"), the name of Heaven.

suspended in the air, as if in the climax of an explosion. The fragments still connected by invisible threads but already flying off in
all directions. A model to be assembled without an instruction
manual.*

Thus (who could even imagine it, minds all still accustomed,
through inherited rituals, to the European parsimony wherein all
tradition is maintained across generations, all of it measured in
lustrous centuries and not in rapidly molding lustrums) the new
and nouveau-riche surnames begin to object to the prestige of the
first and freshly anointed nobles of the brand new yet also savage
and wild State still in liquefaction. And soon the credentials and
achievements of recent ancestors seem to matter less and less and
no longer bequeath such luster and power to their children. Thus,
the youngest Melvills and Gansevoorts are questioned by the new
and exceedingly numerous upper class (it's so easy to make yourself
rich in lands where everything is yet to be made; all you need is
good aim to hit the target of good businesses or bad investment
partners), and the reclamation of lands and privileges begins. And
the prevailing idea is that everything is there for the taking for whoever arrives first or for whoever is first to stake a claim among those
who arrive first. Maps and land deeds fade away every night and
are redrawn the next morning, like twice or thrice told, like never
entirely finished novels. Alliances are agreed to to thereby have reasons to find disagreement. The air reeks of gunpowder and the ink
never dries on violated treaties or violent death certificates where
the causes of death tend to be synthesized as "conflict of interest."

Thus, faced with the abuse of neighbors who defecate at their
gates or trespass on their properties, the Gansevoorts behave like

---

* A new style for beginning to write things, yes. A style that I want to be mine for
the things I'll end up writing. A style that no longer runs through what is written but
through how it is written. The present of a style that might be the style of the future,
knowing that all style is but the result of new language being added to an old expression.
Or vice versa.

calculating strategists while the Melvills decide to recklessly gamble and take considered risks, using their privileged position in the labyrinth of customs law and good information regarding the safest shipping routes to evade pursuit by the spiteful British Armada.

That climate of intrigue and deception is the context for the formation and deformation of Allan Melvill, who before long is sent by his father, Thomas Melvill (preferring, he insists on it, to throw him right into the action before he wastes time going to college), to Paris.

Again, the aforementioned: Grand Tour.*

There ("in high style" and "in the most exalted circles" while he spends a small fortune on the genealogical tracing of ancestors who link his blood to that of kings) Allan Melvill circulates through diplomatic and social circles. Allan Melvill among *les meilleurs milieux*. And before long Allan Melvill attracts attention for his wit and good looks and good taste and eye for selecting products and merchandise that will fascinate the most affluent people on the other side of the ocean but, also, for the way in which he squanders money to finance transactions that always end up benefitting his partners. Treacherous accomplices who, first, let and even prompt him to embark on bad deals that, after watching him sink, will benefit them when the tides wash his cargo up on their shores and Allan Melvill finds himself forced to liquidate it at cost.†

---

* And I insist on this point and moment, because it will be the time and the places to which my father will return to again and again (lucid and in good health or hallucinating in his terminal illness) as the core of his entire existence. Everything led there, everything sprang from there. And my father remained forever, more surrendered than trapped, in the amber of that ambiguous and mysterious part of his life, understanding it (if he'd been able to edit it, aware that when one travels one becomes a caricature of oneself) as his whole life.

† To which is added the public humiliation that several of my father's awful transactions and unfortunate decisions (to the benefit and delight of those who take advantage of his desperation) appear clearly detailed in the memoirs of traders and even in Stock Exchange statements or in pamphlets that describe the "amazing offers" of his merchandise (imported from Europe and after he covered all the transportation and customs expenses) that ends up being acquired by none other than his competitors and even his friends.

And yet, even though he's almost ready to be embargoed, none of that prevents Allan Melvill (in 1813 and as if it were the acquisition of the most esteemed merchandise) from kicking off the courtship of Maria Gansevoort. A young woman he meets through her older brother, Peter Gansevoort, with whom he'd planned a real-estate investment that never comes to fruition.* Maria Gansevoort is young yet mature for her years, an impeccable hostess with a refined sense of humor, a polished piano player and obsessive reader of the Bible in Dutch and English.† And, beyond the fact that her brother considers her "not to possess the beauty of a Helen," Peter Gansevoort also admits that "she could be more attractive if she dedicated her mind to studies useful in the improvement of her person."

Allan Melvill and Maria Gansevoort are married in October of 1814 and the former moves into the mansion belonging to his mother-in-law, Catherine Van Schaick Gansevoort. Into the house haunted by the ghost of The Hero of Fort Stanwix.‡ And in Albany, Allan Melvill opens his first lingerie shop. At first, things don't go badly for him, but soon he gets bored of the same faces and conversations that, before long, he can predict as if he were reading them in the not-at-all diverting diversions of the most uninspired writers. In Albany, there's neither adventure nor surprise

---

* My poor uncle, who, as bequeathed by my father, will take me in and even agree to finance the printing of my late poems, thinking that in that way he'll "keep me sane" and calm "my tormented and unpredictable temperament."
† Telling stories of amazing travels in the voice of my father and the recitation of episodes from the Old Testament in the voice of my mother. Not battling each other but (marine monsters in both) coexisting and blending together: the mortal yet divine audacity of an almost desperate search for the chance reward sailing hand-in-hand with the strict and Calvinist and reformist and protestant fear of the inevitable encounter with the reefs of the deserved punishment at the hands of a God with unforgiving tendencies. Again, there and from there, from both: my style, the style of all that is mine.
‡ The unsettling sensation of inhabiting (for the first time, though it won't be the last for me, as I've said already) a museum in which you're not entirely sure if you're a disgraceful handsy visitor or an untouchable exhibition piece.

nor risk. It doesn't take Allan Melvill long to realize that the future is downriver and on the opposite shore: on the island of Manhattan, where the buildings grow taller and taller, because the sky is the limit for that city and for the people who live in it and make it grow day by day.*

There, Allan Melvill takes out the first of many loans to establish himself as "an importer of French goods and Commission merchant," at 123 Pearl Street, and he notes in his travelogues that, between 1800 and 1822, he travels "by land 24,425 miles, by water 48,460 miles," and spends "days at sea etc. 643." Before long, his older brother and occasional business partner, Thomas Jr., ends up in debtors' prison for suspicious transactions in his accounting books. And the unpaid loans and outstanding debts begin to involve the Gansevoorts too (on account of Maria's inheritance, Maria who doesn't take long to start suffering from migraines and depression and raises her eight children with a firm hand to the point of assembling them around her bed, standing still and in absolute silence, when she takes her afternoon nap) while Allan Melvill commends himself unto "future favors" with "patience, resignation and perseverance."

Then the epidemics empty the streets of New York and keep the ships in port and (according to the winds that blow, ascending in opulence or falling into near misery, depending on the run of luck the head of the family is on) he has to busy himself with moving to a new house or a new neighborhood and with switching schools and servants who, inevitably, disappear like characters in a melodrama who are eliminated because they no longer serve any useful purpose or, even worse, because their presence is no longer plau-

---

* "A city of unexampled growth & prosperity, & unrivalled local resources and foreign intercourse, which must become the great Emporium of the western World," he explains in a letter to potential European partners.

sible or sustainable.* And the children of the marriage† get accustomed to the idea of brief journeys between the same few streets that, nevertheless, end up far better at insulating one world from another than the most stormy of seas.‡

Then, the battles of pending promissory notes and unpaid installments, of unkept promises and borrowed lies. And Allan Melvill always asking for more time and a cease-fire, because he was awaiting (and here, almost conspiratorial, he lowered his voice and glanced side to side and spoke out of the corner of an almost-closed mouth) the help of a "confidential connexion" whose

---

* Mysteriously and to everyone's surprise, I excel in arithmetic and receive first premium in my class and am awarded a copy of my first book (*The London Carcanet: Containing Select Passages from the Most Distinguished Writers*) accompanied by a plaque that congratulates me for being "first best in his class in ciphering books." And it is there (the teacher, Henry, made a mistake when commissioning the engraving) where I read (and I must admit that I've struggled to read ever since I contracted scarlet fever in my infancy, and I think it's because of an alteration to my pupils) my last name written as Melville for the first time.

† Again: my arrival to the world took place on Sunday, August 1st, 1819, at 11:30 P.M., in the family home at number 6 Pearl St., a few days after my due date but without complications, according to what Dr. Wright Post put down in his files. I am named Herman in honor of my mother's older brother. And I am baptized in the South Reformed Dutch Church by Reverend Mr. J. M. Mathews, who during the ceremony asks my parents if they are aware that "all children are conceived and born into sin, and as such they are subject to all the miseries and punishment, and that's why they are consecrated in Christ thanks to this ritual." Both of them answer yes without really understanding what they're answering to and what the priest is referring to, and the priest probably doesn't really know either. And Grandmother Gansevoort, freshly arrived from Albany, brings four gallons of rum that they toast with in celebration until the wee hours of the morning as cholera spreads throughout the city. Later, it will also be put down in my father's records that my first words won't be random but an already more or less well-formed and floating sentence: "Pa now got a 'ittle Boy."

‡ Idea for a story/novel: a succession of houses and schools that the young hero goes in and out of as a result of his father's bad fortune. The houses and schools as the true protagonists of the story, while the people who inhabit or frequent them end up being simple and fleeting settings in ever more frenetic and desperate movements, as if ravaged by typhoons or what the Japanese call tsunamis. Warning to myself: having learned how to think too much and with great bitterness at too tender an age, I've also learned to not think too much (at least until much later) about the delight of times prior to my arrival to the world, before my father turned into a being broken in every sense and before we were all expelled from the big city; because when I do think about it, something seems to climb up into my throat and almost strangle me.

"highly respectable name" he would never reveal "at the express request of my well-known associate." And in that way making (wasn't Allan Melvill, after all, the son of the Hero of the Tea Party and the son-in-law of the Hero of Fort Stanwix?) his creditors imagine the surnames of local heads of state and even foreign aristocrats.*

By 1827, everyone has gotten tired of listening to him and buying his drinks and Allan Melvill is on the brink of a nervous breakdown and all promise of a confidential connexion has ended in public isolation.

Allan Melvill is worse than pestilential.

Allan Melvill is pestilent.

And people smell Allan Melvill coming on avenues and in ballrooms whose doors have been taken off their hinges and piled in some bedroom to better guarantee the circulation of gossip throughout the party: acquaintances who cross the street when they see him coming or pretend not to know him, groups of guests who reconfigure and close ranks to discourage any attempt he might make to join them, preferring to talk about him than to talk to him.

Soon, Allan Melvill is left with no way forward but to leave the great city of the great future and return to the small city of the great past.†

---

* Few things end up being easier than for one man to make another man believe that he is in possession of the greatest and most decisive (though nonexistent) of secrets.

† And I've made it this far and I'll stop here and won't elaborate (I prefer not to) further on my father's comings and goings as it relates to his increasingly inactive professional activities and decreasingly good results. All those additions and subtractions. All those ever-larger quantities backed by ever-fewer family members whose names and relationships now produce in me a migraine akin to the one lying in wait at the lush and as if telescopic bottoms of bottles on whose mouth, clutching them by the neck, I rest my eye to see if I can see something worth putting in writing. It turns out to be almost as exhausting and distressing to trace his downward spiral as, I suppose, it was for my father to know himself pursued and persecuted. For me (his creation now recreating him), the

only thing of interest and importance and that, I think, has true dramatic and narrative validity is, first, my final voyage at his side, aboard the *Swiftsure*, from New York to Albany. And, soon thereafter, the exceedingly symbolic eternity of my father crossing the frozen Hudson River on foot, the night of Saturday, December 10th, 1831, and the subsequent and long and fevered and hallucinated days that led to his death a half-hour before midnight on Saturday, January 28th, 1832.

Now it's autumn and the invisible engines of cold are kicking into gear and the tree-green paintbrushes are drying.

In Albany, the Widow of the Hero of Fort Stanwix, Catherine Van Schaick Gansevoort, is not in good health. Every night, she insists, the shade of her deceased husband visits her, waving to her with sword unsheathed from a hilltop, gesturing for her to join him under a sky stained red by artillery fire. But she's not ready to depart yet, she says. She's worried about her daughter and grand-children. And she has to keep battling her son-in-law, Allan Melvill, who ceaselessly besieges and beseeches her with increasingly absurd and desperate requests regarding the revision of wills and advances of inheritance.

Soon, her home* has been invaded by an army of Melvills (boys and girls running the halls and climbing up and sliding down the banisters) under the command of a general, their father, who lacks any sense of strategy beyond ordering successive retreats. Her

---

* 46 North Market St.

increasingly impoverished, in every sense, daughter limits herself to smiling with the corners of her once-adorable mouth down-turned and to playing sorrowful sonatas on the piano (as if the keys were a sort of medium or ventriloquist's dummy that alone were capable of intoning the truth that she doesn't dare admit) that, to top it off, is always missing a decisive note (the piano was damaged in what's already known in the family as "The Great Escape from New York"). And the old woman can't stop fixating on and, anxious and unable to think of anything else, anticipating the moment when the score will be played and there won't be any way left to fix it.

Soon it's decided in a secret tribal meeting that the Melvill clan will have to move and another house* is rented for them and Allan Melvill gets a job as a clerk at a clothing store. Humiliation and descent to reality and being put in his place, which don't stop him from continuing to concoct grand plans for a gleaming tomorrow where, he promises vainly and in vain, definitive success and the clearing of his honor and name await.

His son (who tries to spend as much time as possible in the classrooms of the Albany Academy) listens to him with a combination of admiration and fear and feels as if he were still in the hold of the *Swiftsure*, waiting for the passing of a storm that lingers on even now that the sun shines in the sky.†

The complicated words and supposedly salvatory moves and twisting rationale of his father (while always further indebting himself to his family and his wife's family) at times remind him of the stories of *One Thousand and One Nights*, where the wicked sultans have been replaced by scornful relatives.

---

* 338 North Market St.
† Which might be worse: because sometimes it's better for the weather to go hand-in-hand with our mood instead of completely opposing it and leaving it to its own devices and fate.

Then, the death of the Widow of the Hero of Fort Stanwix does nothing but worsen Allan Melvill's situation. Peter (Maria Gansevoort Melvill's older brother) inherits the responsibility of administering the family's assets and that door slams definitively shut; and Allan Melvill is thus left with no option but to go to Boston to beg for help from his own family. He gets enough money from them to pay off one of his debts and allow him "to reenter and be back in circulation," and he holds onto a few bills so he can return to New York, at the beginning of December, a little over a year after his departure, and attempt to get one of his businesses going again.

But back in Manhattan, nobody trusts him anymore and all they show him (one after another, unfurling them across desks like the hides of animals hunted long ago or like maps of lost battles whose defeat he still has to answer for) are past-due promissory notes, their fading letters only silenced by being buried under the numbers of the amounts owed.

Allan Melvill promises, between tentative bows and broken smiles, he'll take care of all by the next morning, but once again makes for the docks that very night, thinking how, at this point, he could almost be considered a must-see and always-reliable tourist attraction or circus sideshow: The Fleeing Man.

And Allan Melvill embarks (this time alone and missing so much the company of his son) for Albany aboard the *Constellation*.*

Allan Melvill, like Odysseus, needs to return home.

Going home is all he wants, the only thing that matters.†

---

* A magnificent name for a ship, aboard which he travels for the last time, barely afloat, taking on water, the black hole of an eclipsed man.

† Life is but a journey whose destination is the home you've left behind; but, even still, my temptation to then attribute to my father thoughts and ideas like those of the protagonist of that story by Nat H.: my father arriving to Albany but not returning home, hiding, instead, in a nearby room and watching us through lace curtains, spying on us between blind slats and ajar doors. But no: that wouldn't be fair. My father just wants to return home; because only by returning will he feel that he'll never be forced to leave again.

Thus, Allan Melvill thinks of his return (along with his family, to whom he owes so much, to whom he feels so indebted) as a decisive undertaking, a successful transaction, a business deal that brings his run of bad luck to an end. If he makes it back to his beautiful home, nothing else will go wrong, Allan Melvill thinks, almost magically, the way the almost unthinkably desperate or the mystics suspended atop pillars with views of the abyss think.

But the *Constellation* sails up the Hudson to Poughkeepsie and can go no farther—the river has frozen. Much earlier than ever before. Nobody really understands how or why except Allan Melvill, who can't help but understand and accept it as another manifestation of his misfortune and an ominous sign dedicated to him alone: even the forces of nature are arrayed against him. But not even that will be able to stop him, he says to himself. And, of course, there's nothing more dangerous for a hapless wastrel than to convince himself that he is or might become a hero.

Allan Melvill decides to continue on by land, renting an open one-horse wagon and making it as far as Rhinebeck, where he spends the night. The next morning, he hires another wagon (two-horse, open, and it snows and the cold cuts like the edges of a book with pages that turn too fast but take so long to be written) and, shivering, Allan Melvill makes it to the streets of the town of Hudson,* where he spends that night, waiting for the storm to abate. And a two-horse sleigh (covered this time) the next day; and Allan Melvill arrives, according to his journal, "at ¼ before 5" to the outskirts of Greenbush, across the river from Albany. Tomorrow, this place will be overrun by skaters young and old, cutting lines into the ice. Some moving clockwise and others moving counterclockwise, intuitively synchronized, as if obeying a consanguineous and unconscious dictate of

---

* I never liked the idea of towns and rivers sharing a name. The unpleasant sensation that the person in charge of naming places has lost all creativity or gotten bored of the job.

the species that transcends all names. Now, on the other hand, the landscape is like the whitest of blank pages and time appears to have stopped its turnings and displacements. From there, Allan Melvill stares out at the lights of the open arms of the candelabras in the bay windows on the other side of the river. And among them (brighter than all the rest, like one of those fundamental stars by which even the most confused captains manage to orient themselves) he thinks he can pick out the one in his own house.

Then (night falls without warning, like one of those elliptical music-hall backdrops that, with a harsh and descending sound, suddenly transport the actors from a forest to a temple collapsing on its faithful or to the most angelic skies), Allan Melvill decides to walk across the frozen waters of the Hudson River, there before him, motionless, as if posing for a portrait. It's not a great distance,* nobody would consider it an epic odyssey, though it is a long walk in the cold and the dark. But it's clear that, for the purposes of the story of our story, that distance is equal to the one across which, almost infinite, the loving forces that separate the sun from the other stars stretch out.†

Before walking across the waters,‡ Allan Melvill (feeling that he's on the brink of an experiment but with so little experience,

---

* A little less than half a mile, a little over five hundred meters. Or maybe double that. Could there exist some precise man-made instrument that faithfully measures the ever-unfaithful distance that separates exact desperation from diffuse love? The number of feet matters less than the difficulty of walking his feet across ice, and the cold in his body, and the wind in his face and in his heart and the snow in his disheveled head. In any case, the memory of distances and sizes tends to be imprecise and so it is that our parents who, once giants, with time end up for us almost dwarves both physically and mentally.

† But let it never be forgotten that, while it's true that in many lands the visible world appears to welcome that form of love, the invisible spheres that also comprise and spin ceaselessly inside it (which it's only fitting to imagine like those little spheres of colored glass with what look like petals of nebulas inside them, like those marbles that make you feel like you're holding the eye of a whole universe in the palm of your hand) have been molded by the hands of the most pure and gripping terror.

‡ The waters of that river into which my father threw me more than once so I would learn to swim. And I wonder where that atavistic impulse comes from that makes all

barely an expert on the margins of a new science, not entirely sure whether he's a scientist or a specimen) writes down in his journal that the incidental expenses incurred on his trip to New York add up to seventy-five cents while what he spent on his return to Albany was less than forty-two cents.

And that's the last note written by his own hand in the records of Allan Melvill.

---

fathers believe that the best way to teach their children something is to throw them through the air so that they land in a place where it will be impossible for them to survive and from which they will invariably need to be rescued. Might the idea be that, in the water, human beings automatically activate the memory that returns them to their fluid origins, regaining an awareness that their bodies are nothing but the solid vehicles that liquids avail themselves of to move from one place to the other? Who knows, someone who isn't me can figure it out.

What comes next is what remains.

The cold that won't quit.

The ice that will never melt.

The unforgettable memory.

The birth of the dying life of Allan Melvill who, guided by the glow of lamps and candles in the houses of Albany, makes it to his house on Market St. That world barely illuminated* by the impossibility of a two-days-from-new moon that's like the fingernail clipping of a giant tossed into the heavens to hang among the stars.

Allan Melvill arrives home, and his family welcomes him like a titan who's accomplished the most impossible of feats. Not because they believe it, but because he—their father and husband—appears so desperate for them to see and acknowledge him as such and to believe in him.

---

* First you need darkness to then perceive light. Darkness that really isn't dark but a different variety of light.

Allan Melvill tells them of his crossing of the Hudson as if he were returning from a voyage to Earth's poles. He speaks of hearing mysterious voices tempting him, of messages seeming to come from The Beyond, of red eyes blinking in the darkness, of withstanding a blizzard wind capable of sweeping everything away, screaming that he would never surrender, never retreat.*

From this side of things, Maria Gansevoort Melvill decides not to ask him about lost or found money, she doesn't want to spoil the festive mood. And they all dance around him as Allan Melvill strikes heroic poses, like one of those mythological statues that he admired in European museums so many years ago now, and he smiles and can't stop smiling and doesn't really understand why he's smiling.

That smile that refuses to leave his face in the subsequent days and that (to the increasing worry of his wife and growing disquiet of his children) has acquired the tension of a frozen and sardonic and too-many-toothed grin and is accompanied by an all-consuming fever that rises and falls but never entirely dissipates.

Thus, Allan Melvill keeps going to work and seems almost frenetic in his interactions with customers to whom he tries to sell anything he can, including things they don't want or need, invoking the Christmas spirit. Allan Melvill, who takes advantage of the moments the store empties out to compose long and rambling letters to his creditors in New York wherein he promises treasures hidden among the vestiges of civilizations yet to be discovered and among the wonders that he came to know in a Venetian *palazzo*: "I've seen them . . . I've been there, and with your financing I can

---

* Here I remember the German legend of that rider who, in the middle of the night, crossed the frozen Lake Constance on horseback and who, upon arriving to an inn and being informed that what he'd believed to be a plain was a frozen lake, had fainted, terrified by the temerity of what, unbeknownst to him, he'd bumbled into. One version even says that the rider dies, struck down by his own involuntary and private and unknowing feat.

return and get us a great deal ... All these marvels are within my reach, and I'm certain that obtaining patents for them couldn't be more difficult than the miracle of walking across the waters of the Hudson River ... I swear, I saw them, they work," he writes in large letters with no attention given to syntax and orthography and logic.

In the increasingly rare moments when he appears to regain some use of his reason, Allan Melvill opens Maria Gansevoort Melvill's family Bible and memorizes Psalm 55 and recites it over and over (he even puts music to it at the piano that, more than playing, he punishes) with a voice that moves from roar to whisper.* "My heart is sore pained within me: And the terrors of death are fallen upon me. / Fearfulness and trembling are come upon me, and horror hath overwhelmed me. / And I said, Oh, that I had the wings of a dove! For then I would fly away, and be at rest. / Lo, then I would wander far off, and remain in the wilderness. Selah.† / I would hasten my escape from the windy storm and tempest," intones Allan Melvill more and more out of tune.‡

Letters from the time exchanged between acquaintances and family members (some of them, though they would never admit it, find any excuse to come see the show that breaks the monotony of provincial winter) describe him almost as a freak. And they refer

---

* I, Herman, joined his tribulations, my shouts rising along with his, my oaths mixed with his; and I shouted louder, and sealed my oath more forcefully because of the terror I felt in my soul.

† Hearing it, I ask what Selah means and my mother explains to me that it is a Hebrew term that she doesn't really know how to translate; but that it could mean "stop and listen"; and that it could come to be understood as a liturgical musical mark between the recitation of one psalm and another. And, as my mother explains this to me, my father scream-sings songs that don't seem to have anything religious about them, the same ones that I heard not long ago in the hold of the *Swiftsure*, when our whole world began to sink and we understood that there wouldn't be enough lifeboats for everyone to reach the island that we believed welcoming and deserted but where we would be surrounded by the cannibals pursuing my father, resolved to get their pound of flesh.

‡ Later my mother would note in the margins of that page of her Bible that "This Chapter was mark'd a few days before my dear Allan by reason of severe suffering was deprive'd of his Intellect. God moves in a mysterious way."

to the "state of constant excitement" and the "inability to sleep" of someone who, when at last he agrees to lie down, "appears to sleep with open eyes that move incessantly" even "manifesting an alienation of Mind." Soon, the family doctor deems him "very sick by a variety of causes" and "beyond any cure." And he laments that, if Allan Melvill survives the intensity of his shivering and the volume of his howling in incomprehensible tongues, he'll present "the melancholy spectacle of a deranged man."*

One morning they find Allan Melvill with his steel Catalan knife open† and his hands covered with blood. They think that he has tried to commit suicide, and nobody heeds his explanations that all he was trying to do was modify and lengthen his fate line.

Then, as much for his own safety as for everyone else's, they decide to tie Allan Melvill to his bed.‡

---

* Here I allow myself to transcribe a fragment of a letter from my uncle, Thomas Melvill, Jr., because it strikes me as worthy of attention and even of a somewhat admirable prose: "In short my dear sir, Hope, is no longer permitted of his recovery, in the opinion of the attending Physicians and indeed,—oh, how hard for a brother to say!—I ought not to hope for it.—for,—in all human probability—he would live, a Maniac!"

† Which he was given when in Europe on his Grand Tour ("My protective and blessed blade and, ah, if this knife could talk . . ." my father said) and which I keep in a drawer of my desk and use to turn the pages of other people's books that, on more than one occasion, I have to stop myself from stabbing.

‡ Ahab shouting things like "Ego non baptize te in nominee patris, sed in nominee diaboli!" and imagining his wife telling his son what the boy's demented father was like. Ahab tied to his hammock, cinched in a straitjacket, his human and clever madness that, when believed to have disappeared, had really just been transfigured into a subtler form. Not dissipating but contracting, like the mighty Hudson River does sometimes, running through narrow stretches but of unfathomable volume, through gorges, amid the indifference of the mountains. That river that my father crossed, walking on the water, like a Messiah giving in to all temptation and with no faithful flock and in whom no one believed.

Selah.

T henceforth, Allan Melvill's moments of lucidity are few and illuminate next to nothing. They're nothing but an intermittent succession of matches lit in a drafty room and lack the determination of a candle or the constancy of a lamp. When these moments of sanity take time and place (ever fewer, ever briefer, like a handful of watchmen on the ship deck who never manage to raise the alarm for the approaching giant wave or sharp iceberg or gelatinous and tentacular monster of an unpronounceable name), Allan Melvill can't stop sobbing and lamenting all the ill he has wrought; the way he's squandered the fortunes of his family and his in-laws and of his sister Nancy Wroe Melvill.* Allan Melvill never stops

---

* Engaged to one of the prominent Shaws, Lamuel, a future judge (but Nancy dies before the wedding) to whom I will dedicate my first book. Which doesn't prevent, in the eyes of Allan Melvill, the Shaws from becoming the forced benefactors of the Melvills. Me included because (in a curious plot twist of the kind considered unrealistic in fiction but that never stop happening in reality) the daughter of the Judge Shaw, Elizabeth "Lizzie" Shaw, product of his prior marriage to Elizabeth Knapp Shaw, will end up becoming my wife. In the beginning, Judge Shaw will oppose his favorite daughter marrying a writer (or, perhaps, marrying the son of that father); but he'll end up not only financing my first home in Manhattan but also the publication of my books (among my

moaning about the immense love he feels for his children and his wife, a love that, nevertheless, won't help keep the fire in the fireplace lit during winter.

"There are strange times in this complex and difficult thing we call *life* in which man takes the entire universe as a lame joke, even though he can't see any humor in it and is totally convinced that the joke is at his expense," Allan Melvill laments in increasingly rambling phrases, as if he were reading them in the air. Before long, (though they don't admit it aloud but only with their downcast eyes) his wife and children prefer him delirious and demented to rational when it comes to enumerating all the ways he misused his supposed irrational talent for business, tormenting himself but actually tormenting all of them with the "injustice of his bad luck, because of the punishing curse that's hounded him for so long."

Allan Melvill is there, bound hand and foot. The man once so worldly (and who left testimony of the many wonders that he visited so far from home in a notebook bombastically titled *Recapitulations of Voyages and Travels from 1800 to 1822, both inclusive*) now confined to a small room with the curtains drawn and, as his only view, facing him, the increasingly antiquated landscape of his own two portraits.

The first, young and glowing and all promise, but small in size (possibly prophetic in that contradiction of dimension and intention) and almost full body and giving the feeling of wanting to escape the borders imposed by the exaggerated frame. And the second, from just a decade later, but as if already offering testimony of another era and far smaller and more formal and easier to mistake

most gratifying reads are the diverse range of documents whereon it says, "Financed by Judge Shaw" or "Paid for by Judge Shaw," ha!), as well as several of my trips to Europe and the Middle East. Far from Lizzie, whom I'll so passionately torment toward the end of my life (when her successive inheritances saved us from absolute ruin and allowed me to keep acquiring books and nautical stamps), the way only a writer who no longer writes because nobody reads him can.

for so many other portraits of the time: chest up and, though of greater magnitude and volume, displaying a somber and trapped expression, against a dark backdrop and trying, in vain, to appear dignified and respectable.*

Allan Melvill speaks to those two Allan Melvills who, one beside the other, could be understood as similar to those ads in magazines that juxtapose a *Before* and *After* to thereby demonstrate the curative effects of some new and miraculous elixir of more than dubious results. Just that in Allan Melvill's case, the portraits were reversed: the first to be painted and smaller one, the *Before*, showing the strong and healthy individual in excellent spirits; while the second and larger one, the *After*, offers a degraded man of a taciturn air.

And to the *Before* and *After* is now added a third portrait, a consumed and consummate *Now*: Allan Melvill tied to the bed. A living model of an almost spectral dead nature for whom the physical world of solid objects seems displaced, slipping away, floating in an ether of blind visions, under those stars where a whole slithering universe of serpentine creatures hiss in one undulating voice.

---

* My own portrait (which Joseph Eaton will be commissioned to paint in 1870 as a gift from my brother-in-law) looks, it couldn't be otherwise, more like the second portrait of my father than the first. And the light that illuminates my face there and that appears to emanate from it, barely alters the melancholy already present in that other portrait of me painted, gratis, by Asa Twitchell, in 1846-1847: when the success of my first novel turned me, for a brief time, into a desirable subject for painters as optimistic as they were mistaken in their predictions, fantasizing about immortalizing themselves by immortalizing me. They, like me, departing early from one port to arrive late to the other. And no, there was no painter to paint what would have, perhaps, been my best portrait: the landscape of the shadowy bedroom of a dying man, tied to his bed like a helm, a boy at his feet, taking notes and writing and narrating. A son telling the tale the father will never tell.

N ow, the sound of his moon-colored madman's face.*

And it's his entranced voice that his young son, at the foot of his bed, can't stop hearing. A voice that feels toxic and disorienting,[†] like the echo of sirens nesting in his father's throat.[‡]

---

* His face beardless and, maybe that's why I took it upon myself, as soon as I left my youth behind, to grow one. To differentiate myself from him. To be someone else. Here's one (another) of my enumerative plotlines to outline there: the history of my beard leaping from portrait to photographs and to portrait once more and to photographs and to portrait again and to one final photograph where I appear as if watching from a great distance, from the other side of a river far wider and faster-flowing than the Hudson and whose ever-raging waters would be hard pressed to still themselves to allow one to cross them.

† More than two decades later, in a novel, I'll write that the father of the book's aristocratic and decadent protagonist "had died of a fever; and, as is not uncommon in such maladies, toward his end, he at intervals lowly wandered in his mind."

‡ Is the madness of my father the origin of the madness of my son? Transmitting from one generation to the next in different ways and taking different forms? My madness (less obvious and perhaps more ambiguous, yet still easily detectible) has been poured into my books, which, for one pygmy among the most slavish and servile critics, read more and more like the products of an unhinged mind. Madness that, maybe, had a far more destructive influence on the brief lives of my sons, who were unable to *channel* or *conjure* it through writing.

One writes, yes, to put into writing and thereby exorcise or neutralize something that many people, wretches and not scriveners and not even readers, end up using to cross out

There and then, Allan Melvill's words composing The White Delirium over and over again: variations on the aria of their voyage together aboard the *Swiftsure* and of his solo voyage aboard the *Constellation** and (repeating himself endlessly like two mirrors facing each other in a single landscape) his impassioned crossing of the frozen Hudson River and, between one shore and the other, the hallucinated adventure of his Grand Tour.

---

their lives because they never learned from the true and instructive errors of fiction's exceedingly real creatures.

* My father confuses the names of the two ships over and over again, and, more than once, blends them together into a third that sounds to me like *Peck Wood* or something like that. But maybe most important of all: my father had never seemed to me as disturbingly happy (could there be anything sadder than this?) as he did during the great delirium of his death throes.

† My father cries out strange things but things (if you give them their due; and I do and I copy them down, as if they were formulas of the most inexact sciences, in my algebra notebook with a sailboat on its cover) that function as a sort of self-diagnosis far more precise than the diagnoses of the "specialists" who visit him and who, lost, seek in the beats of his heart an explanation for the palpitations of his brain. To wit: "All my means are sane, my motive and my objective mad"; or "Madman! look through my eyes if thou hast none of thine own"; or "I am madness maddened! That wild madness that's only calm to comprehend itself"; or "there is no folly of the beast of the earth which is not infinitely outdone by the madness of men"; or "There is a wisdom that is woe; but there is a woe that is madness"; or "All that most maddens and torments; all that stirs up the lees of things; all truth with malice in it; all that cracks the sinews and cakes the brain; all the subtle demonisms of life and thought . . . Am I mad? Anyway there's something on his mind, as sure as there must be something on a deck when it cracks"; or "I felt a melting in me. No more my splintered heart and maddened hand were turned against the wolfish world"; "So man's insanity is heaven's sense; and wandering from all mortal reason, man comes at last to that celestial thought, which, to reason, is absurd and frantic; and weal or woe, feels then uncompromised, indifferent as his God"; or "Venice . . . Shit . . . I am still only in Venice"; or "The horror! The horror!"; to later descend to the perhaps earthlier, but, also, less inspired with a "There is all the difference in the world between paying and being paid, Herman . . . The act of paying is perhaps the most uncomfortable affliction . . . But being paid—what will compare with it? The urbane activity with which a man receives money is really marvelous, considering that we so earnestly believe money to be the root of all earthly ills, and that on no account can a monied man enter heaven. Ah! How cheerfully we consign ourselves to perdition! Ah, Melvill! Ah, humanity!"

‡ My father sometimes caressed himself lasciviously and said strange names: Ella Elle Lei and Ta Lei Sei and Lady Kismet and Madame Mirror and Cosmo The Magnificent II and "Nicolás Cueva on the other side of a window." And at first I can't help but think

And his cries are ever longer[†] and his words ever wilder[‡] and, yes, soon there would be a last word and a last cry and a last breath and closed eyes and an open window that nobody remembers opening.

And he, Herman, his 'ittle Boy, joined his tribulations. So, again, the cries of the boy rose up alongside those of his father, their oaths swirling together, as if in a landscape of air above the whitest beach where the perturbations of memory are linked to the intermittencies of the heart.

And (now, there and then, what he can only put into words and footnote much later) the boy cried out louder and swore his oath more forcefully because of the terror he felt in his soul. The oath to keep his father alive however he can;[*] because it was clear that his father wouldn't be able to keep himself alive to keep it.[†]

That terror (his father as a symbol of everything symbolizable; more intuiting than knowing and the boy stating, again, that real places don't appear on any map, that the most marvelous things are the ones that are hard to name, and that the most profound memories don't tend to produce the most inspired epitaphs) that

---

that they are, again, kabbalistic sounds or biblical passages or psalms or psalmodies; but no, because then my father kept talking and telling and . . .

* And I hope I'm not disturbing his rest; but after all I'm merely respecting his wishes. And perhaps everything I'll write thenceforth won't be anchored in reality so that, when it casts off, it can strike out for the imagined, which is nothing but what might have been and, from there, what is and what will be.

† Allan Melvill dies on Saturday, January 28th, 1832, a half hour before midnight, and two months before turning fifty. His funeral took place on January 31st in the sitting room of the Market St. house with just close family in attendance: a final celebration in honor of the man who could not attend though his body was present. And, there and then, as if in a subtle yet powerful physio-chemical reaction, Maria Gansevoort Melvill mutates and ceases to be a feeble wife and becomes a more powerful widow and more exacting mother and occasional amputator of the fantasies and dreams of her progeny, attempting thereby to prevent the poison of the father's frustrations from jumping and shriveling the hearts and minds of her little ones. And Allan Melvill is buried in the Dutch Church section of the Common Albany Cemetery. There someone recalls that (according to Allan Melvill's genealogical investigations during his Grand Tour) the motto on the family crest is *Denique Coelum*: "Heaven at last."

only seems to wane, over the years, by evoking those nights.*
Nights that fall and rise again here, obeying that master and father and captivating character whom the captivated writer-son so
loves, and who now, captive, he makes speak and hears again as
the author of his days.†

---

* Should I clarify here, as if it were a confession, that I didn't dare embrace his body
but did embrace the coffin that contained it, to try to stay afloat and keep from sinking
into my deep sorrow?
† All living beings (from the most unknown to the most illustrious, be they animal or
human or belonging to the intangible yet real and winding sphere of the spirits) deserve
and are worthy, I think, of someone giving a structure to and telling the tale of their lives.
Every existence, even the most apparently (but only apparently) insignificant (as much
the one that unfurls from the colorful dust on the wings of a butterfly as the one that
spouts from the spiracle of a leviathan), should be told; because we ignore the many ways
in which this could end up influencing or affecting the universal epic of the greatest men
and women yet to come and live. Thus, perhaps, in a very distant future or, maybe, on
other planets, the books will be immensely small, and their words replaced by symbols.
And all books will be one, because they'll tell a single plot that will include, simultaneously, all stories. A story that symbolizes everything in the same way that I endowed a
single and unrepeatable whale and a singular and incomparable captain with so many
different meanings. But going even further . . . Telling (because really it is always the
children who end up writing their haunted parents while those parents read them fairy
tales) how the voice of an immense delirious father tells: with no beginning, no middle,
no end, no suspense, no moral, no causes, no effects. And all of that (in a way the truest
and most invaluable of inheritances) being heard and understood by all the little children
as the depths of many marvelous moments seen all at one time.
    To be able to carry out and finish this pilgriming yet also anchored idea of mine,
I would ask the person to whom my biography will one day be assigned to, reaching
this point in the story, specify something like "Since twelve-year-old Herman had been
withdrawn from school the previous October, he was in the house all during the last
weeks of his father's life. Whatever horror the young Herman saw and heard during the
days before and after Allan Melvill's death (and what influence that might have had on
someone at such a tender and permeable age) was not recorded. And yet . . ."

II

GLACIOLOGY
OR,
THE TRANSPARENCY OF THE ICE

And therefore I looked into the great pity of a person's life on this earth. I don't mean that we all end up dead, that's not the great pity. I mean that he couldn't tell me what he was dreaming, and I couldn't tell him what was real.

DENIS JOHNSON

"Car Crash While Hitchhiking"

Jesus' Son

Listen, Herman: first one foot and, making sure the ice won't break, only then the other.

And then, out on the ice now, keeping your balance and taking a few cautious steps; the way one enters an unknown house or leaves a known house to venture out into an unknown world. Because, of course, the feeling is at once very foreign and familiar: suddenly we're somewhere we've never been though we've been there so many times or somewhere we dreamed of going (and in that way went) so many times.

But never *like this*.

The feeling of writing or saying something that was never said or written, though you never stopped thinking about it in the same language and same words as always.

Walking is the known.

The ice is the unknown.

Walking on the ice and thinking about things you only think about when walking on ice.

For that reason, again, first one foot and then the other.

Taking care not to break anything fragile or precious in the darkness or, much less, to crack the ice that holds you up and that you're advancing across on your way back home, back to your always-subsequent point of departure.

With the same devoted attention with which you'll someday dance, calculating each step and turn and bow. Like in a minuet, like in a quadrille, like in those dances and contradanzas that I so enjoyed and for which I was so admired in the best ballrooms of Paris and London.

And thus you find your footing out there, atop that solidity that once was liquid and, if all goes well and follows its natural course, will become so once again.

And thenceforth to advance with feet slightly splayed, for stability, like penguins who know the ice so well, Herman.

I wish I could get up to show you how right here.

Or better: to go down to the street together, not running, walking slowly, to explain it to you in situ: on the bank of the river, beside the frozen Hudson.

To take you to see the ice, yes.

Not so you can come to know it, because you already do; because, unless you're a savage in some prehistoric and tropical village, clearly you know what ice is.

But this ice is different, it's a river of ice.

A river made of ice.

A frozen river.

A glacial river that, suddenly, is like a winding horizontal iceberg.

A river that has paused so that we can better appreciate what a river is.

A river in repose.

A river posing.

A river like a museum piece titled *Frozen River*.

A river that is like the portrait of a river / mixed technique: water and cold. (315 mi / 507 km–14,000 sq mi / 36,000 km².)

A river (the same river we crossed so many times in a boat, the river I once threw you into so you would learn to swim with that exceedingly paternal combination of love and malice) that, in a way, has forgotten that it's a river in order to remember how to become something else.

A river that's also a bridge over itself from which nobody will ever be able to throw themselves into that same river.

A river that—paradox—left without going anywhere but that will return with spring.

And, oh, how I would love to still be here, at that time, to greet it: hearing its yawn from out in the garden as it's waking up, rising from its bed as if after a long and slow convalescence, listening to how the river creaks and cracks and breaks into pieces in order to, whole again, fully flow once more.

But, I'm sorry, I can't, I won't be able to do it then just as I can't do it now.

Move.

And it's not that I can't because I don't want to.

No no no.

Someone has tied me to this bed and at times I'm furious and at other times I'm grateful for it: thus, immobilized, I'm free from doing anything, from not doing anything right. In this way, I can no longer do everything wrong, as usual. Bound and dying, I'm held in higher esteem than I've been in a long, long time. Elevated now by that eminence that at the outset can only raise a glass (to your health!) to the infirm and terminal imminence of the end.

Thus I rest, not ready for battle but for truce, yet so soon to peacefully rest, to rest in peace.

S ometimes I think of myself in a frozen third person as well as in a warm first person. I don't think I'm the only one (or, who knows, perhaps this . . . *device*, the difference-similitude between something experienced and the experience, between the *I* and the *he*, will someday be of some use to you, Herman). It's probably something (a mental construct as invisible as it is decisive in the physical and corporeal world?) that's activated in your early youth, when you remember your late infancy. When you feel so tempted and need so badly to believe that you're the protagonist of the great novel of your life and at the same time, as a defense mechanism, just in case, you might prefer to have your story told rather than to tell it yourself. And thus, in a way, to avoid absolute responsibility for your own and most guilty and shameful acts and sins, sharing their commission with an invisible entity or author who moves us from here to there. With successive failures, of course, that feeling becomes more intense, and you want to see yourself as if you were someone else, as if those things (the most terrible things) were happening to a different person. And then blaming them on fortune or fate while evoking that unrecoverable and initial seduction of feeling more audacious and well-cast and yourself than ever.

It's like this, Herman: when I'm outside myself (and this fever has done nothing but intensify the symptom), I'm relieved by once again being able to think of myself as someone not outside of himself but as someone capable of carrying out lucid enterprises and accepting reasonable challenges that otherwise . . .

Not as if I were watching myself from outside but as if I were reading myself at a slight remove. Not overly pronounced but decisive when it comes to gaining some crucial and even strategic perspective on my own person, to better observe myself and my actions (a remove like the width of a frozen river that separates one bank from the other).

To be a good character despite my bad actions.

Thenceforth, now, the opportunity to first introduce myself (*You lot can refer to my person as that of Allan Melvill* . . . or *Call me Allan* . . . or something like that); and later transform myself into the voice that narrates everything around it, until it ends up drawing in the whole universe, until there's no longer any line between the story and the one telling it.

To be witness to my own protagonism.

To be hunter of a symbol symbolizing everything.

To be witness in order to bear witness.

As if, in a way, my life were being projected before my eyes, like everything that Cosmo The Magnificent II projected for me (clothespins holding my eyelids open to train my pupils) during not the most extensive (but, yes, the most secret and unconfessable and improbable as it was real) period I spent in the underwater chambers of his Venetian *palazzo* while on my Grand Tour.

Sometimes the feeling is even more unsettling: that third-person I (that *life* of mine) seems to me to be, also, appended with explanatory footnotes. Clarifications (whose origin or author I can't identify or recognize in the shadows of the orchestra pit or backstage and behind the scenes) that comment on my writing and dialogue and that seem to know so much about the particularities of my identity or the characteristics of the part I have to play (and maybe it's the case, Herman, that here I'm remembering something Nico C. once told me about the singular manner he and his kind had of expressing themselves and . . .).

For example:

Record and archive, even if you prefer not to:
It is Saturday night, December 10ᵗʰ, 1831, and Allan Melvill crosses the frozen Hudson River on foot.

And all this information comes to me as if in spasms, in brief paragraphs, like messages from very far away that sometimes I struggle to hear, see, read, and that, to more easily classify them, from now on, I'll distinguish with asterisks.

At first, I thought of using something like this: †

But that symbol is too reminiscent of a dagger and a dagger reminds me of a knife, and a knife reminds me of . . .

So, better, I think, to just use asterisks.

Asterisks like snowflakes or like one of those bacteria that wink at you through the microscope and that now, with infectious enthusiasm, dance inside me and make me dance and shake, as if possessed, in bed, bound hand and foot, looking up at the ceiling of this room, like *Le Fou* on the Tarot card with neither destiny nor destination: someone who bumbles along without looking where he's walking, on the edge of an abyss, eyes fixed on the sky, starless, because the stars, the black stars, are his eyes. And they're eyes that have seen too much and would give anything to stop seeing what they saw and keep seeing.

And on that same card, at my feet, instead of a little dreamed dog that could well be named Argos or Ajax, I see you.

There you are, Herman: awake, trying in vain to get me to stop so you can help me fall asleep and take me away from my hallucinatory reveries.

Listen, Herman: this sound that I make now, with a click at the tip of my tongue, as if it were flowing from the point of a pen onto paper, is the sound of a pause and an asterisk.

Like this: *

That asterisk that also precedes and separates each of the entries that I reaped out in the world to sow inside my penmanship exercise book, from back when I first began to write.

I still keep it, Herman.

There, my handwriting, first childish and round, then angular and youthful, and finally, rushed and tremulous.

It's there, in the top drawer of the desk in my study. Find it and get it and bring it and open it and, no doubt, there will be enough blank pages left, at the end, for you to begin (if you want, and I hope you do) to take my statement and become the transcriber of my memory.

Herman: you recording all these random and fevered words to lower their temperature a little and maybe make some sense of them.

But, I acknowledge, it will be an impossible task for someone of your age and vocabulary and limitations. But maybe you can trap one idea here and another there and, with time, after many years, out of the ruins and some lost jewel among the unearthed bones, you'll be able to reconstruct the splendor of my defeat.

I remember having written down there, in my exercise book, at your age, things like:

* *I will respect my Elders if I want to be respected.*

* *DICTATE: Heaven—Hell—blue sky—pain—green field—cold steel rail—smile—veil—heroes—ghosts—hot ashes—trees—hot air—cool breeze—cold comfort—change—war—cage—lead role*

* *With early Virtue plant thy breast / The specious Arts of Vice detest.*

* *Education. Forms the mind and the manners.*

* *Money runs everything.*

* *This advantage resides in all disgraces, it humbles us, & makes us wise; / And he who can acquire such Virtues, wins / An ample reward for all his pains.*

* *A generous Friendship that knows no cold, / Burns with a love, shines with a Resentment / One should be our interest and our passions; / My Friend should despise the man who wounds me.*

* *Art and Science come together in Nature.*

* *Honor and Fame, with Diademas & Imperios, are the Goals of Men of Ambition; but he who is the Master of a sublime pen transcends all.*

* *Let us be better in the Time we are given. There won't be Time for regret in the grave.*

Don't stop moving, but where to?

* There they are (from now on, each paragraph gets an asterisk, Herman), moving ceaselessly in all possible directions. Closer to vice than to virtue and with so much regret and art and science and, yes, love, all these phrases and thoughts (that I know by heart) and many more besides. And that now (it's odd or perfectly logical) I can't help but understand as some kind of intuitive autobiography in advance. As if, putting all of that in writing, I had already unwittingly made use of some divinatory ability. As if they were epigraphs. Among many but never too many epigraphs (or, better, among *extracts*; because that is a word that makes me think more of faraway perfumes like the ones I trade in whose olfactory character changes once combined with the fragrance of your own nontransferable skin, achieving something unique and impossible to reproduce: your own essence). Extracts of others at the beginning of the novel of your own life. A life that, from here onward, I choose to use Science to synthesize in order to—with all the Art I can muster—give account of my Nature.

* So I propose here the creation (though I couldn't be sure that it doesn't already exist and, yes, Nico C. informed me that it does, in the same way that next season's fashionable frock coats and hats will, inevitably, be the distortion of an echo of past colors and cuts) of a science called *Glaciology*.

But, pay attention and take heed, adapting it exclusively to my needs and interests. Thus the statements contained in the extracts that follow (disorganized yet authentic) should not be taken, invariably, as the ultimate and most meritorious gospel of glaciology. Just the opposite. The only interest or value of these extracts, with respect to the authors, generally ancient, and to poets and painters already cited and yet to come, consists in how they convey a succinct image, like the flight of a bird, of everything that's been said, thought, imagined, and sung in thousands of different ways across nations and generations (even ours, Herman) about ice and its transparency.

Thus, coming up, the systematic yet exceedingly personal study (based on a general examination of ice) of this particular variety of the species that was the ice that I walked across, days ago, the fateful night of Saturday the 10th of December of 1831.

Gelum mellvillium.

The private miracle of the once-and-for-all heroic Allan Melvill walking across the frozen waters of the Hudson River to get home.

Listen, Herman.

Lend your attention at least to this man to whom nobody would dare lend anything anymore and for whom all debts have come due.

* We've already struck bravely out across the ice of that night; soon we'll lose ourselves in its vastness with neither shores nor harbors. But before that (before your father's fever-consumed body ends up melting everything and sinking into the coldest depths), it would be appropriate from the outset to give our attention to one almost-indispensable matter so that we can understand perfectly the more than peculiar revelations that the ice will afford us and the allusions of every kind that we'll have to make with respect to its shape and substance.

What I would like to offer you now, Herman, is a systematic exhibition of ice in all its genres.

It's no mean feat.

It's like attempting nothing less than classifying the random components and scattered fragments of the most compact Chaos.

And yet: the different species of ice require a kind of classification accessible to everyone, even if, for the moment, it's but a sketch that future scholars will complete.

And since no better man has yet undertaken it (I need to convince myself, despite Nico C.'s mockery), I offer my modest services.

I'm not promising anything exhaustive, given that any human undertaking that deems itself complete is, for that very reason, necessarily imperfect. I won't attempt to attain a detailed physiochemical description of its frozen and diverse varieties or, at least not here and now, a general description.

My purpose is, simply and modestly, to sketch out a systemization of Glaciology.

I'm the architect, not the builder.

But it's also true, I must confess, that I aspire (and respire, exhaling clouds of cold vapor from my mouth and nose) to be, at least, crowned as that devoted minstrel composing and singing the exploits of the Prince of the Powers of Ice.

* But, oh, it's a very complex task. No ordinary classifier of fabrics would have any reason to be (it was neither the idea nor the purpose of my life, much less at the hour of my death, which I sense approaching so quickly and as if on the razor-sharp blades of frozen skates) up to the breadth or length or height of such an undertaking, Herman. My scissors no longer cut, my needles no longer sew, my buttons no longer button.

And yet, I'll try, because, already being the most triumphant of wastrels, there's nothing left for me to waste or lose. And when you have nothing to lose, in a way, you're already beyond defeat.

In a territory with neither name nor map.

Suspended and in suspense.

As if frozen.

And, oh, tell me, Herman: who is that in a corner of the room, seeming to float there, fluttering around my portrait that's also yours? Is it maybe Nico C.? Has he come back for me? His cape floating, as if under frozen water, unfurled like wings? Is he there or on the other side of the window, like that night in Puig de l'Àliga, when at first I mistook him for the banging of tree branches in the wind, asking me to let him in, his hands so cold and transparent and emulating the most refined of ice? Can you see him too? Or am I raving? . . . Oh, but I don't want to stray too far from the matter at hand . . .

The ice.

The Ice.

Because wandering across its fateful surface, slipping and falling and getting back up, freezing your hands in its ineffable origins, is a terrible thing. Because its surface is, in truth, the highest and most elevated part of its profundity.

I am referring here to The Original Ice. The Ice (and not the dust) whence we came and The Ice to which we will return, The Ice of the deepest and most cosmic of space. The Ice that preceded the Light That God Let Be and The Ice that shall return when our sun goes out and cover the entire surface of our planet like a mask that clings to and sinks its fangs into the face it masks.

* To begin with: the imprecise and undefined condition of this science of Glaciology is attested to from the start by the fact that in many places the key and primary point of *what* ice *is*—of its unmistakable appearance, of the many names it wears for the peoples who live in and build their dwellings out of it, and of what order it belongs to, and . . . —remains unresolved.

* Now I can't help but imagine Nico C. listening to me with one of his characteristic smiles. Cold smiles that burned. Smiles that sometimes made you shudder, and others lit you up like a bonfire.

Smiles of teeth so white, a dazzling reminder and perfect preview of the skeleton beneath the skin and muscles: teeth as the only part of our bones that demand to be seen while we're living and are indispensable for keeping us alive, to chew our food (did you know, Herman, that George Washington supposedly had false teeth made of wood that he carved himself? I don't know if it's true, that's what I was told by your grandfather, who met him, who never stopped talking about how he met him, to the point where you felt like you'd met him too or wished you never would) and restrain and contain our brazen bones, always fighting to escape their tortured prison of aches and pains.

And now, yes, I'm no longer imagining but clearly hearing his voice and encyclopedic compulsion and referential mania: Nico C. sighing in my head a "But Allan, how do you not know that *Glaciology* is a known and studied field? And has been for a while now. An interdisciplinary science that soon, with the discovery of ice on the moon and Saturn and Jupiter and Uranus, will be elevated to *Astroglaciology* . . . Not exactly novel, your thing. It's something being studied, while you speak to your son as if speaking to me, right now, by tracing the different glaciations and analyzing the nature, alpine or continental, of glaciers, and, very soon, races to conquer the poles will begin and . . . Did you know that if all the glaciers melted at the same time, the sea level would rise seventy meters? Did you know that the oldest sample of ice will be dated at 750,000 years old? Do you need me to help you with a bibliography? Here, in my own library, I have incunable copies of *Descriptio montium glacialium Helveticorum* by Johann Heinrich Hottinger, of *L'histoire naturelle de la Suisse* by Johann Jakob Scheuchzer, several books by Mikhail Vasilyevich Lomonosov . . . And I also have copies of books that haven't yet been written, incunable and unborn, by John Muir (who will postulate that it is glaciers that, through their expansive movement, draw and mold and sculpt the landscape) and by Louis Agassiz and by François-Alphonse Forel and by Freddo Sorbet and Albert Heim and by Leonard Snart ... And, oh, I was there, too, among the eternal and Antarctic snows in the southern reaches of my continent, and I heard those immense white birds sing their mad *Tekeli-li! Tekeli-li!*, flapping and soaring over walls tattooed with characters that could only come from the most pyramidal Egyptian or ancient Arabic. And I also went down to the subglacial Vostok Lake, where men won't arrive until 1970; and, there, I could feel the sleeping breath and rapid ocular and tentacular movement of all those microorganisms waiting to rise to the surface, so eager to travel in the air of the future and to enter the lungs of future people to invade and infect them with hitherto dormant biblical plagues and thereby bring about their premature departure, suddenly taking their breath away and ..."

And then, now, I interrupt Nico C. and scream at him (don't be frightened by my screams, Herman; and, also, there's no need for you to note down all these strange-named authors and books) that on all the shelves of his labyrinthine library and in all his information and knowledge of past or future millennia there's not enough space or capacity to store and contain the exact nature and composition of the ice that I crossed several nights ago with only the singular and untransferable heat that drives a man to return to the warmth of home.

Because, I'm sorry (and it's an *I'm sorry* that apologizes but does so with the most joyous and not at all guilty of sensibilities), I realize now that my *Glaciology* is, in truth, in reality, *Melvillology*.

And, yes, it's a science that's mine and mine alone.

And its theorems and equations are rooted in the (necessarily) precise inexactitude of the most mortal yet, also, for that very reason, most living feelings.

And, for once, knowing that he'll never be able to experience that desperate love for his family that I felt that night (floating above me now, my guilt that he's guilty of causing), Nico C. falls silent and dissolves and melts away.

* The ice, then. The temperature at which ice is made and at which ice is unmade.

The ice that, by definition, is water in a solid state but that is really so many other things, so many other ices.

The ice that takes up more space than the water from which it originates in the same way that the cold of sorrow always tends to be greater than the icy spark that ignites it.

The ice in the heart provoked by a cool glance.

The ice in the veins.

The ice that I study and expound upon here (thinking of Earth's poles or of the moons of distant stars) as if it were at once the eternal problem and the final solution.

The ice that freezes in a variety of structures or differentiated crystalline phases to be memorized: histrionic and hexagonal and Dante-esque and cubic and epidemic and rhomboidal and cyclothymic and tetragonal and edible and orthorhombic and mutating and monocyclic and amorphous and symbolic and maniacal and referential.

The ice that has a strong tendency toward fluidity in time (marking its passing by freezing and melting and how is it that there are no ice clocks the way there are water and sand clocks?) and that some even consider part of the mineral family.

The ice that retreats from salt but, slipping in through a crack, can level mountains when it expands.

The ice that preserves ancestral and interstellar creatures or monstruous marvels of our time, like that monstrosity galvanized and stitched together using parts of men ("Have you read that popular novel, Allan? It's not bad at all . . . No . . . You can't have read it, because it hasn't been written yet . . . It was written . . . sorry . . . it will be written by the female *companion* of a good poet and best friend . . . Barely older than a girl, running away in the name of forbidden love to wind up clinging to the heart of another dead poet, who not even the flames will extinguish or consume, in a future year, in a year without summer when the skies over Lac de Genève will be blotted out by ash spewing from Mount Tambora and falling to the ground like pieces of clouds. And her novel is, will be, constructed out of pieces. And I love this insistence among fictions of the fantastic on being composed of letters, newspaper articles, journal entries . . . As if in that way the authors thought that would make them seem more plausible and realistic, when actually, without realizing it, all they're doing is denouncing the easily torn fabric of our misnamed reality and of the supposedly real . . . But it doesn't matter. What does matter, what will matter in this book that I'm telling you about is that the idea of the fantastic is built on a kind of technological foundation. And this, I think, is a good sign that the times are changing for the better, improving, or, at least, getting more interesting . . . More or less firm or affirmative formulas instead of dubious evanescent myths. The palpable miracles of science replacing the intangible miracles of religion," Nico C. said to me).

The ice that invites you to come out and play and, also, to stay inside and delve deep into the most interior of lives.

The ice that can be reward and punishment in equal measure.

The ice that preserves our food but also covers and completely conceals it, until, lost in the clearing of a forgotten forest, we lie down to be rocked to sleep by the coldest lullaby, never to wake again and, with any luck, to only be discovered with the coming of spring or after thousands of summers, intact, our skin the color of the ice.

* What is the color of ice? Hard to say definitively. People (without really thinking about it, automatically associating ice with snow) tend to think and say *white*. And, then, to stick out their tongues to catch those first snowflakes or to lie down on the covered ground to angelically open and close their arms and legs or to, with a glee approaching that of the most playful gods, to sculpt figures not of divine clay but of celestial snow.

Maybe it would be best just to say that ice is the color of ice.

A misty transparency, like an uncut diamond or winter views through a fogged-up window.

But the truth is that (if pursuing and attaining true chromatic precision) the ice of maximum purity is blue. This is because snow, when it freezes, when it gets so cold that it's impossible for it to keep being snow, traps air bubbles inside it.

Or something like that.

Nico C. explained it to me (while expounding on "red and yellow and green photons" and "chromatic molecules" and "dispersive particles" and "the snowy light of the sun"; and I thought not about what he was saying but about him saying all of it to me) as we walked, our footsteps rhyming, through a frozen Piazza San Marco and the arias of the gondoliers scarcely warmed the frigidity of the canals they glided through, breaking the ice with their oars as if they were lances or harpoons.

"Which doesn't prevent (Nico C. continued) there from being, in polar regions, a hopeful green ice and even a burning bloodred ice, due to almost-dissolved algae particles in the water or to the presence of a variety of microorganisms on the suddenly temperamental ice floes."

I ask him how he knows, how he could know.

"I saw it," Nico C. says to me, closing his eyes not to stop seeing but to remember better. "I saw it," he repeats.

And, then, Nico C. opens his blue eyes so they can pierce the eyes of the now-in-third-person Allan Melvill and keeps telling him about the color blue. About its "wavelength" and its standard variant and the etymology of *azul* as being Hispanic Arabic or Arabic more broadly or Sanskrit or even as coming from the Greek lexeme. And about blue as a result of the European combination of *bleu* and *blewe* and *blao*.

And Nico C. smiles as (here *I* am back again) he tells me that, in Japanese, they call it *blue to green*. And I don't ask him anymore how he knows so many languages for fear of his answer or because (as he tends to do or not do) he won't answer except with that smile. A smile from which, between rows of small and sharp teeth, all the knowledge in the world ceaselessly spills.

And smiling Nico C. tells me that, originally, blue pigment was extracted from lapis lazuli and other minerals and plants. And that it is one of the four primary colors (and I tell him, with absurd pride, that I already knew that; but that there aren't four primary colors, there are three, and Nico C. tells me that there is a fourth primary color but that "your pupils aren't yet capable of perceiving it"). And then he adds that within a decade blue will *also* be considered a "psychologically cold" and "subtractive secondary" color and, as with Jehovah, "contracting to become infinite." And that among its many shades (cornflower, steel, Alice, navy, cobalt, Klein, Egyptian, electric, Munsell, marine, ultramarine, French, maya, Prussian, blueberry, periwinkle, turquoise, indigo, sapphire, azure, cerulean, YInMn . . .) his favorite, "for obvious reasons," is "Electromagnetic Spectral Blue, which resembles the blue of the Olympic swimming pools of the future." (Allan Melvill asks Nico C. what that shade of blue is; "Look into my eyes and then close yours," Nico C. tells Allan Melvill; and, again, the feeling that the first person is reduced to the third and that seconds stretch out into hours, into entire nights; and that the body of Allan Melvill is part of the body of Nico C.)

And Nico C. reveals that there is a color blindness to blue. And that, due to its poor linguistic representation in the ancient world, philologists (what might that be? I wonder) came to believe that in those days the Greeks and Romans suffered, because of some kind of optic-genetic disorder, from "tritanomaly" which made it hard for them to appreciate the sky and the sea, which they always assigned a kind of roiling jet black or the bloody brown of good wine (and Nico C. adds that "it won't be long before someone explains why the one and the other, the sea and the sky, are blue).

And then Nico C. explains the divine differences between the dancing blue of Vishnu and the plumed blue of Huitzilopochtli and the watchful blue of Śakra and the medicinal blue of Bhaisajya-guru Buddha and the recurrent blue of the veils of the violated and unconsenting Virgin Mary.

And Nico C. confesses that for him letters have colors, thus there's the blue of steely x, the blue of thundercloud z, the blue of huckleberry k, and the blue that blends with pearl to achieve the precise shade of the letter c.

And Nico C. distinguishes the blue in the blood ("the real color of blood, Allan") of all those people convinced or trying to convince you that God has chosen them to reign over the Earth (and who, unlike the peasants and workers, spend little time in the sun and so much in candlelight, and their pallor is such that it reveals their azure circulatory systems, which can only be irrefutable evidence of class and aristocracy).

And Nico C. points out that blue is the preferred color of flags and uniforms. And that there aren't many traces of blue in prehistoric paintings, but that blue abounds in the palaces and tombs of Thebes and Babylon and Knossos and Pompeii, and in Byzantium and in Islam and in the striking ruins of the Constantinople hippodrome. And that in the Middle Ages (with the exception of the beturbaned Tuareg) blue lost ground in the robes of princes of the Church and in their cathedrals right up until the reconstruction of the Basilica of Saint-Denis and the installation of *vitraux* in Chatres or in the Sainte-Chapelle. And that soon the paintings of King Arthur begin to present him dressed in blue, and Louis IX likes the idea, and ultramarine blue becomes the star of Renaissance painting and of the azure and dynastic porcelain of China. And that the exploitation of *Isatis tinctoria* or woad brings down the cost but enriches the possibilities. And that then, beginning in the seventeenth century, European chemists launch themselves into the quasi-alchemical pursuit of the "perfect blue," trying to recover the formula lost in the disorienting Luxor sands for synthetic Egyptian blue. And that, by pure accident, a German pharmacist illuminates Prussian blue. And that it's then imported to Nagasaki with great success, which leads to that painting of the giant wave that within a few years a painter named Katsushika Hokusai will begin to paint ("a painting that reminds me so much of that curl on your forehead, my dear Allan"). A blue that will be greatly appreciated by a group later known as the Impressionists "and also by my favorite abstract expressionist: the visionary of extraterrestrial horizons and dead by suicide Mark Rothko, who will make even more obvious his love for blue by renouncing it completely in a chapel of the future, in a city that's American yet somehow foreign, the air riddled with lead and dust and three languages all at once."

And listen to Allan Melvill listening to Nico C. referring to the blues and to blue jeans and to a titanic blue iceberg that'll sink a supposedly unsinkable ship bigger than a castle and to the burning hot *blue movies* ("Soon Cosmo will show you what a movie is and will be. Our favorite is about ice and snow and miracles") and to the sad blue of dead bodies.

And among all those blues, Herman, one is missing: my blue.

The *so blue* Melvill Blue: the blue of the ice of the frozen Hudson River that I crossed on foot in order to, between one bank and the other, keep from falling down and losing my mind.

* A mind that, in a way, here and now, I'm trying to recover, Herman.

Come and see, ladies and gentlemen: Allan Melvill, as if horizontally crucified, on sheets that nobody would consider holy or worth guarding to worship as religious relics (a couple washes in boiling water would suffice to exorcise their demons so his abandoned wife would be able to use them again without fear of possession).

And, sure, I suppose the way I express myself (but actually, so far, quite akin to Nico C.'s way of expressing himself, Nico C. whom I'll soon introduce you to, Herman, in a clearer way and in greater detail) won't be the most calming for you.

Forgive me.

And I hope that these lists of slightly capricious information regarding the capricious behaviors and variable tonalities of ice don't have a toxic and deforming effect on a mind in formation such as yours. And that they don't cause irreparable damage or constitute the worst of influences as it relates to your mode and style of expressing yourself, verbally or in writing, in a not-too-distant future . . .

You've said more than once that you like reading and writing, Herman. If so, please be merciful when it comes to the senselessness and confusion your father is going through right now, crossing a frozen river, trying to get back home . . .

Sure, what you say is true: I'm already here. But only in body; my soul is still out there, suspended between one shore and the other: between the shore of sanity and the shore of madness.

And, between the one and the other, that flaming and frozen torrent that is Nico C.

*Nico C., then. Because, Herman, you've probably been wondering for a while now who—or *what*—was and is Nico C.

And it's not easy to describe him, because, to begin with, Nico C. is another form of ice, of my ice, of The Ice in which I now burn and in which I've burned since I met him.

Terrible rumors of every variety never cease to exaggerate and make more menacing the true stories of certain lethal and sinful encounters. Because not only do legendary voices sprout naturally from the body of all surprising and terrible events (just as a wounded tree provides sustenance to its fungus), but also, in the frozen life, extravagant voices abound whenever you give them a reality they can latch onto and first bleed dry and then burn to ash.

It's no shock, then, that having spread by moving through salons and parties in palaces the world over, the increasingly complex rumors regarding Nico C. were enriched with all kinds of morbid and amorphous and vile insinuations regarding his thaumaturgical abilities. Murmurs and twittering gossip that ended up investing him with novel terrors and tantalizing perversions unrelated to anything of the visible world. One of the extravagant hypotheses in those antiquated and superstitious minds (again, I insist, like any child of the Colonies, I can't help simultaneously disdaining and envying them; because there's nothing more wishfully credulous than the mentality of European nobles and aristocrats obliged to

believe that they are quasi-divine beings) was that Nico C. had
been spotted in multiple places (at receptions and celebrations), of
opposite latitudes and longitudes, at the *same time*. Naïve as these
minds had to be, such an idea (as you'll soon see, Herman) was not
lacking slightly more than a touch of probability. Because just as
the secrets in the behavior of ocean currents have never yet been
faithfully pinned down by even the most erudite research, likewise
the hidden byways of Nico C. (and of his kind), were and will forever remain unknown. And from there, the most curious and con-
tradictory speculations sprang; above all regarding the mysterious
means, after sinking to tremendous depths or ascending to great
heights, that allowed Nico C. and those of his kind to travel with
enormous speed to the most faraway places. Coming and going.
Now you see them, now you don't, now you see them again, and
let's see how they went and in what way they came back. Some
went further still and said that the omni-absent Nico C. was not
only ubiquitous but also immortal (given that immortality is nothing but ubiquity in time); and that proof of it was the appearance of
his face and name in paintings and memories and even in ancient
sculptures. (And I can attest to this. Visiting public and secret museums in Nico C.'s company, I discovered his face in the faces of
emperors and martyrs and even in the faces of mythological beings,
framed in silver and gold, in light and shadow.)

But, setting these extraordinary conjectures aside, there was
more than enough in Nico C.'s appearance and immediate presence to spark the imagination with startling power. Nico C. was
the most beautiful being anyone had ever seen, and legion were the
men and women who pursued him with impassioned monomania.
Some men and women, in the desperation of their abandon, had
even been driven to operatic suicide, throwing themselves into the
mouths of volcanos, and to monastic reclusion, and even to the

mutilation of their extremities, offering them up for his return and the return of his affections. Others had fought duels or poisoned rivals, convincing themselves that in that way they could possess him. The ones who had tried to kill him (because if I can't have him, nobody can, they cried) had lost their lives or won their deaths in the attempt. Many, on the other hand, chose the somewhat safer and less exhibitionistic option of, alone after withdrawing from all social activity, going mad with no hope of ever coming back.

And I've already told you a great deal; but there hasn't yet been a glimpse of the vaster, darker, deeper side of Nico C. (as well as his reasons for choosing me) in this part of the glaciological Melvillology.

It's pointless to divulge the most profound things; and all truth is profound, Herman.

Let us leave, then, the infirm heart of this room in this Albany house and strike out, O noble, broken souls, for the immense halls of the Old World where, far below the fantastic towers of the human surface, is buried the root not of the glory of man but of the beings who transcend him, the ones who came before and will outlive us in all their terrible presence, residing in the most virile pomp and circumstance: Nico C.! A relic buried beneath antiquities and enthroned atop torsos of statues! Thus, on a broken throne, the great gods mock that captive king (or at least that's what we mortals want to believe). Nico C., like a caryatid, keeping still and patiently seated, holding the accumulated cornices of the centuries over his frozen visage. Come down there, ye most downcast and proudest of souls! Question that proud and cold and blue king! He has a familiar air, yes, because though nobody looks like him, we all wish we were him or like him. Nico C. who, for everyone, always ended up resembling, in a mysterious and surprising way, the Great Devil Errant of the Ices of Life. How to pin down where Nico

C. carved out that subterranean track that runs through all of us, guided by the ever shifting and muffled sound his scepter makes? Who doesn't feel the irresistible arm pulling you along?

For my part, I surrendered to the abandon of the circumstances and gave myself to Nico C. as I'd never given myself to anything or anyone before.

And Nico C. accepted my gift the way one accepts a sacrifice, a sunset, a greeting, a snowfall, a river without a bridge because the bridge was the river and the river was Nico C.

* And, of course, the deceptive transparency of Nico C. was the transparency of ice. The transparency of something that freezes and burns simultaneously. A transparency I clung to and found terrifying. An almost-impossible-to-explain transparency. Even though, for many natural objects, the transparent emphasizes their beauty by refining it, as if imparting some special virtue; even though in the highest and most indissoluble and insoluble mysteries of the most august religions, the transparent is a symbol of divine purity and power; even though in the Apocalypse of St. John, tunics of an almost translucent white are worn by the redeemed and the twenty-four elders are thusly attired before the great white throne and The One who sits there ("What're you talking about? What've you been drinking?" Nico C. interrupts); despite all these accumulated associations with and within all that is sweet, vulnerable, and sublime, something elusive always hides in the private idea of this color that's not a color; something that instills more panic in the soul than the horrifying red of spilled blood. This elusive quality makes thinking about the transparent, when separate from the most pleasing associations and connected to some in-itself terrible object, exacerbate the terror to the maximal degree. Could the transparent then be the power to see all (power sees all) or

the powerlessness of knowing ourselves fully seen? Could it be that the transparent casts a shadow with its vagueness across the void, the unforgiving vastness of the universe, and stabs us in the back with the thought of nothingness, like when, provincials of Ursa Minor, we stare out at the cosmopolitan and lacteal depths of a spilled Milky Way? Might the transparent actually be a color fallen from the sky? Or perhaps, in its essence, transparency isn't so much a color as it is the visible absence of color and, at the same time, the fusion of all colors, which would explain why such a vacuity (silent and simultaneously pullulating with meaning) exists in a panorama paralyzed by a shudder-inducing atheism toward all color? And when we consider that other theory of the naturalist philosophers which holds that all the other earthly colors, all majestic or striking ornamentation (the sweet shades of nightfall in forests, the dusty golden silk of butterflies, those other butterflies that are the cheeks of children like you, Herman, and the butterflies that find no place in the dreams of the wise Chinese of the past or in the nets of Russian writers of the future whom Nico C. read to me), would be but clever ruses. Burning deceptions not inherent to real substances but superimposed over them from the outside, such that *Divina Naturaleza* would be painted as a prostitute with a flaming body and a frozen heart whose incentives only cover the inner sepulcher and final resting place. And when we go further and consider the mystical cosmetic that produces each and every one of its shades (light's great beginning is colorless and if it didn't operate through a medium, it would drape everything, even the most brilliant and fragrant flowers whose scents are their colors, in its neutral and odorless hue), when we get into all of this, I say, the paralyzed universe arises before us like the most polychrome and suppurating of lepers. And akin to those future Arctic explorers who refuse to wear tinted eyeglasses (and Nico C.

claimed to have been one of them, but with intact and invulnerable eyes, capable of the most nocturnal of visions), the unfortunate nonbeliever stares to the point of blindness at the monumental blue and transparent shroud that falls across and eventually envelopes every landscape.

Nico C. was, for me, the symbol of all these things, yes.

How can the ferocity of my obsession with frozen transparency surprise you, Herman?

I've learned that the ancient Romans used a small white stone to represent a good day and a black stone to represent a bad one. There's no information, however, about them using transparent stones to represent anything. I postulate here (like an aristocrat from my bed-rostrum, its wooden headboard carved with the date of my marriage to Maria and our interlaced initials and the successive birthdates and names of our sons and daughters) the glacial and Melvillogical certainty that transparent stones are used to represent unforgettable days.

Days like the day I met Nico C.

* Like this, then: Let there be light so that we might know darkness.

The very particular half-light of certain European palaces or mansions. The weak light of a few candles dwindling in immense spaces whose function is not entirely clear: could it be to illuminate the darkness or to darken it, making its diminished power more obvious?

In any case, now and then, the ballroom is full of people who appear to melt into the walls and furnishings. The feeling of floating in the skies or sinking to the bottom of the sea. Muted voices that every so often crackle with a burst of laughter that sounds more desperate than happy. And looks that pierce like pins or daggers or, in the best of cases, like thorns of withering roses. Everyone is there to see or be seen, though it's no mean feat to capture details and twisted smiles or fake moles or motheaten wigs in the eternal twilight of that space as immense as the belly of a leviathan.

Better that way.

And now everyone looks at Allan Melvill, who just entered with that combination of shyness and arrogance that characterizes all New-World natives passing through these spaces. Atmospheres where you glimpse the once gleaming past (everyone here appears to have, yes, a shining past but, also, the least lustrous of futures) clinging tooth and nail to a far less glorious present.

And they all turn (turn on their heels, like in bad novels) to see him walk through those opening doors.

And Allan Melvill gives a bow and it's unclear if it's meant to honor or mock them. Because Allan Melvill still hasn't recovered from the surprise of how provincial all these vintage aristocrats are: all they do is talk about themselves and for them the world doesn't appear to stretch beyond their properties or the pigeon-hole of their faded coats of arms that are no longer brandished or ennobled on the battlefield. While, Allan Melvill thinks, the flashing new barons of a thundering America seem to think just the opposite, understanding their nation as a kind of diving board or canon from which to launch themselves, right now, without delay, into the conquest of the planet. That's how Allan Melvill thinks and wants to feel and be felt. Like the most conquering of conquistadors.

And, watching from one side of the ballroom, the only person who appears truly interested in him and even happy about his appearance and presence is that pale young man with white hair who appears to have made the nature of ice his own: someone who appears deceptively transparent and yet, it's impossible to tell what he's hiding beneath that cold exterior. And the young man (who, looked at closely, seems not to have a fixed time, his face passing from one age to another with each word that spills from his red lips) approaches Allan Melvill and introduces himself in an English that has a ring of the artificiality of something consciously learned by someone foreign and distant and far beyond the simple variations of accent. The precise English and refined French he speaks are languages without inflection, of an almost soulless correctness, and as if devoid of all personality, sounding more like something read in silence than spoken aloud. And in which, first in one and then in the other and then in a third, Spanish (which Allan Melvill doesn't understand), what he says now (so that Allan Melvill reads it in the heavy air that hasn't known open curtains and windows in a long time) is:

"Welcome, my name is Nicolás Cueva."

"Nicholas?" Allan Melvill asks.

"No: Nicolás," Nicolás Cueva repeats. "But my friends, and I hope that you might be one, usually call me Nico C."

And he reaches out a hand that, more than a hand, resembles a delicate and dangerous albino animal, a hand asking for another hand, and that other hand belongs to Allan Melvill.

* And it's clear, Herman, that maybe it's not very wise for you to hear what I'm saying. I'm sure that your mother (who has naïvely left you here, at the foot of my bed, as a sentry, to watch over me and attend to my needs) never suspected that I would submit you to the story of all of this, of my ... let's call it, in capital letters (the grave capital letters marked by a sharper voice, as I mark them now), WHITE DELIRIUM.

White Delirium.

White.

And transparent.

And frozen.

And I raise my voice and then, from there on high, I scream.

And have no fear, Herman.

Don't run.

Don't go, please.

Come back.

* You'll have plenty of time to go once I'm gone, Herman.

You'll go as I once went.

To travel.

To go on a journey.

And I have always (I'm lying, not always; I'm only thinking of these things now, dis-eased, physically bound and mentally unleashed, understanding language as a virus from beyond this world for the first time) found those two ways of expressing the same thing as both amusing and intriguing: *to travel*, where it's you who does the action, and to go *on a journey*, where things are no longer quite so clear; where there's no longer a precise separation between the *journey* and the *traveler*; where you're no longer making the journey *happen* for yourself, instead, the journey is *happening* through you. Suddenly, you're a part of the journey because inevitably the journey will *travel* you. Not only will the outside landscape shift but the inner world will as well.

Thus, the difference between the common *traveler* and the select few who are *well-traveled*.

That's what *happened* to me, Herman. That's how I *happened*.

That's how it happens to me now when I retravel my journeys by remembering and trying to make some sense of their trajectory and of my trajectory while traveling them. And I take it up and retrace it, thinking of my past in a way that so far I've never thought of my present. The geometry of space applied to the optical errors of time and the proof that the past, ever fleeting, never stops moving. My memories of those journeys belong to me because I belong to them. But it's a strange form of belonging and of ownership. A *foreign* form. Something *your own* (because it's you who traveled) but, at the same time, not exactly something *you own*. In a way, it's like one of those chests full of little drawers and secret compartments that you never stop discovering and never fully use or in which, later, so long after returning home, you discover a letter, a dried flower, a scented kerchief that someone dropped so someone else would pick it up. Something akin, also, to those cabinets of curiosities overflowing with wonders.

And, yes, most people travel in search of pleasures and comforts (and to, in the end, though they'd never admit it, experience the happiness of first starting to return and then actually being back home) and only a few do so with a curiosity almost ineffable to their loved ones: to go very far away and find that something that, they already know, they'll never find in their own city and home. That something that, to find it, you have to go out looking for it.

And, again, I never stopped to think like this.

I never understood words as entities that applied to this kind of idea (for me, words have always been, merely, the names of people and places, verbs conjugated for simple and primary actions, ways of being more or less courteous or striking up a romantic or business relationship). I never again expressed myself to myself in the sophisticated and deliberate way I did back then, when I traveled, when I was the most traveled of travelers.

* And now I discover that I've regained something of that way of seeing and understanding things when I remember all of that, Herman. The fever of the past sweating beside the fever of the present. Suddenly, once again. Then, everything once figurative departs and returns as abstract, and the Grand Tour of Europe of my youth is suddenly far more than an itinerary and a succession of hotels and modes of transport and postcards and journal notes.

And the intensity of the phenomenon became (went and came) far more powerful when it involved leaving this immense new country. A nation like a planet. It wasn't easy to cross its borders because, to the west, America was everywhere and ceaselessly beginning again so it never had to end. Thus, the only possible option was to point the prow east. From Boston to New York and from there to Europe even though . . .

* . . . every tale of a journey is a deception. Sure: you can specify a route by enumerating cities and rehashing the order in which you visited them. But the essence of that journey will always remain diffuse and fluid, like everything that you see while in motion.

More water than ice, yes.

With time (I'm sure, an idea to commercialize, take note, Herman, this may be useful within a few years) people will be able to buy and sell nametags for all the secret sites and grand capitals they pass through and even for the luxury hotels they visit. And add them next to their surname or initials on their luggage, affixing them there (as if they were the happiest of scars and broken spears protruding from the back of a biblical beast or, sometimes, when it's a trip that would be better to forget, like menacing and rippling tattoos, already almost features of the hardened skin or the torn tarpaulins of a freakshow) to configure a kind of nomad and portable memoir. And later caressing them as if they were the most beloved of pets, the best of all possible company. Sitting down to look at them, back at home, void of content yet full of memory; thinking about when the moment might come to dress those suitcases and trunks up on the inside with our clothes and go somewhere far away, as far as possible. Because in the most and best hidden compartments of all imperfect trips (the ones booked to save on money and documentation) the possibility of a perfect escape always rears its head and demands acknowledgement. The temptation to never go home and from then on every journey, with no returns, would be one-way.

* On my Grand Tour, I felt like that, I felt that.

And it was Nico C. (and Nico C.'s world, which appeared not to figure on any official atlas but seemed to bite the neck and feed off of that known world) who made me feel it.

And what's that feeling you get when, with perspective, you realize that the most important part of your life was, in a way, outside of what your life had been before and would be thereafter.

The journeys that in my hypothetical biography (or, who knows, maybe in your future biography) wouldn't take up more than four or five lines without anything too eye-catching and accompanied by a couple of dates and minimal details about one of the business deals I tried to make during my stay in Europe. Those journeys that now (paradoxically less of a traveler than ever, bound to my bed and speaking not in foreign languages but in almost personal tongues) stretch and expand and fill the space that belongs to them and that they deserve.

And that space knows neither borders nor nationalities and it was Nico C. who explained to me that "countries are nothing but different masks for trying, in vain, to hide the true face of the world. A face that laughs at the longitudes and latitudes imposed by men to convince themselves that they're not lost and that they know the way back to that more or less common artifice, to that agreed-on mirage that, to find calm and not feel so lost, they've taken to calling *home*."

Which doesn't necessarily imply that I (I, who, I hope, don't now belong, infected, to the order of the species of Nico C.; I, who, resisted with a final jolt of reason or, who knows, madness) won't be as precise as I can in hand and in mind when it comes to times and locations.

Mine is not (understand and forgive me, Herman) a quirk of style or an aesthetic choice. It is, simply, my commitment to trying to be as realistic as possible. Not that false reality of *realist* novels (in which everything reads and is structured in such a convenient way and with dramatic *crescendos* and placid valleys and such perfectly placed *allegros* and *agitatos*, like in the score of a symphony) but the disorder constantly interrupted by zones of silence and resumed with the most polished of harmonies or the most discordant of notes.

True reality, though you may really doubt that all of this is truly real.

The life lived and not lived.

And—looking at you look at me, Herman, with eyes in which I believe I can anticipate the very singular wisdom you'll one day possess—I can't help but think that everything I'm theorizing about *novel* and *reality* is not something I think but something you'll one day think. And that now I'm nothing more than a specter for whom you're a medium or you're a specter for whom I'm a medium. Either way: because now it's time to try to give an account (ellipses and advances and retreats will abound, Herman, that you can indicate, or not, using suspension points, as if leaping from one to the next, as if they were stones in the narrowest and shallowest stretch of an already melted river of a future summer) of the phantasmagoria and masquerade of my days and nights with Nico C., on my Grand Tour, so long ago that it seems as if it were right now.

And I must ask a favor, Herman: go up to the attic and get my traveling trunk and bring it here and open it before me. Even though I don't have nametags for the places I visited, it'll help me to remember more and better. My trunk will open like a door or a tomb where an archeologist of the self will unearth first a temple that conceals beneath it a still more ancient shrine and, deeper down, hides (irrefutable proof of intelligent life on other planets) a monolith, overflowing with voices and outside of time, that is nothing more and nothing less than the signal commemorating the most important event of our life to be transmitted to the stars. Of that blessed moment that (in general, with the running and falling of the years, depends on the day or on our mood) seems and appears to us as something prehistoric or something that hasn't yet happened or hasn't yet stopped happening.

* In the same way that an architect might have an architectural vision and a doctor a medical perception and a chef a gastronomical elaboration when it comes to their respective assessments of reality, understanding the reality of each as the one that's familiar to them and about which they know something/more (I suppose that only writers, if they're any good, can consent to the cursed blessing or blessed curse of a potentially maddening plural point of view above and beyond the strictures of their profession), my recollection of my Grand Tour will inevitably be textile. Feeling and weighing it like a fabric unto itself. Something that begins with the soft and possibly predictable texture of virgin silk to, subsequently, shift its condition on the loom and mutate into something closer to a fabric used for the weaving of ceremonial tunics or guillotining curtains. Another shade: Subterranean Blue Velvet, or something like that. The blue of the deepest and most magnificent ices. An element that's liquid and mineral and harmonious and dissonant

all at once. Something that looks like a shade descended from on high or a substance pulled up from the depths. Ideal for worshipping or being punished by deities of such sonorously consonant names. Perfect for enveloping or preserving the stuff of dreams and preventing them from melting away or being forgotten.

Thus, what I unfurl first is a certain predictable normality of my travels.

The Atlantic crossing of the ocean.

The strolls across the deck and the bows to the captain, whom you hear coming before you see him: he has a pegleg and, when some passenger gets up the nerve to ask him how he lost it, he makes reference to battles of ever-changing names or to some duel with a marine beast, or he limits himself to smiling with the most eloquent of silences. The songs of sailors swinging from the tops of the masts. The affected laughs (that more than really laughing seem as if they were practicing laughs to be laughed in a soon-to-debut show in wedding halls of London and Paris) of the young heiresses traveling in groups and closely watched over by aunts and mothers and hunting some ancient title of European nobility that'll elevate their ranking in the mansions to the north of the *nouveau-riche* Manhattan. The foreigners returning home and already exaggerating their adventures in the, for them, so savage New World and buying trophies that include Sioux feathers and bottles of something that's not yet named bourbon and even a handful of gold nuggets pulled from the teeth of riverbanks in a febrile North Carolina. The circular storms and the straight-line stillness and the onboard priest kneeling and praying for the return of favorable winds and the numbered days. The nausea and the discreet vomiting overboard and the inexplicable rushes of euphoria and the moments of profound melancholy that, sometimes, produce the irresistible urge to throw yourself into the waters, as if responding to the silent call of invisible sirens. The rats conversing with the dolphins. The occasional random pieces of the jigsaw puzzle of some glacier. The shapes of clouds (some of them repeat over and over) like tattoos on the shoulders of the sky. The game of chess between a father and a son. The salty wind on your face and the sun setting behind you to rise on that liquid horizon where the moment grows ever closer when someone will shout "Land ho!" the way once upon a time someone grunted, in the first of all languages, that grunt equivalent to "Fire!" And before long, you discover that looking at the sea is the same as looking at a fire blazing in a fireplace (thinking about how both water and fire think, because both make you think so much when you stare at them, thinking about fire and about water).

And there I am.

So far from home and closer and closer to myself, telling myself that it was during those days, as if in flames and on the waters, that I was truly born. I'm going to Europe to become *someone*. Finally with some direction, because up until that point, I feel that all I've done is walk in circles, around a small and provincial space. Now, at last, I've broken the chains of the gravitational force of that comfortable and familiar orbit. Now I'm going out into the world and the world is coming out to meet me, Herman.

And the first thing I do (though many people will think that, again, once more, I'm misspending my money) is pay a genealogical researcher in Kew Gardens to trace the origins of my clan. Only with my feet set firmly in the past, I think, will I be able to gather momentum to project myself into the future. My own name reclaimed in order to impose it (name as brand) on the name of everyone else. *Nomen est omen* and, thus, thence, it doesn't take long to have the memory disinterred before me of one Galfridus of Melville, baron of Malaville in Normandy, a Scottish noble under the reigns of David I and Malcolm IV and William the Lion. And, yes, his name has an *e* and mine does not; but no matter, either way, it's a minor detail attributable to so many things swept away or carried in by the winds of History. And, sure, maybe I've let my enthusiasm and a certain voracity typical of Americans get the best of me and have also included the nobles Melville of Raith and of Monimail among the branches and leaves of my family tree. And among all of them, of course, over the centuries there's also some inevitable traitor, accused of conspiring with the English invaders and summarily executed, which, I think, only makes my lineage more charming. And then Melvilles as devout advisors to the reigns of Mary and Elizabeth and ambassadors in England and even one descendent (Elizabeth Melville, Lady Culross), who becomes the first female Scottish writer to have her writing printed as the author of the "small epic" *Ane Godlie Dreame*. And later, the Latin poet and polemicist Andrew Melville and his nephew James, "of a prolific prose and author of a much-admired *Autobiography and Diary*." And then, later, the theologian Thomas penning his *Observations of Light and Colours*, based on his mastery of the art of oil and watercolor painting (and I wonder whether among his pages he dedicates any reflection to the luminosity of the transparent). And as you see, Herman, writers and artists abound. And, enthused, I visit the recently restored Melville Castle and present myself as a legitimate descendant of the people who now own it: the exceedingly respectable Dundas family. And they invite me to spend the night with them and welcome me as one of their own and ask me for a parchment with the seal of my family coat of arms: a hound's head over a red and white plait and circled by a belt with a big buckle and the Elysian motto *Denique Coelum*. And, yes, I feel that I'm in Heaven at last, but ignoring that the distance that separates it from the far more appealing and entertaining Hell (and yet, there are many people who believe in Heaven without feeling obligated to believe in its complementary counterpart) is significantly less than what's assumed and the border far more porous than what's thought. More membrane than border, Herman. Something as thin and flimsy as the eyelids that separate light from shadow and that, if you keep them half-closed, you can perceive equally the possibility of the luminous and the certainty of the darkness.

And then I opened my eyes wide shut and shut my eyes wide open.

Watch me cross that line and push past that limit, Herman.

Watch me pass through everything to separate myself from everyone: walking on the flames and answering the call of Nico C. the way I would later walk across a river of ice to burn, the way I burn now, engulfed in fevers and chills and unforgettable memories.

Denique Infernum.

* If Heaven is the place where nothing ever happens, then Hell is the place where everything is always happening.

Then, now, Allan Melvill descending into the depths of a salon in a *palazzo* of Venice, in the Isola della Croce, everywhere and nowhere.

In truth, all of Venice lies in the depths, because it was built atop liquid lowlands, carved out by the cold tongue of the last glaciation, Nico C. tells him.

Venice and its red nights.

Venice smolders, Venice burns.

Venice is for Allan Melvill the suffocating sensation of an impossible-to-suffocate fire even though it's surrounded by water.

Venice like an underwater animal, the belfries like harpoons in its back.

Now, there outside, *acqua alta* and the rising sea coming in under the doors and through the windows like an undesired yet entertaining guest; and the novel sensation of feeling submarine and amphibious; and Allan Melvill, stretched out on a divan, dreaming waking dreams.

Just arriving here in the company of Nico C. (in a gondola recalling a duck with jet black plumage) brought Cosmo The Magnificent II, lord and master of the place, out to greet them on the esplanade: all of him stuffed into a suit of impermeable material the likes of which Allan Melvill had never seen or touched and that he immediately understood as worth importing. Wearing something on his feet that resembled duck or frog feet. His face behind glasses that clung to his face like an inseparable part of his eyes. And, on his back, like a backpack, a pair of metal tanks with a tube coming out of them and running to his mouth, which makes it a little difficult to understand what Cosmo The Magnificent II says next: "Original design by Leonardo, the only man more magnificent than I, but, it must be said, *only slightly* more magnificent . . . But he's no longer with us and I'm still here. I'm named Cosmo because I'm as cosmopolitan as I am cosmic; though I need to leave my *palazzo* less and less: because it's here, *proprio qui*, that the indivisible nucleus of the universe takes time and place, where all things and all times converge . . . Welcome to my home! Enter freely. And take care upon your departure to leave behind some of the happiness you brought with you."

And Cosmo The Magnificent II says this last bit and he and Nico C. burst out laughing, as if sharing some secret joke whose punchline only they are privy to.

And Allan Melvill just smiles to avoid appearing ignorant or impolite.

Cosmo The Magnificent II shows them to their room (for a while now, Allan Melvill no longer thinks or prefers not to think about how nobody seems to consider it pertinent to offer him and

Nico C. separate bedrooms, even if only separated by a door) and invites them to toast their arrival.

"What I've served in your glass, Allan ... Uh ... How to explain it? Nico has told me that you're an expert in the procurement and selling of luxury items and exquisite merchandise. Well, what you're about to taste is a liquor but also a fragrance ... And a place ... And a remembrance and a dream and an invention ... And this is the only bottle that exists, blown by the maestro of glass and mirrors Sudarg of Bokay. It was developed by medieval monks from a secret recipe of which only a few of the ingredients mentioned in different *vade mecums* are known ... Like the intermingled and misplaced pieces of a puzzle. I've discovered the shape and color of only three of them and I prefer not to continue my research, because it's not for dignified people to attempt to reveal the magic of a secret or the secret of magic: a pinch of the sands of Zerzura, sweat of lustful virgins, and the tears of Cetus, that sea monster that Perseus had to slay to save Andromeda ... And it's so powerful and intoxicating that it only takes a few drops to sweep you away without you moving from wherever you happen to stand; and, once you've tasted it, you'll never stop missing it. Maybe that's why it's called Canzoni Tristi and why its bouquet evokes the most burning of ices."

Outside, across the high waters, across the crests of the flood, the maddening African *sirocco* blows: Sirius escaping his leash to fog and frazzle the minds of men.

And I, Allan Melvill, drink and inhale ("Death to the chronology," Cosmo The Magnificent II exclaims as a kind of toast) and then everything experienced up until that point on my Grand Tour seems to rearrange itself, like postcards being shuffled with the same deftness that others devote to illusionist illusions or games of chance that are never that magic or that random. There's no trick here nor was there one there. And suddenly, I felt as if the entire history of the human race was tattooed across my face and was, at the same time, my own history.

I couldn't comprehend the exact reason (though I experienced and suffered a sudden awareness of it) why the dictatorial stage directors that are Moirai and the Parcae had theretofore assigned me such a lackluster role, while letting others play sublime characters in great tragedies, or brief and easy parts in salon comedies, or monologues more absurd than comical in farses. Suddenly, it was as if I'd been elevated from minor character to dazzling lead. And even though I couldn't explain the exact reason (now that I'm a prisoner, bound to this bed, I remember all the circumstances of my carefree abandon from back in those days), I think I discern something among the props and springs that, skillfully concealed under various costumes, induced me to play that part, while deceiving me with the chimera of a choice made of my own free will and judgment.

Primary among those reasons was the overwhelming idea of Nico C. occupying every last corner of my thoughts. A being so extraordinary and enigmatic, arousing a curiosity and fascination I'd never felt before. And, later, the choppy seas and untamed territories where Nico C. set his shadow of light to spin—illuminating thousands of landscapes and winds—only fed my longing. For other men, perhaps, none of that would've been an incitement. But I was tormented by an irrepressible longing for exotic and faraway things. I felt I was inhabiting a predictable life and surrendered to the exile of the unforeseen, of sailing forbidden oceans and exploring wild coastlines. I told myself (contrary to what our religion dictates) that it wasn't a sin to ignore the good if I then perceived the horror. And that it was even worthy and in a way sacred to be able to live on good terms with it, as long as the horror allowed me to.

For all these reasons, I welcomed the journey and the escape and Nico C. as my captain.

Then, the great gates of the world of wonders opened before me and, among the mind-bending imaginings that propelled me toward my goal, oscillating in my soul, two-by-two, came an interminable procession of possible miracles. And through them, a giant ghost, hooded and tall, approached, reaching up into the air like a mountain of snow and stretching out across the ground like a meadow of ice.

And in his hand he held a blade.

And, blessed and serene, like the most obliging of masters with his servants, with that blade he shaved me.

* And Allan Melvill, approaching him with a sudden passion, said to Nico C.: "Few are the profound beings I've met who have something to say to this world . . . Will you one day abandon me?" "I would prefer not to abandon you," Nico C. answered, softly emphasizing the *not*, with that accent of his. And he added: "Take any path you choose, and ten to one it'll lead you to a valley and leave you by a placid pool. A pleasant place, yes, but so safe in its normality. Whereas one out of ten paths . . . There's magic in it. It allows for the most distracted of men to sink into the deepest and most oceanic and stormy of daydreams: set that man on his feet, set his feet in motion, and they'll inevitably lead him to water, if there's water anywhere in that region: but those waters will be of unpredictable behavior and will never know stillness. Yes, as everyone everywhere knows, meditation and water are forever wedded. And the product of that meditation between the invisible and the liquid is the solidity of the ice . . . Look, Allan: it's starting to snow . . . Look, Allan: it's snowing in Venice."

* Thus, the snow in Venice was the continuation but not the consequence (it was a snowfall like the first snowfall in history, chronol-

ogy had died by order of Cosmo The Magnificent II) of the snow in Boston and Albany and New York. Nor of the snow in London and, there, the huge squirrels of Hyde Park; so big (the direct descendants of the squirrels that Henry VIII once hunted there with a crossbow) that they looked like squirrels wrapped in coats of squirrel fur with green sleeves. And, by night, the ballrooms where the lasses of the aristocracy were pale and beautiful, but their teeth resembled country manors abandoned years ago and their dresses were decades behind, which didn't deprive them of the visual ostentation of precipitous necklines that refused to diminish or cover up the spirit of more licentious times. And there were moments when, he could swear, those creaky suits of armor positioned in different corners of rooms appeared to move, as if somebody were inside them. And, there, everyone performing complex waltzes: arms loose and curving and interlinking like swans' necks; and me, causing a stir, Herman. Because the way I danced those choreographies was respectful and yet, at the same time, it had about a certain ferocity of parts untamed that stopped just shy of indecent.

And, again, it is there that I meet Nico C. so that he might know me.

And we talk while, in the corners of the ballroom, everyone talks about us.

And Nico C. invites me to dance a dance that he teaches me as we dance it.

"A dance for men, a dance of my homeland," he says in my ear.

Dancing with Nico C. is like dancing with a spider: he has too many legs and I too few.

And our heavy breathing silencing the whispers of everyone watching us dance, hiding behind fans or feigning scandalized fainting spells.

And I ask Nico C. about his strange accent and Allan Melvill asks him where he was born, and Nico C. answers me and answers Allan Melvill that he doesn't really remember; but that he has spent a lot of time, "lately," at the bottom of the continent, at the end of the world, surrounded by ice, in a metropolis that, "unlike so many other nonexistent ones, whose tempting myths the conquered used to take revenge against their conquerors, is real and is called Trapalanda or Errant City, and it never stops moving, and I move with it and it accompanies me wherever I move."

And, moving him and moving us, days and nights later, the snow in Paris and Nico C. and I at the foot of Notre-Dame, on the banks of the Seine, where a lost humpbacked whale has wound up. And the faithful have fallen to their knees beside her, taking her as sign from on high and praying an "Our Father of All the Whales and all the Leviathans in the Ocean, have mercy on our souls, amen."

And the whale accompanying them, singing her last heartbroken song.

And the funereal and final aria of a geyser spouting from an orifice on her back, like the fount of an almost dry and broken voice that will never sing again.

And Nico C. says to me: "Oh . . . Few things are as moving as the need of human beings to see miracles everywhere they look so they can keep believing in the impossible . . . Whales and earthbound mammals, including men, wander sometimes and end up in strange places. These wanderings tend to be an error; but sometimes, and with the right guide, they end up the most enriching of experiences."

And then Nico C. says the strangest thing he's said yet:

"Do you dare enter? Do you have the courage to cross over?" Nico C. smiles and points at the whale.

And we enter her and with her we cross over.

* Later, in Venice, time passes and doesn't pass and seems to fold in on itself. Allan Melvill and Nico C. walking across frozen beaches of floating cemeteries and glass factories. And the *palazzo* of Cosmo The Magnificent II (Cosmo, who, Nico C. explains to Allan Melvill, is "one of us, one of the ones who you, I believe, might end up becoming if you really want to"), appears to grow more and more rooms. And so, to keep from getting lost, Allan Melvill looks at and studies the ever-shifting scale model in the middle of one hall that displays a longitudinal cross-section of the building.

And me, Allan Melvill, taking notes, Herman: I believe that my diagrams and itineraries are there, in my notebook. Though my clumsy sketches will never give you an idea of what it was like and what it felt like to walk through that place: all those sounds in the shadows, sounds not only of whirring machines in perpetual motion, but, also, unhinged screams and half-stifled cries and the varied melody of a solitary piano piece that lulled you to sleep but never allowed you to stop hearing and revering it. All of that and more as if rising from the metallic insides of some ghostly engine and superimposed over the timeless breathing of a singular and supposedly extinct beast, inside of which I lost myself and never stopped finding new marvels.

And suddenly, descending a staircase that, I could swear, hadn't been there days before, a zoo of free-ranging animals ("A *palazoo*," Nico C. jokes when I mention it to him). But all of them (including gorillas and elephants and lions and a two-necked giraffe and a turtle from the Galapagos Islands, its shell decorated with precious stones, and a tiger whose stripes reminded me of the bars of a cage that, perhaps, was my own and that I'd entered of my own free

will), all of them behaving in an almost human way in their civility
(I'm referring here to civil people, of course).

And then a room full of chairs facing a taut white curtain where
there was . . . projected? . . . the huge face of a man, driven to desperation by debt, in the middle of a bridge over a river and under
the falling snow, wishing he'd never existed. And I look at him and
hear him and feel his despair and his desire to jump and to put an
end to all of it and to himself as something I might end up feeling
myself.

And, farther down, a kind of colossal aquarium where there
swam the palest of fish: a kilometer long and with three rows of
teeth ("*Guarda Il Terribile Pesce-cane, L'Attila dei pesci e dei pescatori,
native dell'Isola delle Api Industriose!*" exclaims Cosmo The Magnificent II.) A beast of the waters singing in a liquid human voice a
song of good parents and their lying children (or vice versa) and
sending up its prayers to a sort of incorporeal yet omnipresent deity
or "Big Sky": something or someone who doesn't watch over us but
does, every so often, look down on us with a gaze between sympa-
thetic and dismissive.

And, oh, the many and increasingly numerous secret rooms and,
inside them, the secrets spoken from the burnished throats of automata with names like Ella-Elle-Lei and Madame Mirror and
Ta-Lei-Sei and Lady Kismet. And me playing with them, though,
really, it is they who play with me, trapping me between their legs
and wrapping their arms around me. All of them going in and out
of swimming pools and, apparently, immune to rust or fatigue after
all the ecstasy they bestow on me. Do I penetrate them, or do they
entrap me? Either way, it doesn't matter when what we're talking
about is perfect mechanics applied to a generally imprecise and
unpredictable act, because it is fueled by feelings. No: it's not love.
It's not even making love. And sometimes (and then the formula

of the mechanical and utilitarian is transformed into something else, into inexact science, into impassioned unconsciousness), Nico C. and Cosmo The Magnificent II join us and we're all one. And then the entire *palazzo* seems to tremble like a ship in a tempest and to want to cast off its moorings and get lost at sea, lost like me, though in Venice I feel more in my place and time than anywhere I've ever been before.

And Cosmo The Magnificent II talking all the time, but more than talking, delivering disquisitions, about the relativity of time: about the paradox of how one sibling who is born five years before another is five times older at the other's birth and how that distance diminishes as the years pass. "The explanation is simple and terrible: each of your remaining summers will be winter: because each one is, progressively yet reductively, a shrinking part of your thin and finite existence: the time of nobody, which is also our timeless time, expands such that your human time contracts, like a sickness and not like a cure," Cosmo The Magnificent II recites, marveling then about the "relativity" of how something described as immediate in a letter takes weeks and even months to reach its recipient, who, upon receiving it, experiences it as something that just happened, because they're only just learning about it. And Cosmo The Magnificent II almost howls, "a time will come when good and bad news will be known as it is happening and this, though convenient, won't necessarily be a good thing; because it'll be conceived and composed continuously without any reflection or care; and then the present will be a continuous thing with no caution or concern for what it was and what it will be."

And suddenly, as if overcome by the power of his own ideas, Cosmo The Magnificent II seems to run out of energy, like one of his automata, and, not expecting a response, almost sighs: "And, oh, my dear Allan Melvill: if you could see everything I see, everything

I saw, everything I will see . . . All of it, simultaneously . . . All of it would be lost in time, like laughter melting in the snow."

* And then Nico C. leading Allan Melvill out of the room and almost apologizing for Cosmo The Magnificent II's soliloquies.

"He's been alive too long; his energy is almost depleted; he's the oldest one of us I've met," Nico C. explains to me. And he adds: "He's no longer what he once was and is increasingly prone to outbursts and accidents . . . Not long ago he completely lost control of his brigade of *scopautomi*, his sweeper automata, and flooded and almost submerged the *palazzo* . . . And yet Cosmo The Magnificent II is so much more than any other . . . He's one of the founders of the cosmogeny that governs our orbits, Allan."

And then Nico C. warns me about the risks of his condition, about the dangers of proposing "a new form first of understanding and then of narrating things that alter the texture of the fabric of History . . . That's why I brought you to Venice, to enlighten you: because in Venice, even the strangest thing seems and is plausible, because Venice is in itself a true impossibility."

And we went out walking and came to the Grand Canal (to the *Canal Grando*, the *Canalasso*) and discovered that it was frozen.

"Allow me to explain it to you in a clearer and more practical way . . . Hear me once more, I'll give you the most profound explanation not with words but with deeds. All visible objects, my friend, are but cardboard masks. But in every event, in the living act, in the resolved action, something unknown yet always reasonable projects its features across that unreasoning mask. And man wants to lash out, has to lash out against that mask! I invite you to be part of a maskless world, Allan," Nico C. says to me.

And Nico C. walks across the water, across the ice.

Or maybe, I'm not sure, the water freezes behind his steps, with each step that he takes.

* Things that Allan Melvill thinks after getting to know Nico C., after recognizing the true face beneath his mask.

Things Allan Melvill never thought about because he never thought like that before.

Suddenly, the language with which his mind expresses itself is so different from the one with which his mouth expresses itself (until recently they were the same; as I said: rules of etiquette, pleasantries, innocuous words punctuated by some insult or profanity only when he drank two or three drinks too many and was among friends).

Out of nowhere, ideas presenting themselves no longer as brief and appropriate and simple phrases but languidly stretching out and as if adorned with parentheses and dashes and exceedingly exigent subordinate clauses.

Allan Melvill thinking about abstract questions; not only about himself and his needs, but, also, about the invisible yet exceedingly complex mechanisms that seem to drive or halt all Creation.

Allan Melvill (who doesn't doubt that all of this is due to the influence and proximity of Nico C., who increasingly strikes him as a being not of this world, his glassy eyes and sharp and cutting smile, as if wound and weapon coexisted within it) reflecting on the common hereditary experience of the human species, ceaselessly bearing witness to the magical nature of the transparent. There can be no doubt that the most common feature in the visible appearance of the dead and the one most frightening to those who look at them is their azure and marbled and crystalline pallor; as if in truth that pallor were the sign as much of consternation in the other world as of mortal vacillation in this one, Allan Melvill thinks. That translucent pallor of the dead that significantly suggests the color of the shroud (and for that reason you must take great care when selecting the cloth to wrap the dead in, like when you choose the cloth of the sheets in which you unwrap a young wife on your wedding night, it occurs to me). Not even in our superstitions do we stop covering specters with the same mantle, the ghosts that rise out of an amber mist, I think. But yes, even as these terrors dominate us, the King of Terrors himself rides a pale horse, Herman. Here he comes, hear the galloping and snorting of his mare of the night. Therefore (though the man, with a less melancholic mood, symbolizes with a frigid non-color all the grandiose and beautiful things), nobody could deny that this color, in its deepest spiritual significance, evokes a particular *spectrality* of the soul. But if this point is established without objection, how could the mortal man explain it? Analyzing it seems impossible. Might we have a right to hope for some clue that will lead us to the hidden cause we seek if we cite some cases in which this transparency casts the same, though slightly modified, spell on us (even though, given the circumstances, completely or mostly cleared of all direct association that communicates something terrible)?

Do you understand me, Herman?

Does anything I say make sense?

Have I explained the lesson well enough or will I be failed?

Is my science science?

* Is Nico C. hoping to educate Allan Melvill? Why? To what end? Or, maybe, he understands that proximity to Great Art arouses the senses and stimulates the sensibilities. And it's true that Allan Melvill is not what you might consider cultured. For him, books were always the best place to hide perfumed letters or to dry flowers stolen from the gardens of the sweetest-smelling damsels of

Boston. And reading the Bible, at mass, was always the perfect excuse to know and to be known (he goes to mass not to believe in The Other but to try to get others to believe in him). Subjects of culture were always limited, for him, to fleeting topics of conversation, to what fills the few empty spaces between one whispered rumor and another behind kerchiefs or fans. His specialty has always been the good life and everything that gives it oxygen. His excellent eye for luxury items and his ability to anticipate trends (Allan Melvill isn't so good at managing money, but nobody's perfect). Thus, what many savor in a good wine or perceive on a visit to the studio of a young bohemian with the plaster and marble and color to succeed in the annual salons, Allan Melvill perceives with his fingertips (that's how Nico C. reads: the lines of his almost worn-away fingerprints seeming to voraciously and rapidly feed off the lines of books), as if they had invisible eyes in them that allowed him to detect the best Russian satin or the best linen from the Nile.

Which doesn't imply that Allan Melvill devalues paintings and sculptures (because they looked so good framed by heavy curtains or well-upholstered armchairs) and that he doesn't now feel a shudder looking at the painting that Nico C. points out to him, in London, before Paris and before Venice.

"Ah . . . Fuseli," says Nico C.

"*The Nightmare*," reads Allan Melvill.

"Magnificent example of chiaroscuro," Nico C. continues. "This painting appears . . . will appear on a page of that novel with the living-dead creature that I already told you about. I suppose that when its day comes, you won't read it, but hope is the last thing you lose. Maybe I should tell you that its pages contain very detailed descriptions of imported luxury items or something like that, because is there anything more valuable or desirable than the possibility of a dead man who's been *imported* back into life from the Great Beyond? . . . Ha . . . And look at that painting: don't you find the red brocade canopy and that blanket and those sheets in the background to be really striking? And what could be in those jars on the nightstand? Aphrodisiac powders, some kind of elegant, somewhat illicit sleeping potion; that melodic and melancholic perfume that, I expect, Cosmo will have you smell and drink within the next few days? And, oh, again, the symbolism . . . The symbolism that is our reason to be and not to be . . . What would we be without it? The symbolism that awakens all dreams to all interpretations. Let's put it this way, for example: in this painting, you're the sleeping damsel, and I'm the incubus crouching atop your body . . . And the nightmare, the mare of the night? Let's say that that mare is everything that you don't dare mount, but unbeknownst to you, you're already riding it toward the abyss, Allan."

* Then, a few halls beyond, Allan Melvill and Nico C. pause in front of *Snow Storm: Hannibal and His Army Crossing the Alps*, by J. M. Turner. "That painting that you see on that wall hasn't been painted yet, just as the novel that I mentioned hasn't even occurred to its author yet, but, if you pay attention, it's all happening, Allan . . . But there are times when time freezes and folds in on itself and you can glimpse what will be discovered with the thaw, there, already captured, all times at the same time . . . The dead and the living and those yet to live and yet to die . . . That's why I want you to see it . . . Look at those vibrant colors, they seem to ring out, they seem to speak to each other," says Nico C.

There it is, there he sees what others will one day see: that dark wave-cloud of snow and ice almost closing over the eye of the sun and looming like a wave over the Carthaginian army. The fury of the elements as the manifestation of the wrath of the gods. Or something like that. The same painting, also, as if shaken by strange forces: nontraditional composition, shifting of the axes of perspective, a style ahead of its time that hasn't yet arrived. A little too close to how Allan Melvill has been feeling since he's been accompanying and being accompanied by Nico C. (multi-personal: he accompanies Nico C. and Nico C. accompanies Allan Melvill). Avant-garde, yes, and that's how I would like you to describe and write me, Herman. Me as the worthy winner (though unworthy to others) of the consolation prize so oft not received by one who, in the shadows, congratulates himself, wanting so badly to convince himself that his present defeat will sooner or later be reassessed as a future victory. Hannibal, after all and notwithstanding any storm (his legionnaires in golden armor riding elephants in the dark of night), crossed the Alps the way I crossed a river.

"And to the point, Allan, that indomitable curl on your forehead looks a lot like that storm, doesn't it? Your curl like a nightmare in itself that appears to me in all the paintings and is, no doubt, deserving of being immortalized in painting itself, I think . . . Could this be a manifestation or syndrome of what all of you call *love* . . . of *being in love* . . . of having *fallen in love*? Could it be that I am humanizing that much? Does it maybe mean that I'm entering a new age of splendor and decadence? Could you, Allan, be a good or bad youthful influence on this ancient being of antiquity?" Nico C. says to Allan Melvill, running his hand through his hair, tousling it and then laughing a laugh that's more teeth than sound; while Allan Melvill wonders if he's dreaming or if he's ever been awake.

And so it is that Allan Melvill and his indomitable curl were painted in that small portrait. The portrait surrounded by white lace: as if he were wrapped in a shroud of ice and cold, as if his figure were a stake driven into the heart of an insoluble ice floe. His other I, which looks down at him now, tied to his bed, the curtains drawn and only illuminated by the glow of the fireplace (and a painting is not worthy of being a painting until it's contemplated by the light of a fire that enlivens its figures and moves its shadows). That portrait not fixing me with its gaze but fixed to the wall where it hangs.

* Back to that painting. Again. Not my portrait or the one of Hannibal but Fuseli's, *The Nightmare*. And, oh, my portrait (in its youth and vigor, so fresh, as if just painted) seems to me now, also, like a bad dream; because it's an impossible and irrecoverable dream and thus the most disturbing of all. (And, oh, that paradox that's always unsettled me so much: that every bitter nightmare gave way to the sweetest waking, realizing that wasn't true; and that the sweetest dreams turned into a bitter nightmare when you opened your eyes and understood that none of it was real.)

Here and now, Herman.

In my memory, when I remember it, it's as if I were painting it. Just like it was, but with its symbolism altered though intact in its ability to symbolize. And I am still the damsel. Even more than I was back then. In bed. Not fainting but hallucinating and bound hand and foot. And the horse is my memory of Nico C. galloping with and through me with no reins that could slow our ride. And maybe that little monster is you, my son. Though not crouching atop me but standing at the foot of my deathbed. Not hallucinating me but hallucinating everything you're hearing and writing down now to tell who knows when.

Your first work.

The thing that'll turn you into a writer and me into something written.

* Allan Melvill asks (I ask) Nico C. whether he's a ghost or a vampire. Nico C. smiles and pauses for seconds as long as centuries and (answers me) answers Allan Melvill. And he does so by clarifying that his way of clarifying something is not to make it more comprehensible but "in the characteristic way we have of expressing ourselves: like footnotes, making the impossibility that your kind will understand all of it even more obvious, because it's impossible for you to understand all of it."

And that's how Nico C. speaks to Allan Melvill and speaks to me, with the same tone and cadence of an adult explaining to a child something that he more or less assumes the child knows (or that it will be good for him to learn) about where we're going and where we came from.

Nico C. tells him and tells me:

"I'm neither the one nor the other, Allan—I'm both. Ghosts and vampires are not supernatural or impossible beings but, actually, the most natural constructs of human fear. A way of using fear to frighten away your terror of death (a terror that, no doubt, arises from your insecurity when it comes to thinking of death as a sort of sculptor who strips away all imperfection from the stone until it is polished and reveals absolute purity or, to the contrary, as those cosmetics that get applied to corpses to conceal decay and bad living, wanting to make the fakest and sweetest of sleeping visages appear convincing) as well as a way of thinking that you can go on living after it . . . Death, which, in the eyes of the living, in the act itself of dying, transforms a dirty man into the cleanest of dead, cleansed and sullied by tears . . . False comfort and true lie . . . Like that whole thing about how, you want and need to believe, you're born and die alone. Just the opposite: in the beginning and at the end, there are always other people. True loneliness is something that takes up ample place and a long time

between one end and the other ... Horror and hope ... The Great
Beyond of man is nothing but another chamber in the heights or
in the depths of the ever-teetering house of his ideas. Basements
and attics that are frightening to ascend or descend to. Spaces that
are compact and infrequently visited (because you're all so afraid
of going up or down the stairs), but that are always present in
the architecture of every religion. That's why you humans prefer
to believe in somebody you don't see than to believe in us. That's
why you think you've got us cornered or you attempt to examine
and describe us in pagan legends and in cheap and shabby pulp
novels, when really, valuable and valiant, we're everywhere and in
plain sight. Better like that: our power resides in your desperate
desire to *not* believe in us, to not *believe us*. We are and will become
more popular as fictions and more impossible as realities. It's not
ideal, but it ends up working fine for us. I myself, in appearance
and manner, will be a commonplace, a serial cliché. A role for different actors or playwrights to play or to write with little variation.
And, yes, you'll all be so busy and distracted reading about us or
pretending to be us on the stage, with exaggerated makeup and
false fangs and operatic howls and beyond-the-grave rancor, that
you won't even notice when we finally decide to step forward and
conquer the theater of the world and its horribly cast spectators.
But there's no hurry, we've got time, time does not contain us,
and we're quite content to be as we are: an open secret that all of
you choose or pretend not to hear though it's announced with a
scream. Perfect for me, the effort you all demand of us is so minimal ... How'd it go? ... Ah, yes: *Brevis esse laboro, obscurus fio* ...
And we, of course, have taken great advantage of it and of you, but
in a far subtler and more elegant manner than what you attribute
to us. We don't need your blood, and much less are we interested
in floating around covered in sheets and rattling chains. We don't

feed *on* you, but we do *feed* you. We don't frighten you, but we do make you aware of our act of extreme generosity: the act of *giving* a fright, of causing fear. We're not non-dead nor are we dead who come back. We are, let's say, beings who un-die in the sense that the Christian preacher Ælfric of Eynsham gave us at the end of the tenth century, when he coined the term and adjective *undeadlic* to describe the immortality or impossibility of God dying. An expression that later mutated into *undead* and that describes people brought back to life by a "strange force or entity." Likewise with *revenants*, which just means *returning*, but to whom, perhaps to make that condition more bearable for nearly all the unfortunate others, is then attributed an insatiable thirst and fangs and coffins. And we're diagnosed with allergies to sunlight and to mirrors (there's nothing we enjoy more than looking at ourselves in the mirror, Allan; nothing pleases us more than recreating ourselves, examining our delightful singularity, in the mornings, when all of you look like zombies, do you know what a zombie is, Allan? Have you read *Le Zombi du Grand-Pérou, ou la Comtesse de Cocagne*, another of the many little novels devoted to us that nobody remembers anymore?). And we're set up as foes of mediums and exorcists and so many other Vatican frauds and superstitions that your faith, which should be cause for amusement, actually uses to frighten all of you and keep you in thrall to its power for the glory and benefit of that other rather improbable Holy Spirit and Holy Ghost and Resurrected Undead who, just like his Father, violator of virgins, is somewhat absent when you need him most and—do you all really believe that the symbol to which he was nailed has some kind of effect on us? . . . Oh, it's touching: the invocation of all those instruction manuals for ways to destroy us that you all have invented in order to tolerate just sensing our presence and to convince yourselves that you can expel us at will from your parties. Wanting and wishing to believe that we are devils, when really we're more akin to your angels, but more reliable and worthy and deserving of your faith ... But I fear that it's not and won't be like that, O fearful humans. Ours is the real party and you haven't been invited. And we can't even offer you the consolation of the superhuman. It's all far simpler and more impressive and more humiliating for all of you: we are rare, privileged mutations, evolved organisms, hopeful monsters come originally, perhaps, who knows, from another planet with a name like an onomatopoeia and number, maybe to make it slightly more precise for all of you, riding a meteorite at high speed, leaving a wake of stardust. We're random specimens of a species not yet constituted as such; reproducing with methods more mental than physical; the chosen who choose; *born* before your time when it wasn't yet known if your environment was entirely prepared and ready to receive and accept us, because, of course, this would require that a vast majority allow in and yield to an exceedingly rare and infrequent superiority ... We're like all of you but far better ... But, if you prefer and if it makes more sense to you, so far and almost clandestinely, we're a combination of your imaginative and fearful fantasies. Something (and I'm going to use the Spanish words of the place not where I was born but whence I came, combining the words for ghost and vampire, *fantasma* and *vampiro*) that might be called *fanpiro*."

Then Allan Melvill shudders (I shudder) and (ask) asks Nico C. a question, while thinking something very strange, the strangest thing he and I have ever thought: that he feels and I feel like a character in a novel who—suddenly, without ever having given any indication to the disconcerted reader or having felt any interest in such a thing—wished he was or *could become* (as one possessed) a writer, to give account of the beauty and glory and incredible and irrefutable truth of Nico C.

"And what's it like to be a *fanpiro*," Allan Melvill asks (and I ask), as if already taking notes, the way you're taking notes now, Herman.

And Nico C. (choosing his words with great care, as if they were small fruit picked, one by one and without hurry, from the branches of a tree in the dark) answers both of us:

"Well . . . Among other things, we get neither cold nor wet when it snows, but that doesn't stop us from enjoying the snow . . . And we don't know how to lie . . . Let's say that being a *fanpiro* is a little bit like what you all think being a ghost or a vampire is like, but, contrary to what you want to believe and even wish, with one noticeable and decisive difference: we're far happier to exist and not nearly as weary of being alive as all of you."

* And Allan Melvill (I no longer dare invoke myself here in the first person, out of shame and regret) feels stronger and is happier than ever with Nico C.

And Allan Melvill (who can't help but wonder what it would be like to live without weariness and without lies; and he doubts that that would really be happiness, because he always liked snow, feeling the snow and explaining it as such, because what reason could snow have to exist if it didn't make you cold or get you wet and didn't, also, offer you the pleasure of drying yourself later by the warmth of a fire) prefers not to ask anything further . . .

* . . . because there's no need, because Nico C. keeps answering the questions Allan Melvill thinks but doesn't ask, as they climb the stairs to one of the *palazzo*'s terraces. High up, in a forest of what, I think, are lightning rods.

"Antennas," Nico C. corrects me. "Up here we broadcast and tune in the signals of our love and the messages of our wrath to and from others of our kind in other parts of the world; we're like pirates of the air, always coming aboard, we're the treasure that refuses to be buried, Allan," he adds.

And up there there's also a planetarium and the biggest telescope (like the eye of a cyclops aimed at the heavens) that Allan Melvill has ever seen and, now that I think of it, that is and was the first time I saw a telescope, Herman.

And Nico C. says to Allan Melvill: "Look . . . Why waste time with questions about my origin and about all that lost and regained time when, here, put your eye up to the scope, you can see all of it at the same time. Past and present and future in the frozen vastness of space. The Original Ice to which we'll all, inevitably, return, within millions of millions of years. I can imagine it, because I can see it, Allan: first the stars bursting, extinguishing their light. There won't be any hydrogen left to combine with the helium to locate the stellar cauldrons of the cosmos. Then the stars, jewels hurled against the nebulous ruins, will begin to accelerate in their rotation, spinning like whirling dervishes. And the galaxies will lose shape and the constellations will mingle their myths and it'll no longer be easy to distinguish Cancer from Scorpio and Pegasus from Centaur. All together now and then. And with the decay or not of protons (many of these names will be the ones given to many things and elements not yet named, but already everywhere since the beginning of time, Allan) the majority of the forms of matter will melt and ravenous black holes will reign with mouths always agape devouring any flicker of light. And nothing will make any sense and the dead stars will be like iron whales gravitating magnetically toward their graveyard, until they too collapse in a whirl of vapor leaving everything empty and silent and, who knows, maybe then it'll all begin again and . . . But I've brought you here, Allan, to ask you and find out if you want to be there and then to see all of that with me, at my side, together and inseparable . . . To be clear, I cannot offer to make you one of us . . . All those rumors are not faint but perfectly audible to us; all of your unconfessable wishes; all of that in which you almost desperately want to believe and need to experience as punishment and curse, but that you actually long for, like the most precious of prizes; all those almost-touching longings related to profane trans-mutations that will elevate you and turn you into a member of our species through the exchange of bodily fluids, I fear, have no real foundation, Allan. Likewise, you're not necessary for our sustenance and survival . . . I insist: we're not interested in having you believe in us, after all, we don't believe in you. We don't need you: we don't wish to be considered permissive parents to be tricked or strict parents to whom you end up writing letters explaining why you're so afraid of them; and we don't want you to worship us like obedient or misbehaving children . . . And, oh, again: there's something as ro-mantic as it is pathetic (yet also intriguing for us, I must admit, the best of spectacles and, in a way, so *alimentary* and *nutritious* for us) about your guilty longings to be absorbed and possessed, which you pretend to dissimulate with fear and an exceedingly weak resistance . . . But, I fear, none of that is possible. No: we're not *infectious*. We're self-sufficient, we don't reproduce (your species is not biologically useful to us; we ourselves are and guarantee our own continuation). And much less do we have any appetite or aspiration to mix with you, just as it would never occur to you to get romantically involved with your adored yet inferior pets, right? For us, sex is just sex, and it begins and ends in itself and is something closer to an experi-ment than something to experience. We value it and are, clearly, more than worthy of your desire and admiration when it comes to putting your theories into practice and making them come true by descending to the heights of your ecstasy. We know (it's so easy) how to pleasure you like no other. But for us, passion, true passion, doesn't need the physical, it transcends it. Neither blood nor semen

nor ectoplasm are ingredients for the elaboration of our secret recipe, which is impracticable for anyone else . . . Again: I can't offer to
make you like me, to make you one *of* us. But what I *can* offer you,
Allan, is to be one *with* us. Privileged witness and accomplice: the
balcony with the best acoustics at the Opera, the location with the
best light in the Atelier. Great Art. Something akin to the gift not
of writing us but of reading us. To be *your* book though you're not
my author. Reading, if done well, is the closest thing to writing that
exists, Allan. And I promise to transform you into a distinguished
reader-author: the best and most, yes, *authorized* reader on the face
of the Earth . . . Here and there and everywhere. With me. At my
side."

And Allan Melvill, feeling himself chosen, falls to his knees,
surrendered; and he loses consciousness under the stars, moved
by the love that sets them in motion and immobilizes him as if,
weightless, he were floating in infinity, not with all the time in the
world but with all the time in the universe.

　* Until one night Allan Melvill realizes that, if he stays with Nico
C., there won't be any way of coming back.

It's winter and the impassioned liquidity of his consciousness
turns into the most solid and frozen of guilt.

And Allan Melvill is afraid.

Nico C. frightens him.

And best that you know this now, Herman: when something or
someone frightens you and that fear gets inside you (even if that
something or someone is unaware of it), there's no going back and
all you can do is move forward.

Thus, Allan Melvill believes and convinces himself that he must
escape; because Allan Melvill is afraid instead of coming to terms
with the fact that what he's actually afraid of is the increasingly

proximal condition, of staying with Nico C., of never being afraid again, and of it being like that always and forever, for the centuries of the centuries.

And being without fear, Herman (each and every one of the commandments received by Moses are redacted with the obedient syntax of fear and can be summarized as just one: *Thou Shalt Fear*), is the greatest and most unforgivable of sins.

* Allan Melvill understands then that he's not woven of a resistant fabric. Allan Melvill accepts who and what he is. And Allan Melvill is nothing special (and it would be terrible to be like that forever, he tells himself). And, in the worst case, nothing prevents him from thinking that, sooner rather than later, Nico C. would get tired of him. And who knows (but he doesn't want to know and doesn't dare ask, because *fanpiros* cannot lie) how many preceded him in the position that Nico C. is offering him now (among the many other positions that he'd already given in and submitted himself to, and that Allan Melvill preferred not to think about then and prefers not to remember now). And, oh, Allan Melvill can't help but imagine the sight of broken and used-up bodies along the side of a road or of devastated minds under lock and key in the basements of lunatic asylums. He imagines these things as if they were paintings but paintings that were constantly being retouched, adding new figures, and who might that man with a curl across his forehead hanging from a tree be?

Allan Melvill feels damned and doomed.

Allan Melvill flees.

Allan Melvill steals a gondola and reaches solid ground and makes arrangements and embarks for Barcelona and spends the night in the outskirts high above the city.

In a tavern in Puig de l'Àliga, which its owners refer to as Tibidabo, he asks where that name came from. And a priest, Father Maple, sitting at one of the tables and with the air of having spent decades there, drinking and blessing parishioners with a slow and heavy hand, tossing them *benedicas* with the same indifference with which one throws corn to chickens, explains to him that it comes from *Tibi dabo*, which in Latin means *I will give to you*. That it's taken from an expression found in some verses from the Latin Vulgate Bible of Saint Eusebius Jerome of Stridon, from a passage in Mathew where the Devil, floating across the desert sands, offering all the kingdoms of Earth to Jesus, says to him, "... *et dixit illi haec tibi omnia dabo si cadens adoraveris me*," or, "And saith unto him, all these things will I give thee, if thou wilt fall down and worship me"; adding, in Lucas, "... *et ait ei tibi tabo potestatem hanc universam et gloriam illorum quia mihi tradita sunt et cui volo do illa*," or, "All this power will I give thee, and the glory of them: for that is delivered unto me; and to whomever I will give it."

Or something like that: Allan Melvill hears all of it but doesn't really listen, because he's worried about quieting the fear coursing through his veins and throbbing in his temples.

And hearing it (those words so ancient but seemingly meant for him now and from the beyond of the millennia), Allan Melvill falls to his knees and between sobs confesses everything and begs for salvation. And, even in his desperation, Allan Melvill can't help but notice and disapprove of the coarse and dirty wool of the priest's poorly cut and stitched habit.

Father Maple listens to him and absolves him and, more as a form of forgiveness than of penance, gives Allan Melvill a blade.

And he says to him: "I could give you a crucifix, but I think this blade will be more useful, my son. It's one of several, one for each apostle. It was forged in a Catalonian *farga* after melting the sword that Enric Coriolis de Vallvidrera, a knight templar who was born here, took with him on the Crusades, from which he returned holding a piece of wood from the Messiah's cross. I think you already know what use you must put it to when you are caught by what pursues you, my son . . . Bless you and may God protect you."

And Father Maple says this to Allan Melvill with the sadness of one who knows that God only protects to a certain point, and that Divine Justice is something that in truth it is up to men to impart.

In His Name.

"Men are the weapons that God uses," the priest says to a still kneeling Allan Melvill.

And Father Maple makes the sign of the cross above his head as if shooing away flies.

And, while he's at it and in vain, he tries to adjust that bedeviled curl on Allan Melvill's forehead and, just in case and making no attempt to hide it, to make sure that the filthy and oily light of the febrile Mark of the Beast doesn't shine there, while outside, in the dark, a herd of pigs under the command of a noble and beaming white-haired wild boar snorts.

* That night, Allan Melvill hears a knocking on the window of his room.

And Allan Melvill opens the window to let the darkness in.

And the darkness, when invited in, always enters so that you can enter the darkness.

* Of all the feelings I hope never to feel again, Herman, there's none like burying a blade in the breast of another. Again: the perception . . . the impression of passing through something. The sensing of something that, suddenly, ceases to beat and the stillness and silence becoming so apparent in the hilt that still vibrates like a tuning fork.

And so, feeling my fear crest into ecstasy, I slashed that face again and again, the face of Nico C., with my blade, feeling that in that way I was crossing it out, forgetting it, turning it into another face.

And so, feeling his fear crest into ecstasy, Allan Melvill slashed that face again and again, the face of Nico C., with his blade, feeling that in that way he was crossing it out, forgetting it, turning it into another face.

And I will just say this, which in no way aspires to be an apology or a justification, Herman: contrary to what happens with a bank robbery, a forgery, a fraud, and even a kidnapping, everyone is much closer to murder (the most universal and simplest of crimes, all it needs is a little push to step quickly up to the front of the line) than they think. All it takes is letting yourself go to be brought to it. And to arrive. It is, as I said, much closer than you think, and there's always a space available on a swift-sailing ship that'll carry you to its shores.

I felt it.

I felt *that*.

I felt that thing that so many have felt and will feel, but with aggravating circumstance and transcendence of killing an immortal.

And there were days (when, back home, I used that same hand to sign the documents and invoices that condemned me) when the pen seemed to bleed onto the paper. And now I say that it's all been in vain, that one sin can't wash away another, that the more or less self-imposed penitence of my successive failures (am I committing the sin of pride thinking like this?) never rises to or reaches the cost and value of forgiveness.

Some, in my situation, throw themselves to the seas and rarely disembark at ports because that way they're safer; or they convince themselves that, roaming the waters, their faults on land, if not forgiven, will at least be ignored as long as they stay away from everyone and everything. (It's not true, that thing about how the ports know the names of the seas: it's the seas that know the ports' names and, mingling ones with others, end up mooring waves to their docks and visiting all of them.)

I, more snow and more ice, after crossing the Pyrenees on horse-back (the mare from the Fuseli painting?), made it to Calais and embarked on the first ship to cast off, bound for Veracruz, Mexico. Then I traversed jungles and deserts and cities (I stopped off in Cayo Hueso, ossuary of smugglers; me there, opening and closing my blade and, more than once, tempted to trace the lines of a couple red arroyos, crosses running and overflowing the width and length of my wrists). I crossed paths with multiple tribes, like crews without ships, run aground between absurdly shaped rocks and silent canyons and barely having survived the boarding of their history and the fall of their gods, covering themselves with diseased blankets, their arrows broken, eyes always downcast and addressing me in even more downcast voices and never meeting my eyes ("Ojos Blancos," they called me), as if they knew me to be marked and cursed and not even deserving of their gift of a slow and terrible death, buried up to the neck among voracious anthills or hung from hooks by the nipples. They let me pass because they knew me to be as inoffensive as I was dangerous, lost and with no way back, and possibly pursued by something they didn't want anywhere near them.

And on like that until, at last, I reached Albany, covered in dust, and where, upon seeing me again on its streets and with a changed stride, people barely recognized me, like the most distant and diffuse of portraits in their memories.

I, for my part, surrendered myself to the difficult art of forgetting the unforgettable, mortaring over it with the most predictable and unsurprising of routines. I didn't go back to being who I'd once been for everyone, but I think I faked it with great dedication and true elegance. And it was in that way that I ended up opting for a more sinuous form of expiation and expiration: returning home, courting a young woman, starting a family, building a business, and losing again and again.

And in that way almost convincing myself that Nico C. and the man I was at his side were nothing more than, yes, the painting of another nightmare, about which I remember too many continuous and sordid details for it to be just another framed nightmare.

And, yes, again: I considered ending it all more than once. And, for a few days, I experienced the strange and almost perfect happiness of a suicide victim before the suicide but his mind already made up. That already-dead life (the Bushidō that the best samurais surrender themselves to, ready for battle—and where did this idea come from, why has it occurred to me, what is a samurai and a Bushidō, and what is the provenance of this odd horizontal accent mark that I've never used before?) before the bullet or the noose or the goblet or the knife or the jump, or feeling like a passenger on the platform hearing the train draw ever nearer. But that happiness was cut short when I realized that the train wouldn't stop so I could get on or that I wouldn't end it all by throwing myself in front of it; because my punishment was to continue: to continue being who I was and what I'd become.

And, knowing that none of that would be enough (and thinking that in that way, with the most unnatural of acts, I was restoring a certain lost order, correcting insurmountable errors, and reorienting the trajectory and flow of my life), it was then that I walked, penitent, across the waters of a frozen river whose banks will one day be connected by a bridge whose promise and future I now burn as if it were mine: my bridge, my future, my promise, which, for once, at first I kept in order to burn as I now burn.

* Nico C. being covered by the blue snow.
Nico C. beneath the blue ice.

* Nico C. as creator and creature in that novel that he talked about so much and a copy of which I found in his jacket pocket, giftwrapped, with a card with my name on it. A novel with a surname on the cover that I finally read, trembling, barely leaving my bunk (aboard a cargo ship, traveling almost in hiding, no on-deck social activity) on my trip back to America. Trembling even more when I read that the date it was printed was in the year 1818, more than a decade and a half in the future. And that was why I threw it overboard, tempted to throw myself after it (its letters vibrating outside of time like the future colors of that painting of a triumphant Hannibal), knowing it to be a diabolical and impossible artifact of the blackest of magics. I watched it sink into the warm waters of the Gulf of Mexico, after having read that beginning and that ending that take place in the frozen waters of the North Pole. But, unlike the story told in that book, Nico C. was the one and the other, man and monster, creator and creature, at the same time, indivisible, under the ice but always and forever hanging over me.

* The ice that unifies everything, and that makes all places one, the ice in a forest near the Pyrenees under which Nico C. lies is the same ice as the ice of the frozen Hudson that I walked and walk and will always walk across.
The ice speaking the International Language of the Ice, a dialect of the International Language of the Dead who never die.
The ice that is water's ghost and vampire.

The ice in the ice fields (just like the deserts of sand, their complementary opposites) sounding like an Esperanto, impossible not to understand or meet its demands.

The ice that I carry inside me and that is the ice of the interrupted transfer of the cold essence of Nico C. to my person and that I hope, by some scientific mystery of the laws of heredity or punishment of the laws of the soul (your eyes sometimes remind me of his), I haven't passed down to you, Herman.

The ice that imprisons and from which there is no escape.

The ice to cross like a crusader.

* There is Allan Melvill and there I was and here I am and there I will remain: inside the small diameter of the circle of my private hell, serving my sentence, where it was and is and will always be cold, Herman.

Over and over, I cross the frozen Hudson River.

I move carefully, sometimes almost skating. Some sections of the ropes and chains that bring and lead the barges that carry people across protrude from the ice and I use them as guides. The wind and the snow shut my eyes for me, and I discover that in the middle of the river, a barge has run aground on the ice, and I climb aboard to take a break and rest for a few minutes, and I check my pocket watch and a snowflake falls on its face and crystal on crystal, I think, feeling more fragile and transparent and fleeting than I've ever felt.

And then I remember that man who wished he'd never been born projected on the walls of the Venetian *palazzo*: his desperate face immense like that of a mythological deity who no longer believes in himself because nobody believes in him. And I understand his wish. Not to be. To not have been. To never be. And I feel myself a sinner and, at the same time, like a preacher at his pulpit, warning of the terrors that howl for the souls of men. Of all those men who become fugitives from God, and promising good fortune for those who don't seek a truce in the battle for the truth and yes: kill, burn, destroy the sin to become a patriot in heaven; glory for those who don't let themselves be swept away by the currents of the rivers of the frenetic multitudes; and good fortune and eternal pleasure for those who, in the moment of lying down forever, can with their last sigh say: O, Father, here I die, mortal or immortal! I have fought to be Yours, more than of this world or mine own. But this is nothing: I leave you eternity, because who is man to want to survive his God?

But no.

Not yet.

First I must make it home the way one reaches the lands and promised valleys of Canaan.

Or more and better and earlier still.

There, Paradise at last, I tell myself.

And I reach the other bank and walk down a deserted street and open the door and there all of you are, decorating the tree in the living room and, yes, the Christmas spirit is the most ghostly of all.

And there you are as you still are now, Herman.

And I can't help but think about how children should surpass their parents and wonder if that *surpass* refers, also, to surpassing them in their evil.

And I hope not, and I shudder and keep shuddering at the thought that my river might open onto your seas.

* For a while now, Herman, I struggle to look at myself in those impious self-portraits that are mirrors. I'm not saying that I don't see myself in them, I'm saying that I don't see myself in what they

give back to me with the most mercurial of slaps. I don't recognize and don't want to recognize myself there, in their surface of vertical ice. The effect (having reached the age of those who no longer have age, which is the age that unites all the incurably ill) has intensified in recent days. And, no, Herman: don't bring a mirror near me. I don't want to see myself. I can't stand seeing myself. Mirrors are instruments of self-torture. Sometimes they submit me to the most terrible torment and I can even convince myself that, no, they don't reflect me. And when this happens, when I feel this, I can't help but wonder if that invisibility, that frozen transparency of my emptiness, is the most deserved of punishments or the most unjust of deserts.

* As if, within that emptiness that contains only me, I am allowed (I'm honored, I'm humiliated) to build my own coffin and be forced to inscribe my own name into it.

* A final painting. Not a portrait exactly but one of those broader and more ambitious compositions. Something close to those views of Roman tribunes at their end (not between the sword and the wall but between the hemlock and the column); or of Renaissance nobles with a knife in the back; or of Bonapartist officers beaten and losing a battle whose coordinates would only be understood after the extinguished ceasefire; or of shipwreck survivors on a life raft at the mercy of the waves and the farewells.

Or better: one of those paintings of vertigo that shows the walls and even the ceilings of an archduke's cabinet of art overflowing with masterful oils (temple in ruins or court intrigue or retreat from the front or floating driftwood, any of them, they're all the same) and, among them all, the almost pride and disheveled humility of my own.

In my case, landscape of a locked bedroom but, also, plunder and defeat.

There, entirely out of frame and lying before his two portraits, Allan Melvill, bound with his anguish to his own bed, in the first days of winter of 1831, after having crossed that frozen river, the way other valiant men of great courage crossed Patagonian capes and boreal passes. Allan Melvill frightened and wailing, his body broken and his wounded soul bleeding, one into the other, driving him powerfully mad upon intermingling, right there, as he sails, furiously, aboard his deathbed, beaten by so many blows to the rudder throughout the course of his life. More details from the canvas: through a door left ajar slips in a Christmas glow, red and green. And at the foot of the bed, almost in the shadows, easy to mistake for a pet, a boy with a pen in one hand and a notebook in the other.

Allan Melvill looks at him out of the corner of his eye and prefers not to really look at him. And so, in this possible painting, Allan Melvill looks at the one portrait (hanging beside the other, on one of the walls within that frame) for which, after he posed for it, the painter said that he owed him nothing, that he'd already been paid by an admirer who preferred to remain anonymous. And Allan Melvill begins to shudder again before the gaze of that watercolor. And, if you get really close to that portrait (he thinks as he thought at first but only felt later), he's sure that you can still feel that cold wind whipping that curl against his forehead, moving it, as if it were a whip he were lashing himself with as, again, he crosses the frozen Hudson River.

* Allan Melvill remembers something that once upon a time he learned and wrote down in his notebook. The hypotheses of Heraclitus regarding the impossibility of entirely knowing a shifting river (contrary to the spherical statism proposed by Parmenides of Elea) from which everything flows.

If this is true, if it is true that life is a river that flows, then what is a river that doesn't flow, Herman?

Answer: it is death.

* The final and definitive form of ice (and with this I conclude my glacio-Melvillogical exposition regarding the inappropriate properties of *Gelum Melvillium*) has nothing to do with its molecular shape or composition but with something far more powerful and omnipresent yet more invisible and, as such, closer to the divine: the memory.

Is ice the substance that the memory is made of or is the memory something you envelope in ice to keep from losing it, to keep from losing the memory, to keep it from melting?

I'm not sure that this matters anymore as it relates to my life and what I've decided to take with me or leave behind. And I don't think that it makes sense (neither the one possibility nor the other) to submit it to that mad-scientist mutation (like the one in that book that Nico C. kept talking about and that I finally read) of reconstructing it from pieces and giving it a new reason to be or not to be. Now, the memory is something else, perhaps more enduring and immortal than ice, which comes and goes, functioning like something that'll allow you to, at some point, begin a story from the future, writing it in the present, looking back, Herman, but watching the words say goodbye right in front of you. And whose first and luminous phrase, like that of the Light that was made on the first day, shall be *Call me* . . . Calling itself while also calling to the one who reads it and hears it and sees it and touches it and tastes it and smells it and who (like the ice) then discovers it as the solidified product of something else. Of another variation and subspecies, of what (lacking a better name capable of containing all of it, of freezing and burning at the same time) we've taken to calling *imagination*.

* Imagine the following, Herman. Imagine it first and call it after and, then, deposit it in the frozen vaults of your memory to be able to remember it, along with me, imagining it now.

Imagine what I imagine and what I imagined while I crossed the Hudson River on foot.

Imagine a great future catastrophe, but having it be nothing but the still more powerful echo of those prehistoric glaciers that once upon a time advanced, licking the surface of the Earth so that the first men could advance and cross from one continent to another. But, now, freezing it all with a new form of ice. An artificial ice more purple than blue, pure *mauve*, developed in laboratories whose primary aim will be to use it as a refrigerant and for the preservation of food and even of human bodies for their examination and subsequent resurrection. A kind of ice that turns anything it touches into ice. A violet ice like the yellow gold of Midas. An infectious ice, like a plague, like a virus in flight.

I thought of it like a personal fantasy that dreams of the comfort and distraction of some kind of universal punishment, to thereby mask its private sin and intimate guilt. To wash away that broken-heart's blood and the spilled blood of another heart. And I was almost certain that that scene would be projected (and that it's already been repeated over and over) on the screens of the *palazzo* of Cosmo The Magnificent II. In black and white: the red blood so dark now and looking so much like shadows. Shadows, Herman! That's what it looked like. Shadows stretching out and standing by peaceful waters, but peaceful in that nebulous way that precedes the immediate outbreak of an endless war. And then, the possibility that, I thought, guilt and sin were truly the same thing (and that my crime hadn't been that of killing but of having felt alive for the first time in my life).

And I also thought of that frozen river that I now slide across like the first victim of just such a cataclysm.

And I felt how that ice I was stepping on clung to the soles of my boots and climbed up my legs until it froze first my heart and then my mind.

And here I am, dying, hearing that sound, fluty, like air blown through a metal tube or hollow bone. That sound that is the sound of death approaching, ascending the spiral staircases of my throat. A sound that doesn't keep me from hearing the conversations of your mother and the doctor. For some strange reason, my terminal hearing seems to have increased in power and sensitivity. Suddenly I hear everything: the creak of the tip-toed footsteps across the wood floor, the breathing of the leafless trees, the murmurs about my "condition beyond all human probability" and "A Maniac!" repeating over and over, leaping from mouth to mouth of relatives, suddenly like the most familiar and chilling and recurrent of words.

Here, me deciding what my last words will be; remembering all the ones I copied down in my penmanship exercise book and admiring yet doubting them: because the people who report those last words are never the ones to utter them, they're circumstantial witnesses who (I'm certain) on more than one occasion will have taken advantage of the uninspired and silent final exhalation of an expiring famous person to, surreptitious and secretly, become stowaways of History by slyly slipping their own words into the thenceforth oft-repeated and quotable quote attributed to that illustrious figure. Besides, I'm certain, in that last moment, what interests the dying person least is saying something aloud for everyone else. It must be all internal dialogue, as if at once confiding and receiving the most definitive secrets, impossible to share with or to be understood by the living, who, suddenly, are dead for the dead person. In any case, difficult to surpass the unquestionable and conclusive "*Consummatum est*" of Jesus Christ on the cross (after, also and like me, having walked on water, and I hope that by taking his name in vain and in comparative vanity I am not adding another sin to my record here) or of that haughty sincerity of the "*Non ho scritto neppure la metà delle cose che ho visto*" of the traveler and merchant and imaginative Venetian Marco Polo. (And, since I'm already on the subject, I can't help but remember Nico C. smiling as he asked me how it was that all the people who claimed to have had a near death experience always recounted drifting toward a divine light and never toward an infernal blaze and added: "Oh, the things that all of you believe you believe in, Allan"; and I prefer not to think too much about which of those two possible destinations I'm bound for, when, very soon, I leave this purgatory behind.)

That responsibility and devilry (the choosing of my farewell words) I bequeath to you, Herman. I can't bequeath you much more and, oh, forgive me a final tragic death rattle, a banal and uninspired and exceedingly melodramatic lament to conceal my whole preceding and, I hope, far more interesting White Delirium.

O, pain upon pain! O, Death, why didn't you come on time! If you could have taken me before I fell to ruin (and Allan Melvill can't help but imagine himself closing his eyes forever, back in the arms of Nico C.; and possibly freezing that unexpected crime of passion under the sought-after material crime of successive business failures), your young mother would have had a delightful and dignified mourning, and you and your orphaned sisters and brothers a legendary, venerable father, about whom you would have dreamed in the future years; and all of you would've had sufficient means to live without worries. But, of course, if I'd departed like that, it would've been before I met your mother and before you were born and . . .

I'm rambling.

Fever climbing like a rock pushed up a mountain. Fever finally dropping like the *acqua alta* of Venice and, for a few minutes, giving me a brief breather (a sigh) wherein to wonder if all fantasy might not be the bastard daughter of an omnipresent and unacknowledged failure.

And then, luckily, the fever rises again (and there's something beautiful in this illness: everything appears brighter than it is, everything around you glows as if crowned by the haloes of the saints you sorrowfully praise) and overflows the channels of my past to flood the *piazza* of my present and better that way.

I no longer have to think about what I did and didn't do and about what I shouldn't have done but ended up doing. It hasn't been easy to focus on my already almost-dead life as if it were an object from which to extract everything it has to tell. My life no longer understood as a transparent thing through which not only the past that was but all the pasts that might have been shine, giving way to so many possible never-to-be futures. Maybe if I could consider a future, concretely and individually, as something that a mind vastly superior to mine would be able to discern, the past wouldn't be so seductive to me, and its exigencies would find some equilibrium with what's yet to come. I'm referring, of course (please) to a perception, to the concession, of a *different* past, of a *normal* past. Not a past like mine, which has been part of my present for three decades (it's there when I wake, it's there when I fall asleep, it's even there in many of my dreams: my crime and my shame and my joy and my pleasure), but a past that, yes, has *passed*.

But, for good or ill, there isn't much left ahead of me, Herman. And (I'm so tired, the sweet seaweeds and shipwrecks and bones of animals are waiting to cover me up, under the ice, in the distended riverbed of the Hudson) I beg you to loosen the chains that bind my wrists and to softly send me off. There's one thing I'm glad about now: that you weren't my firstborn, that you won't have to suffer with the stigma of bearing my name by imposition of that absurd custom that seems to demand (given that we, the fathers, are the ones who invent and patent and mark them like head of cattle or racehorses, always at risk of getting impaled on barbwire or breaking down at high speed) that we give our name to anything that it occurs to us to invent . . . And better not to add anything else. I don't want to upset you further. Or (might this be part of my responsibility as a father) should I explain myself? Should I specify texture and density and material of this light cloth of immediate reality that stretches out (carefully, to avoid wrinkling or snagging) like a blanket or a garment to cover the body of the here and now? Lookout, where are you? Where is the last harbor from which we'll never cast off? In what ecstatic ether does this world sail, that the weariest never grow weary of it? Where is the father of the abandoned boy hiding? Will you miss me? Will you feel me everywhere when I'm no longer here? Will you touch me with the fingers of your memory and with the words of your imagination? More in a moment?

Our souls are like those orphans whose single mothers die in childbirth; the secret of our origin lies in that grave and that's where we must go to find it . . .

I can go blind, but if nothing else you'll be able to feel your way. You'll be able to burn, but I can only turn to ash.

Accept the tribute of these poor eyes and the hands that cover them.

The lightning pierces my skull, my eyes ache, my whole ravaged mind seems to have detached and fallen off the edge of the bed to roll across the floor of the room. But, though blind, I'll keep talking with you. And though one be light, one always steps out of the shadows; but I am a shadow that steps out of the light, that steps out of you, Herman. Open your eyes: do I or do I not see? Yes, there, the flames blaze! Or have I been forgiven, and it's not fire but light? Oh you, Magnanimous! Now I'm glorified in my descendants. But I am just your great father . . . And just as human infants, when they nurse, stare past the maternal breast (as if they had two separate existences at once and as they receive that mortal sustenance they also feed off some memory of another world), I feel that you now, Herman, look *to* me but not *at* me. I feel as if you are seeing me now and, at the same time, as if you are already seeing the way you will see and remember me . . . Feeding you to feed me . . . It neither bothers nor, even less, offends me. Just the opposite: inspiring you makes and will make me proud, as only the last thing I have left to be proud of could make me proud. But it also worries me: these are the words of a dark man that the most luminous of children will have to put in writing. I hope I haven't infected you; I hope I haven't chilled your heart and frozen your mind. I hope that my last will is not, involuntarily, your first discouragement. I understand that it isn't just that it falls on the children to atone for their parents' errors and to write better versions of what they did or didn't do, as if they were the ones educating their elders. But this is not a just world and I fear that that was never the idea (that it be just) of its somewhat extravagant and implacable and, yes, childishly immature Creator, whose most sensitive and reflective Son came to justify, with his kindness and sacrifice, so many of his Father's cruel whims.

Thus, it's clear to me that I can't oblige you to do anything, but I can ask something of you, Herman.

I beg you, when the moment comes, wherever you find yourself, near or far, to put this in writing.

In another way and in other places.

In other stories.

Me there, if you prefer, as a veiled reference, like the sigh that blows out a candle, like the voice glimpsed out of the corner of your eye, like the face that you can barely hear in the crowd.

And, please, if at some point my exact memory becomes pertinent, I ask that you try and find a way to let there be light, to let me be remembered like this: crossing the ice of the frozen Hudson River.

And that I don't cross alone but with you; because your company will be what assures me that the clean ice of that night doesn't melt into cloudy water but turns into black ink at the tip of your pen.

And in that way you release and free me.

Let the true harpoon of the son correct the fallible arrow of the father.

Now, again, to the other side, together.

Let's go across, Herman, let's cross over.

First one foot and, making sure the ice doesn't break, only then the other one.

III

THE SON OF THE FATHER

I have no house only a shadow.

But whenever you are in need of a shadow, my shadow is yours.

MALCOLM LOWRY

Under the Volcano

Soon after Allan Melvill's death, his widow Maria Gansevoort becomes, in a way, the great writer of an exceedingly brief body of work, when she decides to add the terminal *e* to her married name. When acquaintances ask her why, she says she thinks the letter adds an elegant final flourish to her signature.* And though she doesn't say as much, Maria Gansevoort naïvely assumes (because she was

---

* I don't know how I know this; but the moment of my final farewell (perhaps another blessed minute or the most cursed of seconds?) will take time and place at 12:30 A.M. on Monday, September 28th, 1891, at seventy-two years of age, in a bed with an iron headboard, forged so differently from my father's deathbed, and me there with my heart dilated and broken. And here comes a new postcard sent to me from the future: my headstone at Woodlawn Cemetery, in the Bronx (between the two graves of my dead sons and to be joined by that of my wife fifteen years later), not displaying a cross but, above my name and dates of arrival and departure, the shape of an unfurled and blank manuscript, without any inscription, and in whose fold visitors will leave pencils and pens. So (wherever I am or might be, I've been accustomed since childhood to orthographical and nominal alteration), it won't surprise me when even the *New York Times*, in the fairly tame yet still thorny obituary (I can read it, in the golden air of a future autumn, a gold like that faded gold on the worn spines and pages of books burned by embracing the sunlight in the homes of their shelves) they dedicate to me, misprints the title of my book as *Mobie-Dick* and my name as Hiram Melville; and that even *Harper's Monthly Magazine* (which published several of my short pieces and poems) rechristens me as Henry. And yet . . .

ignoring the fact that there were many who, upon hearing it, had always written it like that anyway, in the red ink of their accounting books) that it'll help her evade and misdirect her deceased husband's creditors. All of whom, with pending promissory notes and never-canceled loans clutched in their claws, continue to pursue her and her children. Those children for whom (Maria Gansevoort wants and needs to believe) a new name would be an opportunity to start over and to write and read a new and better storyline, with a safer and more peaceful trajectory, across the maps of their lives.*

---

* . . . now yes all of you can or, better, all of you should call me Herman Melville. And there's still a little while to go before what I've just described, before my coming conclusion. This, now, is the beginning of the end, which (unlike what happens in novels with all those ends of the world) is not brief and abrupt but slow and nebulous. Now, on this side of the books, events don't precipitate, they slide, as if along the soft curve of a beach, descending first to the waterline, and then, already in the water, postponing as long as possible that instant when the first small and foamy waves that previously weren't even lapping their knees (suddenly the feet no longer have any footing) come up to their necks; and their shape, the shape of the waves, is already fused and confused with that of the fins of sharks and dolphins. Now, I'm not dead, I'm a living-dead man who, every so often, is granted access to the cursed blessing of one of those postcards from the future, like the one I just mentioned (and, yes, Nature has taught us to accept the two conclusive voids at each extreme of our existence; but how to accept these orifices, like eyes of keyholes, filled to the brim with full life-experiences that cannot have taken time and place yet; what am I to do with them?, I wonder without answer. But a dead person doesn't have to be a dead idea, I think. It's then that, after a long day of making memory, the pieces that compose the landscape of my past seem to resituate themselves to look out (with the fragmented and kaleidoscopic vision of an irritating fly that buzzes incessantly) at a new territory derived from my lived experience. The uninterchangeable pieces of a life that never quite fit together (might that be why one never ends up being a writer but begins being a writer? One, always in process of assembly, never becomes the writer one could become?) or some of which have been lost and so seeing the finished model will forever be impossible. And so it is, and this is my heavy atlas that I can barely keep aloft, like the heavyhearted Atlas. Here, coming up, the coordinates and tides of my existence marked by the magnetism of compasses and lashing cyclones in the sails and the tentacular lines across the paper of my fictions and poems and the stamping of stamps on the records of merchandise coming and going from the docks of Manhattan. The longest footnote of all: my father's madness and the madness many critics diagnosed me with, not so much because of what I wrote in my books but because of how I wrote in my books. And so, for that reason, I allow myself a final typographical innovation among all the formal innovations I've allowed myself throughout my body of work but never in my life. Thus, here you won't find freewheeling juvenile and initiating fragments enumerated from a desk, or a burst of items in lists, or a whirlwind of epigraphs and "extracts," or a snap of parentheses like the opening and closing of claws of crustaceans, or a storm of encyclopedia entries that there's no escaping. None of that, rather, something that's possibly even more capricious, but, I hope, with full consciousness and greater reason to exist. Thus, here, my dead voice will be stronger than my living voice. Which doesn't necessarily imply greater stability or a more fixed structure (even though what comes next has a clear point of departure and a more or less final endpoint). Should I apologize in advance? Again? Since my first stabs at writing, I've suffered, with undisguised pleasure, the impossibility of distilling simpler things into one or two phrases. I've always enjoyed a swelling of the senses and a dilation of the pupils and an expansion of my prose when it comes to attempting to describe The Absolute and thereby attain the abyssal profundity where anything can be a symbol for everything. And warning: once there, nothing interested me less than containing multitudes (though my style has always been marked by a certain referential mania and citation compulsion that leans on the pillars uniting and sustaining the King James Bible and the fury and madness of the royal Macbeth and Lear and by a burning frenzy of metaphors and by the deep conviction that there are certain enterprises for which a careful and well-planned chaos is the best and truest way to achieve them). What I did aim for was to be contained by multitudes. To float (from what point in time does this new signal come? Is it possible that it is broadcast and transmitted so that I receive it from the antennas on the terraces of a Venetian palazzo? Could its influence be why I write like this, that way only I write? Or could it be that now I just think like this because I don't write like this anymore?) and to rise above the unbreathable air heavy with bacteria breathed less and less by fewer and fewer still-breathing people. To be part of all parts, everywhere, the true gift given to all real ghosts: because when you see a ghost it's because, first and foremost, you saw yourself. And as you know: if you have ghosts, you have everything. You have the sudden materiality of something assumed intangible, as only a life that's already passed but suddenly breaks the waters and forges onward—like an omnipotent and imposing figurehead dropping all masks—can be. So it is that now, courtesy of the final typographical innovation that I referred to a few lines back (and at the speed with which the frozen things of yesterday acquire a burning transparency that makes them clearer and more visible and present than ever; the forever rhetorical future, which is nothing but one of the many rhetorical variations of the imagination, will never enjoy such a real quality, I think), the size of my handwriting suddenly rises and grows and . . .

● ● ● grows and rises here until it now attains the same dimension and magnitude as the volume of the brief main text at whose feet I was born (and that in an almost legal and efficient way provided information regarding how my mother made a change to our name) and ended up outliving.

Thus, from down below yet aspiring to the greatest heights, I go: rising and reaching the surface and gasping for air after so long holding my breath and counting on all the time in the world to recount my story.

There I go and here I come: climbing up to the high point of the ship of my life. Scaling the mainmast and seeking and finding support in mizzenmast and staysail and ketches and yawls and rigging and rostrum (oh, the salty taste of these words again in the memory of my mouth). And once there above, to be deaf to all call of sirens, treed in those branches, clinging to the mast, looking out at bowsprit and the little that's left ahead and looking back at the mizzenmast the great deal that's been left behind. And then, from there, leaping and sliding down the ropes of my still-living chronology understood as cosmogeny: my doings and undoings on Earth, like bad stars not to be guided by but, just the opposite, to avoid the route they delineate, like unlucky and bloody lines on the palm of the hand of the heavens. My terrible map to losing myself. My seasick chart. My private *Theatrum Orbis Terrarum*, in whose margins you read that majestic and uppercase HIC SVNT DRACONES, warning of the danger of encountering "serpents so great they can swallow an ox whole," frightening more and better with details about those mythic creatures, to thereby attempt to hide the true fear: the most fearful fear of all, the fear of the unknown, which begins and ends with the minimal geography of knowing thyself, in that zoo where there's only one cage. That fear that opens like a flower with each new life and whose inevitable withering fate is known and accepted but, oh, what's feared most, I repeat, is all that distance between the point of departure and the final destination. The vulnerable life understood as a voyage lacking neither storms of pleasure nor desperate calms, when the sea will be like a water desert or a frenzy of fluids and humors summoning squalls from miles away. What's yet to come and what's already past, whenever (from the beginning and until the end) present happiness depends as much on the past (here it comes!) as on the future (there it goes!); knowing that, if you don't handle it with great care, the past can become the textbook of tyrants and the future the bible of free men.

Or (just like the Bible, which, depending on the time and the mood of the person who opens or closes it on a given day, can end up being both the Word of God channeled through a contemplative and privileged witness, recounting how everything began and will end, as well as, also, resembling nothing more than the haphazard deliriums of a group of anonymous and mad prophets, overrun with violence and senselessness in its structure and logic) vice versa.

And there I go and here I come just to be able to go again.

Just as my father took in a whole universe crossing a river of ice, I now contain my own meager existence, as I sail the streets and avenues and canyons and ravines of the cosmic Manhattan. The place where I was born. I've never understood why such importance is given to the place where we enter the world (which just amounts to the starting point and the opening line that others write); when, really, the place that most and best defines us is the one that we consciously choose or that—surprise!—is chosen for us as our exit (which makes death matter more as a definitive and exceedingly personal part of our work than of our life). In my case, the entrance to my life will also be the exit from my work. For once, a certain structure, a straight linearity in the telling of my story. The same door in the same place.

Thus, I enter and exit and advance and retreat through a point to the south of the insular city of Manhattoes (name of an ancient place and not, as is believed, of its ancient inhabitants, the Wecquaesgeek), stretching out its steel tentacles through which locomotives snort like buffalo, setting out into the vastness of a country that's expanding and populating ceaselessly without that meaning I have any ability to escape the self-imposed solitary confinement in the moors of my mind and memory.

And, of course, this is no mean feat, which is why I rely on the help of the pages of my diary.

In my entry from Tuesday, May 9th, 1865, I reread something I read when I wrote it, almost three decades ago now:

Today the South surrendered to the North. I took a walk in the afternoon.

Apart from what the end of the War means for history and things external to me, little to nothing has really changed since, as it relates to my private and decreasingly transcendent comings and goings.

Walking is one of my two principal occupations.

The second is sitting.

I have maintained with few alterations the itineraries of my strolls when my increasingly frequent and treacherous and from-behind attacks of sciatica allow me to (I think I crossed paths with Walt Whitman yesterday, that man who, with touristic enthusiasm, sings songs to all the seas and all the ships and to valiant captains and intrepid sailors who go under after having done their duty and blah blah blah . . . Walt Whitman, with whom I have so many things in common, the exception being his great ability to sing his own praises and promote himself and even, under a pseudonym, to pen the most laudatory of reviews of his own books . . . But I pretended not to see him and I'm sure that he, if he saw me, didn't recognize me, we never met).

But sometimes I walk too much: I walk so much that I no longer have the strength to return to my point of departure and, who knows, perhaps that's the idea.

But somehow I always find my way back and arrive home shivering and feverish, wearing the strange smile of a man who has returned from strange lands and passed through even stranger seas.

Thus I feel myself an *isolato*: one isolated from everything and everyone, an island unto himself. Like one of those biblical wanderers, like my Ishmael, whose name comes from that of the eldest son of Abraham (Isaac, the youngest, is far better known, first as the divinely demanded sacrificial offering and then for becoming a great patriarch of his people), fruit of the union with his concubine, slave, and pharaoh's daughter, Hagar, and who is marked by the angels and condemned to ceaselessly roam the earth and sail the seas.

Thence I'm like a castaway on a dry dock.

An X on a map that doesn't lead to any treasure but only to an X.

Thence, I begin to suspect that the true motivation for my walks is that of (before and after alighting at my desks in Customs, as if I were the most ill-omened albatross) gaining some perspective in order to, run aground behind my desk, as my castaway father once was, demonstrate and find a way to better appreciate how time's rapid passing contrasts with the increasingly accentuated plodding of my steps.

Thence, when walking, the new buildings are even more imposing. Buildings they call *skyscrapers* (term of a nautical origin, it's not too much to point out). And I'm not sure if I find the fact that their name is so descriptive (the idea that they're so tall they *scrape the sky*) to be inspired or vulgar. I no longer think (or at least I try to think as little as possible) about that kind of thing, about having to decide between writing this or that in one or another way. I no longer think so much as a writer, and yet it's impossible not to describe them even if only for myself: buildings popping up everywhere the way steamy ships were once constructed, bigger and bigger, to the point where I once imagined that if it continued like that (the mode of transport transformed into bridge) pretty soon you would just have to go from stern to prow to cross the entire ocean. Monumental edifices edifying for many but producing in me the sensation of staring up at them from the bottom of an abyss, even though, they tell me (I have no plan to try to verify this), some of them already have mechanical elevators that lift you up to the highest point and drop you down to the lowest. All together and ever closer together. All with names, again, like ships. Some (like everything) better written than others.

Yesterday, having reached that knot where Broadway intersects 5th Avenue, I thought I saw a new building, the tallest in the city, with the shape of frigate prow breaking the waves. And it was that wedge that cut the north wind and lifted the skirts of passing women such that office workers whistled at them like sailors. Awestruck by that sublime vision (of the building more than of the women's legs, of course), I said to myself that I must be dreaming. And then I woke up at the foot of my desk, as if I'd suffered a brief fainting spell, which I hid from my Customs colleagues by pretending to look for a pen on the floor (I've resisted the temptation of the new typewriters and of the masticating-skull sound of their rapid typing, convincing so many that to write faster is to write better). A (another) parentheses instead of having suffered, perhaps, a mild episode of epilepsy (a term that comes from the Greek επιληψία and which means *interception* or *error* or *lack* or *interruption* or *deficiency* or stopping something in its path or interrupting a line of communication or capturing something before it reaches its destination or something like that; and, yes, if I were afflicted by something, nothing could better define the symptoms of my illness, I think).

Thence, on whatever pretext, I left my post and walked to that same place, the one of my vision. And all I found was a sunny plot emptier than the moon. Or maybe there were other buildings there. What matters: nothing I saw resembled my vision. And I couldn't help but wonder if all of this might not be a delayed yet permanent result of the accident (when I flew through the air, I was so happy for those few seconds when I was no longer part of the earth) I had so many years ago now, riding my carriage in Arrowhead, on the Pittsfield farm, in Berkshire, near Mount Greylock, whose silhouette reminded me so much of that of a whale. That property purchased with the money from the inheritance of my wife, Lizzie, and the more or less exact location where, once upon a time, our America ended and where now it only just begins. A place where I tried to turn myself (without much luck or dedication) into a country husband and only managed to discover that my favorite spot on the entire property was by the fireplace. There, where, for many, my personality changed forever and after which I was never entirely myself again and, also, where I wrote a good portion of everything I've written.

Or maybe all of that (that vision of the city) was just the product of some hereditary disorder passed down by my disordered father, who left behind no inheritance at all: the activity of some strange virus contracted and bequeathed by him or (how did that thing about the *fanpiros* go?) signed, sealed, and delivered by the man named Nico C., as some kind of bad-luck succession from the figure of my father, as his impious and hidden patrimony. Or even, who knows, something exotic unwittingly imported from one of the voyages of my youth, long dormant and now developed and ready to subdue me. Or, maybe, a shard extracted from the explosion of one of those lost dispatches from that always foreign and exotic land that is the future and that every so often dances before my eyes; but, in what I just saw, the people walking in front of that building were wearing clothing not dissimilar to that of today. (Other mirages or oases of that kind that have reached me, seem, on the other hand, to come from a millennial future; like the one where I clearly saw, as if I were reading it, a school of paleontologists extracting the bones of a colossal and extinct *Physeter* from the ice of a glacier and—oh, astonishing hubris and vanity on my part?—christening it in my honor as *Livyatan melvillei*.) It's all the same: in any case, some and others seeking me out like mislaid records of something yet to come and, in a way, requiring my authorization to pass through customs. I, of course, grant them entry without delay, I welcome them, I invite them to be and into being. And it's clear that the lack of concentration of my somewhat disconcerted hospitality has caused a kind of knock-on effect. I receive more and more of these to-be-written missives, unable to discern if they're irrefutable demonstrations of genius or of damage, unable to tell if they're gift or punishment. A gift that I can't enjoy, but a gift that enjoys me, a gift that possesses me like a concave succubus or a convex incubus. Something that makes me feel like an onboard officer shouting from the deck that there are posts available for any who want to sign up to follow my orders and disorders and strike out on an adventure but warning all the potential brave volunteers that there's no guarantee of a safe and healthy return.

So now I walk to Trinity Church and its cemetery and, again, another temporal shift: suddenly everything appears to be covered as if by volcanic ash, and from inside the church rings out a choir singing that old fishermen's hymn: *Hear Us O Lord from Heaven Thy Dwelling Place*, voices like nets cast into ultramarine foam. And a few streets down, smoke rises from an immense crater, and I can't tell if it's an echo off the wall of a cave of Prehistory or the open mouth of a scream yet to be screamed and painted. And the air reeks of airport (what *is* an airport?, what *will* an airport *be*?) and is full of papers and flames. And the sky, where people float (but no, they don't float, they fall, like flocks of Icaruses, feather-stripped and melting), is furrowed by inexplicable white lines (reminding me of the lines of lashes poorly scarred by saltwater on the flensed back of some sun-bronzed and weather-beaten Argonaut). And the ground is littered with books, broken and flapping like dislocated jawbones. One of them, in black letters scrawled across a yellow background, bears the title *Evasion* on its cover. Another reveals the broken and incomplete ... *im Yang and the Imaginar* ... Another is a notebook like the one I had as a boy on whose cover, in handwriting as childish as it is solemn, reads something that could well be the title of one of my stories that nobody seems to understand but me: *Master Advice of a Man Who Sleeps on the Floor.* And I bend down to pick up another one (and this only casts further doubt on my futuristic abilities and reinforces the possibility of my hubristic madness), a book with a missing cover; but on its title page I read that it's the second volume of what appears to be a more than two-thousand-page biography of me, as if my life had so much to tell and yet to tell. And in one part, I read that my Captain Ahab was the inspiration for someone called Captain Hook and my white whale for a time-devouring crocodile (what are they referring to? who are they talking about?) And therein it concludes: "Herman Melville is far and away the most original genius that America has produced, and it is a National reproach that he should be so completely neglected by his contemporaries."

If this is true, if such a thing were to one day take place, I'm not sure (though I *am* sure that no nation can consider itself true and worthy of the respect and fear of all others until it has produced fictions of its own that help it believe in itself and other nations of the world to believe in it, and that I wanted and believed myself to be part of that process so that I could believe in myself) if the sudden materialization of this book so that, here and now, I could read that line is a merciful comfort or the most perverse punishment: what's the point of knowing yourself appreciated and understood when you're no longer there to don that crown of laurels after wearing a crown of thorns for so many years? For it's widely known that art dealers tend to require a genius to fall so that, later, they can grant themselves the privilege of propping him back up, once he's already dead, once the medium will be the one to profit off the achievements of the ghost. Thus, it ends up being far more lucrative to rediscover (when the rediscovered individual is no longer there and his body of work is complete) than to discover—with all the hazards that that entails—an artist when he's still alive and still creating, with no need for others to *interpret* him, and still able to contradict his exegetes and appropriators.

And then I scream the same thing at that book that, desperate, I'd screamed so many times at my own books:

"Book! You lie; books should know their place and just give us the words, so that we, their readers, can complete them with our thoughts and ideas, and clearly I'm not without sin on this point ... All that's truly great and terrible in man has never been expressed in words or in books ...! And I want to convince myself now that genius is full to bursting with trash and that all mortal glory is pure sickness, and that art is nothing more than the objectification of emotion and that there's no quality in this world that isn't what it is but by pure contrast; because nobody exists in himself, and the soul cannot hide, and the truth is not in words but in things. If the reason is judged, no writer has ever produced characters as inconsistent as his own nature. That's why no little wisdom is required of readers so that they might infallibly discriminate in a novel between the inconsistencies of the creation and those of the life ... The great crime and unforgivable sin of novels is that of convincing us that our lives have a logic and an order that doesn't exist. Lives are, really, books of stories. They are born and they die, yes, but between one point and the other they begin and end multiple times and, sometimes, their discrete parts and doors are closed in order to leave their endings open. And it's from a supposedly faithful memory that all these treacherous excretions of false or distorted recollections (I am proof that the supposed grace of being occasionally able to see the future doesn't preclude, in my case and in everyone's, the disgrace of perpetually *not seeing* the past and, as such, upon remembering it, succumbing to the temptation and desire to see it again the way you wanted to see it) end up spilling out. And yet, that almost need, looking back, to discover the story, to find a *narrative* that explains and justifies us to ourselves: a thread of fate correcting and redacting all sequence (*A* and *B* and then *C*) into transcendent consequence (*A* and thus *B* and thus *C*) and, hopeful, believing in vain that in that way we give meaning to yesterday. But no. The past is a flagless ship; aboard it we sail in a different way. And it's always ready for the piratical boarding of everything in canon range and grappling-hook reach. That's why I'm not entirely convinced that anyone actually decides anything in the here and now and, much less, that they do so based on some previous experience. We never manage to become experts or intrepid captains of our own fortune or misfortune. I'm increasingly convinced that we are adrift and that, to keep from running aground or shipwrecking or drowning in the present, we retrospectively invent and believe and need to believe in those decisions: looking back to feel that we're the masters of our lives and that life has some plan or map or reason. As if we were writers of our own existence. But, oh, those of us who write know this is no mean feat. Because whenever you write a book you're really writing two books: the one that people will read and that is presumed correct and that other one, perhaps far more exhaustive yet infinitely better and more revelatory as it pertains to the true intentions of the person who writes it. That book written first in blood that flows from the heart to the brain (the book that you wanted and conceived of writing, so different from the one you wrote) and that will never end up being printed in ink . . . Like elsewhere, experience is the only guide here; but as the experience of one man cannot be applicable to all others, it would be absurd to base it on that. But the whole world is absurd, with many absurd people in it . . . This mortal man who has such joy and sorrow in him, this mortal man whose life is described in this biography cannot be real. With books, with a book like you, it's the same. Goddamn you and goddamn that version of me whose story you tell and whose life you sail through and cast away!"

And then (I experience another small jump, like riding the crest of a high and expansive wave, like taking a deep drag of opium smoke, like that flip I feel in my stomach when I take a curve at high speed, peddling one of those trendy new bicycles built for two, feeling as if my mind were going very far away) I discover that I've been screaming all of the above at a small group of people who have gathered around me. And in their hands they're clutching small metal plaques, which they point at me, and on which appear to blink small eyes of red light. Some of them turn their backs to me, holding the same small objects affixed to the ends of small harpoons. Others throw coins at me. And one says to another: "Look . . . He's like that mad captain from that thing . . . That one chasing the white whale . . . What was his name? . . . In that thing we saw on TV."

And (what *is* TV, what *will* TV *be*?) I scream at them that they're no longer human, that they no longer have memory, that they're not even capable of remembering something they just saw or lived. And, among them (for some strange reason they all have their mouths and noses covered, like stagecoach robbers staging a robbery), most unsettling of all: a man of an indeterminate age. His face (the only one exposed) furrowed by thin scars, like a spiderweb, as if covered by the virginal veil of a widowed bride. His features seem to break apart and come back together in successive not ages but epochs as he stares at me, smiling, lips so red in a face so white and with an abundant halo of almost-transparent hair, giving off that secret phosphorescent glow of certain fish I once saw in the oceanic depths of Oceania. And I feel that that being (for some reason I struggle to think of him as a *man*) is speaking to me without making a sound, though his voice echoes in my head. A voice whose sound has about it a quality of silence that allows you to hear everything a normal voice silences: the stillness of the air, the movement of the breath, the oxygen entering and exiting the lungs of those who, unlike the owner of that secret voice, inhaled and exhaled. A voice at once dead and more alive than any other. A voice of a transparent color saying: "Yes, right . . . Exactly . . . Of course . . . I agree completely . . . I couldn't have put it better myself . . . Worthy descendent . . . That's it . . . Bravo . . . Encore . . ."

And, yes, this is one of those particular moments and strange occasions in this strange thing we call *life* in which a man has no choice but to see the whole universe as a great, lame joke, all the while suspecting that the joke is being made at his and only his expense.

And (nothing happens or can happen by chance) I check and see that this whole scene unfolds on Gansevoort St., thusly named in honor of my heroic grandfather (though, when asked about it, I said it was a name belonging to a family that'd fallen on hard times).

And, even in my desperation, I tell myself that the careful perception of this thematic design and the treasuring of episodes like this in the memory is what really and truly ends up composing any biography written by others or anyone's autobiography, beyond the deceptive precision of names and dates and places and testimonies.

And I run away from there, dodging vehicles that nobody in their right mind would ever get into, while, at my feet, the ground seems to tremble as if from the deep and hot breathing of a creature dwelling beneath it, and overhead, the blue sky is streaked with white lines, like foam on the crest of a wave about to break.

And then the air seems to vibrate again (and it's filled with a music of aquatic rhythms and an old earthy voice that ceaselessly repeats "*Oh Lordy, Lord, trouble so hard . . .*") and I make it home and go up the stairs and lie down and I discover that I'm still carrying that torn book in my hands.

And science holds that you never sleep better and more deeply than with a book on your chest; but when I wake up, that torn book, like so many other things, is no longer there. And the terrifying and fleeting power that allowed me to glimpse its words that described how, in the end, my work transcended my life (is the work the child that one bids farewell to at the docks, or does one end up being the child of the work that one leaves behind, so that others can celebrate or condemn it? or is it perhaps that the true objective is truly none other than achieving and adopting the most untethered and mutual of orphanhoods, and saving yourself or whatever you can of your life and work, and here comes the typhoon?).

Everyone take cover, just in case, come what may or whatever may come.

The same thing happens now (for what remains and among the remnants of my life that I live as if untethered from time; from that time of nobody, which is time without time, and which expands so that everyone else's time contracts, like a sickness and not a cure) with almost my entire existence.

But in the inverse direction.

All I do is receive complaints regarding delays and losses from the past.

And so, my never-recognized feat of writing and publishing ten books in eleven years that was for me, at one time, cause for pride and that later ended up being almost negated by the equally extreme gesture of going nineteen years without sending a single word to the printer. I could invent (and even come to believe) multiple theories about why I stopped writing; but there is nothing more suspect (above all from the mouth of a writer who no longer writes) than a theory formulated in the wake of practice: one of those exceedingly practical theories.

And so I won't postulate anything on the subject.

And so, merely this complete eloquent silence of mine behind the customs' inspector counter by Battery Park, weighing goods to translate their weight into taxes, as if this were a secret and revelatory part of my body of work.

But here's the key: I've remained silent in order to, in that way, be able to hear a new story.

The true story of a writer who gives up writing fiction.

B ecause what goes unwritten is, also, a very important part of a writer's body of work. And there are few things in that body of work more interesting than the last thing written.

The final sputtering crackle of the fire of the end or the last drops of rain like the almost-secret opening ceremony for a desert.

And, then, that deafening silence.

A silence all your own that almost keeps you from hearing what everyone else is saying.

My case has been no exception.

There you have that relic I brought back on my exodus through the Holy Land and the Pagan Land, where they build columns and pyramids and waning moons and breathe the long and deep and inspiring breath of so many gods: the longest poem in my language, longer than the *Iliad* and the *Aeneid* and where I, giving account of my spiritual odyssey, barely hide under another mask: the mask of a theology student named Clarel. A poem whose publication my family and friends held a collection to finance, thinking that in that

way they would placate my outbursts, believing them to arise from
an almost murderous rage at others when, really, they arise from a
despair with myself, which doesn't even deign to take me as its only
hostage, because it suspects that no ransom will be in the offing.

And then, here comes the last story that I write and rewrite
(writing something many times without ever finishing it is the
most terrible form of not writing) whose symbolism is of a transparency that sometimes discomfits me: the story of a young and
almost beatific sailor condemned to death for disrespecting a superior unsettled by his beauty and popularity among the crew. A
manuscript that (at least this is what I believed at the beginning)
would only be a short poem. A manuscript speaking a language
that has little to do with the language spoken by the manuscripts
of my youth. Here, now, a medullar language and as if from within
the bones, but the bones come from the ribcage of the most colossal and feared of all cetaceans. *Les mots justes* on pages overflowing
with excisions and corrections and parentheses (one of my favorite
orthographical symbols, I don't think there's any need to point that
out at this point; those parentheses that allow you to take some
distance by getting a little closer, one on each side, like hands coming together in the act of prayer and containing the space in which
they commune, together, sin and repentance at once) and, in the
future, the reiterated and unclear clarification of a (*indecipherable
word here*).

But all the preceding is nothing more than part of the scenogra-
phy of the secret saga of a living-dead man, of a soul inside a corpse
that drags its feet, the ghost of a writer who once was the most
vampiric of readers: the private epopee of someone who, every so
often, seeing him walking the streets, gives you the impression that
he's walking backward and in reverse and you identify him as a
"man of letters" whom, every so often, is recalled in some literary

magazine in an essay entitled "And where . . . is Herman Melville?" as if Herman Melville were the name of a ship lost at sea.

Someone who is at most a curious specimen (now and then people have mentioned sightings of "another sailor-writer, like you," but I've never seen him; and I have come to suspect that that other man is me in another time and, without a doubt, he would look down on me without that stopping him from writing things that I might write, things like "the human being on terra firma is nothing more than an unscheduled accident that doesn't stand up to deep analysis" or "At once he became an enigma. One side or the other of his nature was perfectly comprehensible; but both sides together were bewildering") and whose writings nobody reads anymore with the exception of a negligible and possibly romantic ship's crew of admirers who exchange and share his out-of-print books as if they were passwords for a chosen few I fear nobody would choose.

Someone who could never change his name, like the clever Samuel Clemens, and be transformed into a parodic caricature of himself and present himself almost like a regional circus attraction: dressed in white linen with the mane of a toothless lion and an absurd moustache, recounting jokes and counting banknotes with a southern accent and . . . (Though I must admit that the rechristened Mark Twain played a great joke on a dozen friends: sending all of them a telegram that read "flee at once—all is discovered," and, to his surprise, they all left the city without delay. I don't need any warning: I've fled from myself, on my own, motionless, alone.)

Oh, there's nothing I find less attractive than lining up on deck, with officers and subordinates acting like bit players, desperate to get as close as possible to the bridge of the so-called literary scene . . . People who (when they see me anywhere in the vicinity get up the nerve to introduce themselves and declare their admiration) find and describe me as "abnormal, the way geniuses tend to be, and someone who, when you bring up his work, says he doesn't remember anything about it, clarifying that, moreover, he doesn't have a single copy of his own books, of the "children of my mind," among the many in his library" or as "someone whose obscurity as a writer is that of one who fired his arrow and hit the target and with that, regarding his accomplishment from a distance, feels more than satisfied now." Some of them call me "Maestro." And then I think about how all of my maestros are dead and yet (like all true maestros) they keep teaching me, because I never stop asking myself what they would have done in my place in this or that situation. Nat H., the captains of my ships, my shipmates . . . Was my father, in his way, one of them? Another maestro, a condemned and condemnable maestro but a maestro in the end? Might he have actually been the most important one of all? The one who informed and formed and deformed me? . . . As far as these things go, I'm sure, none of them would have taken that kind of admiration seriously (though there are some days when I really long for it and others when I really look down on it). One thing is certain when it comes to my occasional followers: I refuse to be a father to them, I don't want any more children . . . Thus, intimidated by my unpredictable behavior (sometimes I smile at them and even invite them to have a drink, other times I grunt and raise my walking stick over their heads as if suddenly it were a lethal hook), my few followers opt to follow me at a safe distance and as if impelled by the somewhat fanatical pleasure of feeling under the sway of a captain possessed by his obsessions who rarely deigns to leave his cabin and come above deck.

One of them, almost on the sly, photographs me walking along the Staten Island pier. But photographs (much less ones of me, where I always look more like a run-of-the-mill politician than a disaffected writer who doesn't fit any ideology or style) never interested me. Why? A photograph catches an instant; whereas a portrait captures a whole life (if he'd had one taken, I'm sure that any photographer would've put that rebellious curl on my father's head in place or, better, would have moved in for the closest possible close-up). A photograph steals your soul and reduces it to black and white and gray and sepia, while a portrait gives it all its colors back. Comparing the ones and the others, photographs are like narrating aloud in a fast and chemical voice and in an imperfect and industrial way something that, in a portrait, you can only read in silence after its creator has carefully and artistically selected, like a succession of words, each and every one of its brushstrokes.

There are no photographs of fictional characters: there are portraits, illustrations, and interpretations, like those of a reader reading. That's how I would like to be seen: as someone whose existence has been verified, but who, at the same time, is presented as faithfully imprecise and worthy of alterations and restorations.

Someone who, for many, yes, represents the reinstatement and revival of that "melancholy spectacle of deranged man" debuted so long ago and with great success by my father when it came to staging his own resounding failure.

Someone who looks like he's moving though he's standing still.

Someone knowing that his vessel's kingdom is not the seas of this world called Earth, which, really (it would be so much more logical and appropriate from a cartographic point of view), should be called Water.

Someone granted the wish of being born a thousand years ago and of sailing the somber seas in a great ship, going from this land to that, fishing for his lost kingdom, with the uniform and hat of a primitive sailor yet far more expert than the sailors of the present.

Someone secretly buried in the past just to be gloriously exhumed in the future.

Someone whose last impossible-to-execute will would be like that of some respected and ancient monarch named Arminus or Hariman or Heriman or Hairman: to be laid to rest in a ship that gets pulled out to sea to wash up on a beach and run aground in a valley; and there, beside his humble treasures, to sink into the earth and drown under stones, so that the skin of the moss of years and the bones of the forest of centuries swim forever above and between and below his fossilized immortal remains.

Thence and thenceforth, fantasizing the beginnings of my end, again, the sudden temptation to begin walking backward (like a clock that went ahead and now is trying to find the correct time or, better, a wind-up toy: not broken but malfunctioning) to thereby make my eccentricity more eccentric and, maybe, more comprehensible.

To take a spin around my life.

A spin for everyone, on me.

Going back as far as possible and, from there, initiating a long return to the present: not following a determined order but leaping from one year to another, in all directions, like when, on my excursions through New York, those internal incursions seem to accompany me.

Sometimes I retreat or advance years or even decades (enveloped in fog, everything around me like a portable watercolor that bleeds out or coagulates, the world as if glimpsed through the skin of a specter) depending on the street corner I turn down.

Then I pause under the constellations of Grand Central Station (a building I sometimes enter and oftentimes can't find, and maybe that's another of my many losses) and orient myself by them the way I once looked for and found myself under the stars winking down at me at high sea.

Then, again, the buildings look to me like the spines of books in the most disorganized yet revelatory of libraries. Put there not according to any alphabetical order by author or publication or genre or theme but bound together by the different ages of a single face and, yes, weight and fate of the one who reads them. And all those signs (in all the languages and alphabets of the Old World and the Older World) announcing a *Father & Sons*, as if mocking me, as if coming together in a single tongue, protruding to remind me that I no longer have any successor in the story of my story. And that Statue of Liberty a prisoner on the other side of the water, holding a torch aloft when, really, I think, she should be (sometimes my poor vision makes me see her this way) holding a sword.

Then, sometimes, I get lost among the stands of some carnival that docks for a few days on the esplanade (I go there for the conversations among the seagulls, for the scent of wet salt, for the waves' rhythmic and soft embrace of the pier, as if caressing your legs, for hearing that invisible yet constant sound of liquid pulleys inverting the true direction of the tides) and I pause in front of the new attractions, dodging all the running children, dressed in absurd little sailor outfits. There's that automaton (Cosmo The Magnificent, inside his glass fish tank) offering for a few pennies, with a sigh of gears and a metallic smile, your exact weight and imprecise fate (and nothing interests me less than knowing how many pounds I weigh or how many days I have left). I have enough with the precise knowledge of the heavy fate of the child of a ruined family, of the youth who abandons his occupations on land to surrender to the seas, of the writer who no longer writes.

And thus the island of Manhattan leading to the Enchanted Islands and the sails of ships supplanting the candles many light in churches or the coins thrown into a supposedly magic fountain to give thanks for favors or to inspire good fortune.

And, oh, those crews that I was a part of composed of nationalities the world over. All of us sailing with a universal language behind our smiles like a coat of arms and "Harpoons, Gentlemen, Harpoons!" like a motto in our throats. All of us casting off for that soft and horizontal curve of the planet over which, in Antiquity, Egyptian baris and Greek penteconters, Chinese junks, and Viking drakkars fell, so that now we, having cold hard maps, could overcome it, floating across its watery planisphere. I've known no greater camaraderie nor stronger love than that experienced by a group of men with names in every language (calling themselves Santiago or Lorq or Von Ray or Quint or Khan or whatever they pleased in whatever language they preferred) but bound together by the collective and comprehensible-to-all name of their ship. All together confronting internal and external storms. All *mares* felt and deemed a *nostrum*. All squeezed together and strong and amid ecstatic songs melting into the mad frenzy of "the very milk and sperm of kindness"; our heads one with the whale but, separate from all particular regions, with the shared objective of arriving to an oceanic commonplace with the most simultaneously impassioned and Spartan of dedication. And, truly, anyone who wants to see something condemnable or impious in the preceding or who might accuse us of having invented such a "pagan ceremony" for the extraction of spermaceti as a way of hiding some forbidden and condemnable custom, damn them all. They missed it, they never had what we had, they never experienced anything like that. That and this was and is true Democracy. This and that was America. An organic Popular Sentiment born of a Divine Working. This was and is and will ever be the Dignity in the languages of men and the angels no matter their origin. The Idea of America as a great international experiment in a national laboratory bursting with possibilities where anyone could be a more or less mad or sane scientist in their area of expertise (mine was to move incessantly and to then restfully and reflectively analyze the movement of that national marvel).

All of that which, in its wonder, didn't prevent or attenuate my resistance to all authority. Thus my disembarkations. In Brazil and Chile and Peru and the Galapagos Islands and my flight in the Nuku Hiva Bay (all of those places now pins stuck in the great map that hangs on one wall of my study; and if you stare at a map for a certain amount of time, you can attain, I've confirmed it, I've grown addicted to it, the autohypnosis of seeing all those places again, beyond the arbitrary colors that synthesize and represent them there and sometimes include an intentional imprecision left by their cartographers, to detect when they've been plagiarized or copied by others). And, on those indifferent nautical charts that suddenly turn into letters of requited love, my mutinies and desertions on land and sea and my suntanned skin.

Thus too the delicacies of my coexistence with cannibals and their oh-so carnal wives (and, oh, it's far better to sleep beside a sober cannibal than a drunk Catholic). Then, in the vortex of one of the bacchanals, the men (inviting me to drink liquors distilled from the fermentation of fruits of shapes and colors and names unknown to me) told me of grand adventures and initiated me in the mysteries of the god Urkh and his twenty-four warriors coming down from the stars; and the women revealed to me their most and best concealed tattoos (there was a certain automatism in their way of surrendering their bodies that, I suppose, is attained beyond all inhibition and closer to all pleasure). And some and others asked for a story in exchange. And I told them the story of my father. My father who was a cannibal like them, but in a very different and more symbolic way that made his appetite insatiable: my saturnine father who devoured the future of his children, who ate them alive the way the Batak of Sumatra ate their victims alive. I told them of my always unsatisfied-with-himself and unsatisfying-to-every-one-else father who, with nothing left to devour in the coffers of his family members, fell into resentment. I told them about my father crossing a river of ice. And the cannibals (for whom, almost naked and with their own hides as their only protection, winter was an unknown animal) asked me what and how and why is and was ice. And then I discovered, still unpublished, the limitations of every author (how to describe ice to someone who has never known winter?), though at that time I enjoyed the excitement of being pure promise: the glorious days in which you don't know everything you're capable of because you don't yet know everything you're incapable of. It is then and only then that, for an immensely brief time, it's worth trying everything, because everything seems worth it: there's far more open space than there are holes to fill . . . And I told myself that, if I one day wrote a book, I would include in it a history of the azure ice: an examination of a science devoted to the study of ice and its transparent tonalities, just as I would one day do with cetology and the color white, which touches and covers everything.

And, back at home, with my stories about them, about my can-nibals (whom I lyingly told that ice was like the stars), I became an author famous and admired for his voyages. My first books are what people want to read. My first books are products of pure profession, like someone who settles for sawing wood without first ever daring to climb to the top of a tree and from there look out at a New World. My first books have titles that evoke exotic flavors (*Typee* and *Omoo* and *Mardi*) or despotic colors at high sea (*Redburn* and *White-Jacket*) and obey that so characteristically American need to seek out the foreign and the brutal from the safe distance of books and paintings and, no doubt, of whatever other new artistic practice that emerges in the future. To travel far without leaving home and give thanks to all those who give you the happy confirmation that no better place could exist in the universe and that it makes no sense at all to cross the borders of that Eden that is America that, from here onward, after the duel between South and North, will promise to wage all its wars beyond its own unbounded borders, to the east or to the west, as far away as possible, farther still, on the other side of the great waters.

Yes, yes, yes: it was to this Great American Whale that I sang and wrote, dreaming that it would read and hear me.

Hear and read the written letters of my song.

The first of my first books sold well and foretold great things that never entirely materialized.

And, suddenly, *that* book rising up from the deepest depths to the surface.

And it's not just a *serious* book, it's *seriously* a book.

And I won't take its name in vain here.

And suddenly I'm aware that, until that moment, I was nothing more than one of those seeds stored in a jar in the Egyptian pyramids to feed a monarch in the Duat of the Underworld (also called Amenti or Necher-Jertet) and that, only three thousand years later, is planted in American soil, and then . . .

And it's certain that with time there will abound theories regarding the genesis of that book.

Some will postulate a succession of more or less dispersed or coincidental events.

The result of the conjunction of a conversation among sailors (sailors who converse, I've spied on their exchanges in the harbor bars, about extraordinary machines and men in strange suits moving underwater, and I don't understand the attraction of that: liquid sky and watery horizon and here come the waves and what's the charm? where's the progress? what's the point in sailing, having already sunk and without the vivifying fear of shipwreck?) and an article in a journal that led me to learn of the disaster of the *Essex* and the hunt for the albino whale Mocha Dick. I add to all of this my own experiences aboard the whaler *Acushnet* (which was my Yale and my Harvard) and the family legend of one of my uncles, one Captain John D'Wolf, who claimed to have skirted the Kamchatka Peninsula tied to the back of an almost translucent cetacean (or maybe, having been a boy at the time, I misheard, better that way). And, starting from and with all of that and in-depth documentation (I remember with special gratitude *The Whale and His Captors; or, The Whaleman's Adventures, and the Whale's Biography, as Gathered on the Homeward Cruise of the "Commodore Preble"* by Reverend Henry Theodore Cheever) and after a typhoon of epigraphs (whose discovery, arrangement, and rewriting I attribute to a ferret and poor devil and wormy "Sub-Sub-Librarian" exhausted from circulating through all the interminable Vaticans and kiosks of books on Earth, gathering as many allusions as he could find to whales from any volume, sacred or profane; someone so similar to who I am now), I make and let speak and be heard the clear but elusive voice of a narrator.

The voice of someone who begins by identifying himself as once a simple, awestruck sailor who ends up, perhaps, in a gray office, so many years after the recalled events, an awestriking and polyphonic cosmic lexia and captain. The voice that offers a name to be called by, but a name that is perhaps no more than an alias behind which to hide himself from the eyes and ears of everyone. A name to reliably invoke for someone who might be the least reliable of all narrators. A voice ringing out during the launch of a diabolical book (even considered blasphemous by many of its readers, who at the time called for divine punishment to be brought down on me for not having devoted my many gifts to the cause of the Lord) so that I could feel as pure and immaculate as a lamb.

Whereas others opted to point out that its genesis arose from my apocalyptic need to impress and feel myself on a level with my beloved Nat H., admired by everyone else as Nathaniel Hawthorne (who added that *w* to his surname). And accused me of a longing to "either be first among the book-making tribe, or be nowhere" and of having been victim of "a morbid self-esteem, coupled with a most unbounded love of notoriety" with "inflated sentiment" and "an insinuating licentiousness."

It could be that both theories are somewhat accurate.

But there's something more and that something is the most important and, at the same time, the most difficult to pin down and to name. Something as if activating in my mind: a kind of invisible tumor that, suddenly, starts launching and firing harpoons in every sense and direction. Something that sets a fixed course for me, and I can only turn my prow and unfurl my sails. A voyage with no return whose objective is not to sail around the world but to circumnavigate and capture the whole universe. A story that (like in *Don Quixote*, another adventure with an obsessive character obsessed, in truth, with nothing more and nothing less than himself) would be both species and genus; that would contain its own commentary and invent its own rules; that would avail itself of everything already on offer while also anticipating everything yet to come. A catalogue of what had happened and also an instruction manual for what would happen (again: going forward in reverse). Everything in and outside of a book accelerating the particles of all Creation, centrifuging it to recompose it according to its will and determination, like a marine cyclone ascending from the seas into the skies of everything already created and yet to be created, in black and white and in color, in Kansas or some yet-to-be-discovered land called Oz. And, at the same time, a book that would be like the stabilizing ballast inside a ship, empty of oil and cargo, preventing the whole thing from flipping over and sinking, until it finds that secret corner of the ocean where there will be hunting and fishing aplenty to pack the holds and gladden the sailors.

A book that would anticipate all the chases, all the persecutions (real or allegorical) in books that would come in pursuit thereafter, thenceforth, and forever.

A book composed in a, yes, Frankensteinian way. In multiple parts and consisting of various impulses: first and in general a whaling chronicle, then a story of a singular whale, and, finally, the narrator Ishmael and witness to the madness of Ahab melting everything into everything. And all of that (all together and at the same time, as desirous of being influenced as of influencing) setting out and I think managing to confront The Absolute.

A book that set forth to exhaust a theme without worrying about being exhausting; because mine was a book that, in its writing, created its own kind of reader: an inexhaustible reader. A reader that didn't yet exist, because mine was a book like none that theretofore existed. A reader who, in his way, would be another "hopeful monster," a premature mutation, but, I hoped, enduring and, in the end, would impose himself on his increasingly abundant yet increasingly weak species.

A book (a pure style of book, a book of pure style) where many things would end so many others could begin.

And so, if all the world's a stage, managing to create a book that was all the world, while distilling that world down to the bowels of a ship (and, yes, forgive me: I can't help but repeatedly construct the most diverse similes and metaphors related to a ship in the book's margins, on its shores).

And from there onward, at thirty-two years old, though I intuit where I want to go, ever fewer are those who await me at the doors and in the harbors of bookstores, thus *that* book (whose reviews aren't all negative, but yes, good and bad, all seemed to coincide in conveying a certain disquiet and caution when it came to understanding it) will go out of print along with the others I write. My Great White Whale won't be spotted for years, but, oh, will it make a comeback, and when it does . . . Watch out, because here she comes, like a lover dancing out of control: reaching the bottom to rise back up and go down again and without ceasing to demand The Answer and, yes, *Look out, 'cause here she comes, she's coming down fast . . . There she blows! T-h-e-r-e-s-h-e-b-l-o-w-s!* And then she spouts out that pillar of water like a pillar of fire.

And the truth is that (overcoming sporadic explosions of rage or bursts of pride) none of the misunderstanding matters all that much to me. I'm fully aware that mine is already the most solitary of voyages with no coming back, and that, unlike the powerful Xerxes, it makes no sense for me to order the sea lashed for all of my adversities; because I always considered the sea a source of good fortune, deserving of the mooring of my caresses across its inky waters in ink. Many, of course, won't see it that way. The direction I've gone in my writing (after that book, which ends in shipwreck and with a narrator from the future returning to a past that he clings to like a castaway to a coffin) will become less and less attractive to almost everyone who once followed me, their eyes fixed to my pages. All those who now not only don't follow me but don't even come to the port to bid me farewell as I depart, both my direction and my destination being out to sea.

The only one who never abandoned me and will keep accompanying me (and who even approved of my almost demented decision to reinvent myself as a farmer of the land, an experience that only bore fruit in my fairly unconventional friendship with the quasi-hermit Nat H., who lived on his utopist Brook Farm, near my Arrowhead farm, and whom, to his unease, I probably visited too often) is my gentle wife. Elizabeth "Lizzie" Knapp Shaw, daughter of The Good Judge, who never judged me guilty of my excesses (though she didn't approve of them either) and will look after me until the end of her days. And, yes, I've always known that I am not an easy person to love. Which makes me a sort (an unlucky sort?) of challenge; but it's also this challenge that makes people like me more *lovable*: because in a way, their difficulties force people to love them. What people who come to love without making any effort actually want is not complex and time-tested love but simple and automatic affection and exaggerated and ephemeral passion.

Am I happy with my wife and family?

Good question . . .

Let's say that I'm as happy as someone like me could be with his family and his wife. I have come to understand that, for many, we were always what's termed *a good family*. But it's well understood that most families give that impression when viewed from a certain distance and, like what happens with many paintings, if you don't get too close or at least not close enough to see the imperfections of the brushstrokes or successive layers (the penitence of the *pentimento*) and thus, suddenly, the sensation that what theretofore had been figurative was now abstract (like that curl on that forehead suddenly swept away like the cyclopic eye of a hurricane on the mural of my father's Grand Tour). It's clear to me that I could've been a more affectionate and attentive and devoted husband and father. But I never hid the fact that I always felt more fulfilled and happier holding a rope or compass or harpoon than I did holding someone's hands. And it's true that domestic life put a stop to my roving impulses (and that, perhaps, I got married to pacify and repress and even castrate certain inclinations impossible not to feel or experience when you only have the sea as Dionysian lover and literature as the most Apollonian of lovers). And it's also true that home life (which for me quickly became more like desk life, behind a door always locked from inside) forced and helped me to focus almost obsessively on writing: a noble office but in a way as melancholic as only the noblest offices can be; thusly transforming me into a sedentary creature, but only in appearance, because mine is likely the most nomadic mind ever heard of.

And yes: I'm aware too that they, my wife and progeny, were not and are not as happy as they want to be with me. There, in the living room, night after night, asking myself how did I get here, how did I run aground on the shores of that house that never felt like my own (a dwelling place closer to Elsinore than to the *Pequod*) with that family that seems not the most alien and aimless of crews but a group of confused passengers so easy to confuse, feeling the distant yet constant sound of water flowing underground? The water that once was ice and will be ice again, the water that dissolves and the water that removes, the water at the bottom of the ocean, under the rocks and stones and the silence of this island, the water that removes the water, the water anticipating the arrival of the twister to hunt on a perfect day for hunting twisters: over and over again, same as it ever was and is and will be.

And there, too, in the living room but as if it were the bilge, the downcast looks of my frightened children (the children of a spirited dreamer, always, seem condemned to the most dispirited of sleeplessness). And the contained fright of Lizzie (who has taken charge of almost everything, courtesy of successive familial inheritances) when she hears my footsteps on the stairs. My heavy and swaying footsteps, like the ever-remoter memory of my sea legs: the cadence of someone walking across a ship deck, that is, at the same time, the recuperation of the swaying movement of the cradle.

My footsteps returning from gray taverns and white nights when everyone caught up on the latest sailing superstitions. No whistling (because it can change the mood of the winds) or redheads (because their personalities tend to be unstable and undisciplined) or flat-footers (I don't remember the reason why) or women (nothing to explain and disregard all songs of Scylla & Co.) or bananas (many a ship disappeared carrying a load of this fruit that, moreover, attracts dangerous insects and rots everything around it) or rabbits (no idea why) or flowers onboard (because they inspire funerals). And always take care of the resident cat (because they hunt rodents and their tails controlled bad weather). And honor the visit of cormorants (among whose feathers nest the spirits of all the men lost at sea). And never set sail on a Friday (*dies infaustus* according to *The Sailor's Word-Book*, because that was the day that Jesus was crucified) and always set sail on a Sunday (because that was the day that Jesus rose from the dead) and don't think too much about the figure of Christ any other days of the week, because, after all, how can you trust or fully believe in someone who opted for the illusion of walking on water instead of the reality of building a ship with his knowledge of the divine art of carpentry. And tattoo animals on your feet (because they help keep those who can't stay afloat). And never change the name of a ship without first informing Poseidon with the proper ceremony (write the name on a scrap of paper, place it inside a wooden box, burn the box, throw it into the water while it's still burning on a full-moon night). And cross yourself whenever the sun rises red. And, most important of all, pretend to believe in these things when you don't believe in them or pretend not to believe in them when you do believe in them and never stop thinking of new forms of fear (soon, I suppose, nothing will yield worse luck than drinking beside someone who was once a writer who was once a sailor who once had his last name changed).

Taverns where, every so often, I fantasized about leaving and never coming back. Getting on a horse and riding into the West and living off the pennies I would earn to read the news to saloon illiterates. I, once a supposedly realist writer, returning thusly to my origins as a reader of the supposed truths of others and perhaps, once in a great while, daring to slip in the little gold nugget of a lie. But no: the impulse lasted little and no time at all because I was a perpetual crewman of that island and had next to nothing to do inland.

Taverns in which—all together now—everyone sang (they sang strange ballads whose verses I often didn't understand but still enjoyed) to a young and unfortunate gunslinger from the black hills of Dakota and to Sexy Sadie and to a son of Mother Nature and to dear Prudence and to some piglets and to a hunter in Africa and to a blackbird and to an "ocean child with seashell eyes," and to a monkey with nothing to hide, or something like that. And me there among them: asking them if they know something, if the ships of my youth and forever mine are still floating out there (the St. Lawrence, the Acushnet, the Lucy Ann, the Charles and Henry, the United States, because every ship you ever traveled in will always be somewhat yours) and feeling like the new part of a tribe where there was no place for false attributions or true tribulations. The closest thing to sailing again, alongside a band of brothers, few but happy we happy few. And they say hello and I say goodbye (because the chorus of the song being sung now demanded it) but then say hello again; and each of those hellos was the firewater-greeting of another wave down the throat and under and to the bottom without bottom and without goodbye from the past.

Taverns where Russian sailors toasted and invited me to toast with a "Vot zapomni!" first and then translating it for me as "Now remember!" (and me wondering how it was possible that Russians drank to remember when I only drank to try to forget).

Taverns where I almost always managed to lose my memory (almost, I say), seeking out bottles that I emptied to see if they contained a messenger ship, and where I came to believe in the return of the genius that I seemed to regain with each drink but, all the while, knowing that genius was a genie that couldn't be put back in the bottle and that it was already gone, long gone, having years ago granted me all my well- or poorly-formulated yet always-wasted wishes. What is it that's sent me to drink? Simple and complex: the liquid and fluid and immediately deep friendship between those who drink together is not that different from the friendship between shipmates. Because alone you drown your sorrows in alcohol, but with company you swim in ethylic bliss. That almost-impassioned dependency, that automatic fraternal reflex, that way of mutually knowing yourselves to be different parts of the same thing, ignited by the humming purr of rum. That firm feeling of fragile certainty that grows stronger and more irresistible if the public house you frequent (the one I visit most is called The Last or The Lost Stowaway—or is it The Silly Pilgrim?) has the name of a seafaring vessel or echoes of sailing and the atmosphere of a ship's hold afloat in liquor.

And I enter thinking like a seer and blindly quoting that line that goes "enter one in sumptuous armour"; and that I float here merely for the pleasure of, in my quasi-unconscious state, being so conscious of the fact that today I'll sink from the weight and the many different locations of the armor of my yesterday.

And there I go: to one of those taverns, in the middle of my ocean, of my true sweet dwelling place. And then, later, back in the bitter harbor of my home, sitting down at the table as if toppling off the mainmast. And there, filling with potatoes a mouth that never stops opening to blaspheme, attacking a plate of crabs, and answering occasional letters to near strangers, where I explain that "You are young (as I said), but I am not anymore; and with my years, and with my disposition, or better, with my constitution, one ceases to worry about anything but good feelings. Life is so short, and so irrational and ridiculous (looked at from a certain point of view), that one never knows what to do with it unless that is . . . well, you finish the sentence. P. S. *I am not mad.*"

Though that is exactly the verdict of the critics, who diagnose it a monstrous morning hangover without the benefit of the previous night's drunkenness, when, after *Moby-Dick; Or, The Whale* (oh, I've uttered its title), I publish a gothic romance, *Pierre; Or, The Ambiguities.*

A novel with which, naïve of me, I aim to recover the favor of an impressionable audience fond of (like me, why not admit it?) the stories of gothic dynasties in disgrace of Ann Radcliffe and the like. I think of impressionable readers, I think of publishing it anonymously or under a pseudonym: Native of Vermont or, perhaps, Guy Winthrop. To be someone else. To start over. To set sail again. I include in it a father dying amid fevers and the story of that father's youth and his obsession with his own portrait of "ambiguous smile" that he asks to have turned around, because he fears that the look on that face (his) will reveal to his wife his hidden love for a "young Frenchwoman" and so better that he look at the wall, as if in penitence, and not at those who can no longer bear to look at him and, yes, Pierre ends up destroying that painting. I also include the figure of a philosopher, Plotinus Plinlimmon, who sets forth two types of mind to distinguish between the earthly and the celestial: one that is guided by a mortal clock and one that is guided by a divine chronometer.

And "HERMAN MELVILLE CRAZY" is the headline of one of its reviews, which I cut out and carry around in my pocket (the critic made the merciful or ignorant gesture of not mentioning therein the demented precedent of my own father) along with my housekey and documents (nothing documents me better than that half-made manuscript, I think), that perhaps serves in a way to justify the volatile and inflammable conduct that sees me getting myself into trouble in the tavern. Others, I must acknowledge, attempt more sophisticated and perhaps more pitying diagnoses of my novel: "We cannot pass without remark the supersensuousness with which the holy relations of the family are described. But the most immoral *moral* of the story, if it has any moral at all, seems to be the impracticability of virtue; a leering demonical spectre of an idea seems to be speering [that is, querying] at us through the dim darkness. Mr. Melville's chapter on 'Chronometricals and Horo-logicals,' if it has any meaning at all, simply means that virtue and religion are only for gods and not to be attempted by man. But ordinary novel readers will never unkennel this loathsome sugges-tion. Here, it all lies as if a stagnant pool or, better, as if frozen by an intense shiver. And, beneath that impassible layer of ice, everything is muddy, foul, and corrupt. Unprepared and unready reader: If the truth is hidden well in the foul river bottom, then it can only be a fallacious and diabolic truth."

And one of them hits much closer to home than it imagines when it aims and fires and burns with its "His imagination seems to arise and have its hallucinatory origin in something ancestral, perverse, febrile, and maniacal."

Something that, already well along in *Pierre*, in the almost set-piece entitled "Young America in Literature," I intensify and rarify even further. There, suddenly and without warning, I make it so that the protagonist discovers, at the same time as the reader, that he has become a writer (author of a celebrated sonnet entitled "The Tropical Summer," that prompts multiple periodicals to immedi-ately request a portrait of him); but that this also makes him aware that "then is the truest book in the world a lie" and that originality is a talent reserved for God alone. (And it seems a lie and it beggars belief: my Pierre, a fatuous and pathetic creature, understands in just a few hundred pages overflowing with almost absurd episodes what it took me years to understand: books are not instruments for making or changing History; at most, they can become part of and alter the history of books. Homer? The Bible? Shakespeare? Mil-ton? Those are neither books nor authors who wrote them, they're something else; they're epidemic systems of thought, they're the most infectious yet curative of plagues. But here's the paradox: first I had to create Pierre so that Pierre could teach this to me, and I could learn and acknowledge it.) And, there, also, another lesson, a warning that all "ordinary readers of common novels" should have already understood. There, Pierre Glendinning Jr. confesses (with me and with pride) that "Among the various conflicting modes of writing history, there would seem to be two grand practical distinctions, under which all the rest must subordinately range. By the one mode, all contemporaneous circumstances, faces, and events must be set down contemporaneously; by the other, they are only to be set down as a general stream of the narrative shall dictate; for matters which are kindred in time, may be irrelative in themselves. I elect neither of these; I am careless of either; both are well enough in their way; I write precisely as I please."

Which, precisely, doesn't seem right or better to many and, of course, does not please them.

Before long (like Pierre, who "deceives" his editors by submitting an impossible book, "a blasphemous rhapsody" that has nothing to do with what was initially promised and that, of course, is none other than *my* book about him), I'm the most complex of easy targets for all (not all, a few; it's not like I'm *that* worthy of interest either) the young critics. All of them so similar to bloodthirsty slaves in revolt. All of them so eager to make a new name for themselves by unmaking an old name and, oh, the temptation I feel to put one of them in writing as a rescued castaway submitted to the will of a powerful and amoral captain (better not, better for someone else to do it, if possible an ex-sailor who, out of love, will become a successful utopist writer). But yes, so it goes: that novel (satirical and symbolic and speaking a baroque and digressive and vacuous language; in which I deform my own life and that of my father to create a young writer convinced, again, that the most authentic text ever produced by a man—as long as he's not dead when he writes about dying death—could only be a blasphemous deceit, because only God can claim the gift of originality) ends up the most mis-understood of all the misunderstandings that come my way. And nobody manages to perceive (I guess I'm expecting too much from everyone) that, behind all that mess, worthy of the most twisted and melodramatic penny dreadfuls, throbs the book's true secret plotline: my need to find success again, fully aware that such success already was and is and would be impossible for me and, thus, achieving the most successful and fully (in and outside of the book) triumphal narration of a failure. And from that pronounced sub-terranean vertigo, at the end, calculating the catastrophic and suc-cessful result that "Something ever comes of all persistent inquiry; we are not so continually curious for nothing." And specifying that what comes (that truth theretofore exquisitely enveloped in the sedative silks of the lie) does so feeding off of the destructive power of love, always "built upon secrets, as lovely Venice upon invisible and incorruptible piles in the sea." (And, yes, I pass through Ven-ice on my Grand Tour. And there I look for something: *palazzo meraviglioso*, trace or ruins of my father's ecstasy, the confirmation that reality is nothing but a tool for fiction's use. And I don't find anything but churches and liquid necropolises and convents and crystalized factories and uneven paving stones on which to stumble and almost fall to lose time and regain memory. And to tell the truth: I didn't really look that hard either. And I stay in the city for just enough time—very little. I flee from the flotillas of tourists who never stop saying *grazie* and *piazza* and I listen closely to my guide's anecdotes about Lord Byron swimming across the Grand Canal to dive from one lady to another. And I attempt to avoid the sensation of being followed, all the time, by channeled liquid shad-ows. And I compose a brief poem to that impossible yet real land-scape that I don't know if it's a city or an island or a huge, grounded ship, broken into pieces and as if emerging from a fever dream or a frozen nightmare. And I leave imagining so many things, not entirely sure if I would've preferred to discover something real to, then, be able to cover it up forever with the oblivion of blood or to navigate it with the memory of ink.)

And, as far as I recall, there are no great ships to move between continents but only small boats for excursions on the lake in *Pierre*. And yet everything quakes and spins and is devoured by the oceanic depths of the mind, while paraphrased psalms are recited and unbearable truths are intuited before a portrait that recalls the portrait of another father. Another painting, a painting catalogued, in *Pierre*, in unexpected lowercase letters as *No. 99. a stranger's head, by an unknown hand*. A painting that's like the ghost of the one destroyed by Pierre and the one saved by my father. And after that, in the novel, all that's left is to plunge (with an estranged head and an unknowing hand) toward the most final and mad act and to annihilate everything. A heartbreaking and vertiginous ending, overflowing with incestuous madness (a malicious wink on my part, I suppose, at Nat H.'s unconfessable obsessions that I could nevertheless detect; writers are specialists in perceiving everyone else's dark spaces to distract from our own shadows) and violent deaths and creative suicides; as if it were forced and submitted to an imperious need to empty the stage, like a parody of Shakespeare, and to frighten readers.

And enough of this for the moment, enough.

I detest thinking about the titles and themes of my work as if they were accidents written in a ship's log or symptoms exhibited before a medical tribunal to defend myself from those tormented and tormenting reviews, like straitjackets or supposedly therapeutic immersions in freezing water or iron cages in which to imprison a mind that thinks too many mindless things.

I hate thinking about thinking about myself like this.

B ut, oh, there doesn't yet exist a science that permits the freezing of the channels of the brain and forces the dropping of the anchor to prevent thoughts from setting sail and offers the distracting truce of the most intoxicating harbors. And it's also known that a ship in the ice isn't safe from the frozen water's embrace, which can asphyxiate its hull and break it into pieces of wood, lighting the fire in which to burn while awaiting the arrival of the fateful and frozen Atropos.

And thus, I can't stop, I can only continue, I continue.

What comes on the heels of my *Pierre* (my sea monster on Earth, my Kraken) are the strange stories of *The Piazza Tales*. And battlefield poems. And that revolutionary in exile in *Israel Potter*. And desolate slave ships in *Benito Cereno* (more ship names: the *Bachelor's Delight*, the *San Dominick*, the names unto which a seafaring man commends himself and to which he clings when faced with the impossibility of naming each and every wave in those oceans whose names are known but whose borders are so liquid and porous and shifting). And, in *The Confidence-Man: His Masquerade*, a stranger coming aboard, in Mississippi, on April Fool's Day, to make everyone feel guilty for their capacity and need to be deceived, changing masks, again and again, but leaving the mystery of the true face beneath all of them unresolved and offering the warning that "after poring over the best novels professing to portray human nature, the studious youth will still run the risk of being too often at fault upon actually entering the world."

And later the fantasy of a final story, that of Billy Budd, which would turn into this unfinished manuscript that I carry around with me everywhere, which I never finish not because I can't finish it, but because to do so would be to recognize myself as definitively finished. And thus, I never stop thinking about its plot (I already mentioned it: another of my many variations on an aria with a mad onboard officer, about the figure whom you assume should be sound of mind but guiltily and lovingly proceeds to lose it) and I go there to go nowhere and, again, like so long ago: out to sea with nothing to reel me back in.

And, before, me departing on a postponed Grand Tour like that of my father. Yet so different (now so much land where once there was so much water). I'm not young, I'm weary, nothing can occur to me out there. I don't travel to *educate myself* but to confirm a suspicion, not that I no longer have anything to learn, but that I *can* no longer learn anything.

Everything out in the world is just backdrop.

Everything that happens, happens inside me.

Six months in Europe and on the Mediterranean and in the Levant with my father-in-law, The Good Judge Shaw, footing the bill.

And, upon my return, the need to fail again at something: my lectures on diverse subjects, like the statues of Rome (for some reason many of them seem mixed up to me: the small riders of some astride giant horses and the small steeds of others ridden by colossal emperors), are a comprehensible disaster for many of the few impressionable attendees, who find all my impressions incomprehensible.

Then, in 1866, I leave all of that behind and start working at New York Customs (just as Nat H. once worked at Boston Customs; in one way or another, I'm always on his heels) the way one cloisters oneself in a monastery. I barely speak while there; but subsequently, I earn an uncomfortable reputation as one of the few honest inspectors in one of the most corrupt institutions in the city. I'm told that I owe my retention of that position, up until my retirement on the last day of 1885, to the protection of secret admirers; but (like the vague news that reaches me about some kind of revival of my work in England, in some whirling intellectual circles of London) I don't have any clear evidence of it.

And if it turned out to be true, would it feel like justice to me?, like a preview of justice yet-to-come?, like the flickering green light of an orgastic future to row toward against the current of the present?

No.

Absolutely not.

I don't even believe myself fit for the sad honor of being the only man to receive a deserved and redemptive posthumous medal for services rendered unto the Nation of Letters. I don't consider (or I do consider it, almost breaking on the reefs of the sacrilegious) the possibility that my kingdom is not of this world.

I worry about other things, more pressing matters: I don't live for some vast and great tomorrow but for the humblest of small and pleasant of tomorrows.

I don't have high hopes: I've been living in a twilight land for a while now. There's no good news for me to preach, everything seems bathed in a serene glow, awaiting the pulsation of the next heartbeat that might well be the last.

But there's always more, always another.

And while good fortune always speaks the same language, misfortune is a polyglot that ceaselessly seeks out increasingly painful synonyms and new and terrible definitions for its meaning in unpredictable accents.

Thus, contrary to the dictates of that secret law, my sons die before me, and I survive them to feel how my heart doesn't break right away but slowly dilates, little by little, beat by beat, until years later it bursts.

But not yet, not yet.

It still hurts.

T hen, fallen, I go up to my study.

The study.

"Open sesame!" I say.

But nothing opens of its own accord (I open the door) and no un-discovered treasures await me inside, just a space, brimming with emptiness.

The place I go to get away from everything and leave it all behind.

The study where I study myself.

A kind of boat that doesn't move but is no stranger to storms.

And another wuthering gust in reverse: it's clear that my wife, always on the dock of my life and never aboard my work, never understood me, but I never understood her either. There are many couples like this, loves composed in this way that, again, are the ones that, paradoxically, appear stabler when looked at from out-side. Or maybe it's that mutual incomprehension that keeps them together and strong and always alive with the hope of someday illuminating the secret emotion of their connection and then, yes, finally splitting up. I fear that won't be our case: Lizzie and I will always be bordering lands but irremediably foreign to each other, with customs the other deems exotic, separate yet inseparable.

Thus, for some strange reason—why and to what end?—Lizzie will soon take it upon herself to recreate this room (this, in her words, "place of mysteries and fears for me"), piece of furniture by piece of furniture and book by book, when she moves to her widow's house, eight streets from this one, when I'm no longer here so I can be everywhere. What could her intention be? To miss me less when she goes in there or, to the contrary, to feel that now she can shut all of that away under lock and key and never go in there and light the cauldrons of oblivion? The truth is that that place that doesn't yet exist (and that will house my many books and postcards and maps, my marble sculptures, my Polynesian oars, my ink pot and quills, and even a fragment of the first transatlantic cable) already reminds me of one of those exotic dioramas from the Museum of Natural History in New York. Or of the stage and context whereupon to erect one of those wax figures, like the ones in Madame Tussaud's Museum, which I visited in London (and where a good number of the illustrious and infamous individuals recreated there have a far more vital appearance than I and my flesh do). But, of course, both locations lack the main attraction (me) and only exhibit that empty plenum, because (as a small sign informs) it is being restored though who knows what good that will do. Or better: imagining that sepulchral and pharaonic replica of my habitat as a kind of cosmic hotel room/cell where I can spend the right amount of time until my reincarnation/rehabilitation, when I shall return to Earth, to do justice and have justice done unto me, like the most wondrous and powerful of superhuman embryos.

There, in that study, facing the wall, the two portraits of my father: the man himself as his only legacy. There, all those books (the public life of a writer is the books he writes, and the private life of a writer is the books he reads). The mocking enticement, silent yet deafening of all those books of others. The books that I read to keep from thinking about the books I don't write (and I don't even keep copies of my own books, because they're a nuisance, like the birds that follow ships waiting to feed on the trash that gets thrown overboard) and that, every so often, tempt me to drive my father's knife into their spines and breasts. But it's not easy to stab a book with a knife. It's harder than stabbing a man. It would be better to use a small dagger. Or, at least, one of those bottle openers inspired (everything can be told another way, in a new way) by that tool used to extract bullets from old revolutionary muskets and, yes, why not just riddle my library with bullets. Summarily judge it and dispatch it without delay. What's the point of rereading everyone else when I can't write myself? Could it be possible to excise the terrifying gland that makes you a humble and depraved writer to recover the Paradise Lost of when you were a complete and absolute and magnificent pure reader? I don't think so . . .

And no, again: stabbing someone with a knife is not easy and I wonder how my father (who wasn't a strong man) was able to pull it off to eliminate the shadow that pursued him.

Or, who knows, maybe everything he told me before he died was nothing more than an impious fantasy and purely symbolic. Maybe none of it happened. Maybe Nico C. never existed. Nico C. as a metaphor for everything my father longed for and didn't dare become: a doubling of his personality, his own possessing demon.

Or perhaps Nico C. was just the febrile sublimination of one of the many merchants far more astute than my father, always making use and taking advantage of his enthusiasm (and thus, then, my father's great desire to stab him to death).

Or maybe my father read *Frankenstein* (after all and first and foremost a novel about the equally complicated and "creative" relationship between a "father" and a "son" and one that begins and ends with ice and in the ice) on that youthful voyage (or that's what he told me, though the dates don't work and seem impossible, and perhaps he only read it after I was born, in Albany or Manhattan) and experienced the suddenly simultaneously seductive and abandonic (does this word exist or am I inventing it?) mesmeric animation of a literary destiny.

Or that all of it stemmed from an impossible to admit sodomite episode with some artist of questionable talent and decadent spirit (whom maybe he killed, or not, who knows, when the man tried to extort him; something, it occurs to me, that could be taken from one of those sensationalist installments that I've almost gotten addicted to, like the most intoxicating of those drugs that give you a way out, an escape hatch, a journey to faraway lands).

And, then and thenceforth, my father feeling so riddled with guilt for possibly falling victim to the lustful dark arts of some sinuous European fortune-hunter whom he ended up putting an end to (someone resembling that pursuing shadow and that Dionysian character in that touristic and fabulous Italy of *The Marble Faun; or, The Romance of Monti Beni* by Nat H., and, I suppose, I drank too much one night and told my most-admired friend too much; and, here's my warning to the reader and, also, to the writer he may one day become upon emerging from his larva: be careful what you tell one of our kind, because nothing belongs to anyone and everything belongs to everyone).

Or maybe in derangement of his final days, my father found a way to transform it all into a delirious imaginary friend. Into a fabulist confabulation to justify and explain and forgive himself and (in his unconsciousness or hyper-consciousness of it?, without meaning to or out of love for me?) he chose me as his confessor and drew me in and transformed me into the sinful saint that I was right up until I wasn't anymore.

And that it was I (under the influence of his influence) who would end up shoving off the ship of his own shattered literary vocation, which never cast off its moorings or made it out of the shipyard. A vocation that's nothing but the professionalization of this equally mysterious and officious part of the brain we all use, in one way or another, to decide how to tell the story of what didn't happen, how not to tell the story of what did happen, or how to tell the story of what could or should have happened, while attempting to control the direction and speed of things as they occur to us, sometimes feeling the admiral and others the cabin boy. (And thus, if you take this on as a profession, you end up living—beyond all human probability, without the blessing of Reason but with the curse of Anything Is Possible—as A Maniac!)

Vampirizing me or possessing me (or *fanpirizing* me), yes, so that later I could do the same to him.

My father.

My Allan M.

His shameful crime or his criminal shame?

His changeable personality or his somewhat immoveable character?

His fall into temptation or his rise to frustration?

Forgiving him without it implying I understood him?

Which of the two mortal sins?

Who knows, who wants to know . . . It doesn't matter anymore, it's all the same, in the end.

And the intensity of his shame is such that it becomes his legacy.

And I already sensed it and now accept it: him telling me so that I tell the story of Nico C. (true or false) is his true and haunting legacy. Because fatherhood is always a ghost. An ascendent and descendent curse. Something (a familiar form of mutualist parasite, like those filthy cleaning-fish that feed off anything stuck to the backs of whales) transmissible from one generation to the next for shame of shame, the way specters are passed from generation to generation and include a mansion in ruins and a badly scrawled or corrected surname and absurd traditions and the slow and thick stumbling and trampling rush of blood. That familial specter that's nothing but the *interesting* part of that ambiguous Chinese curse/blessing that wishes an interesting life (and thus an interesting ghost) for victims and victimizers—bound together under one name—alike.

But (still a slave to *my own* symbolic impulse, though I no longer put it in practice) maybe the one rambling and raving now, as my father once did, is me. And these occasional apparitions of what is to come or what may come that visit me ever more frequently are nothing but the product of another half-excised excuse: why write when you have access to everything yet to be written?

And then I wonder if thinking like this might just be a way (by revealing its springs and gears, explaining, yes, its ambiguous and multiple symbolism) to ruin a good story. And in so doing, turning myself (and, while I'm at it, castigating and slandering my father) into another of those excessively successful costumbrist and social writers that I so despise. The ones committed to and engaged in, all of them, telling the newly ripe story of the grandeur of this Glorious America that I so love, this America that was doomed to break in two only to make itself whole again. A nation that sometimes reminds me of a great white whale and others of an immense mad captain: hating each other yet knowing themselves inextricable from and indispensable to the other for the colossal birthing of a country, or something like that.

And, yes, without a doubt, I'm the one raving now.

Whatever it is that afflicts or differentiates or distinguishes me from everyone else, I let myself fall into the hammock that I strung up across my study, in front of the fireplace where the fire thinks about who knows what, I think.

And, having arrived there, I let go. Almost like Queequeg let go, not reading or writing (the latter at least, the easiest to do, not to do) as if I were not eating or drinking, wishing that the tattoos of my books could cover up or at least conceal and camouflage the scars of my life. Thinking about how the whales I spotted in my youth are still alive and, long-living and slow, will outlive me in the always-shadowy deeps of the sea, where their essence will never be processed into liquid light on earth.

And me there and here, in the dark, rocking back and forth, hands crossed over my chest, humming an old lullaby, a cradlesong in a coffin-voice. Obeying the antiquated custom (that's beginning to disappear and, yes, many times the novelties of the modern are nothing more than a deterioration of the classic) of sleeping in two stretches, rising in the dark between one and the other to enjoy being awake at that magic hour of the best ideas and best orgasms, to later go back to sleep to dream until morning.

Rocking back and forth and thinking that *Thou shalt not think* is my eleventh commandment, and that *Thou shalt sleep when thou canst* is my twelfth.

My thirteenth commandment (once obeyed the previous two; and so apostolically treacherous and hard to consummate and satisfy) is *Thou shalt think very carefully, asleep or awake, about what dreams may come.*

And with sleepiness comes dreams, the unforgettable and enduring dreams of the sleepless.

The best dreams, because, unlike *sleeping* dreams (the ones to recount later to convince ourselves that in that way we'll preserve them, when the truth is that we're not doing anything but remembering their scattered and impossible-to-reassemble pieces), they don't settle for merely being the story of the dream in the imprecise and confused and forgetful moment of waking: so close yet so far away, dreaming and being dreamed.

Dreams of a striking density that, increasingly, seem solider and more desirable than everything I live in my waking life.

Dreams that are the place where ghosts choose to reveal their existence, the dwelling place where all our dead are still alive and to which, every so often, they invite us to come and listen to them, making us feel, upon opening our eyes, that they've communicated something, paradoxically, *vital* for our *existence* on this side of things.

At my side, beside me, everywhere (in the air, almost like smoke signals, suspended like warm breath in the cold of winter), the words of the dead, the words dictated by the dead, are taking place and finding a voice.

I dream that I write them, I dream that I write.

I write with the permissive authority of dreams, which, in truth, is far closer than we want to believe to the ever-changing structure of our existences, whose only iron and inoxidizable law is that of constant and elastic change, beginning and ending and beginning again and again, sometimes, on the same voyage or in the same day. What we do is nothing more than live rewriting, *truly*, the fictions of our real lives.

Lives that only attain the precision of a useful or, at least, reliable, design with the immoveable perspective of death (that finale that doesn't allow for final corrections or alternate versions) and off of which there, in death, they live on.

Lives in which the only thing that absolutely lasts is absolute death.

There, the merciful dictatorship of the dead.

The dead who notice us so that we notice them (asking ourselves and asking them during one of those increasingly popular *seances* what they would think of this or that or what they would have done in a given situation) and whom we sometimes try to forget only to realize that they won't forget us and all they do is remind us that we'll never be able to forget them.

The dead, in whom (and this *is* a miracle) we believe even though we don't believe in God.

The dead, to whom we owe the truth because to the living we owe only respect (and who said that?, Voltaire?, my memory no longer is what it once was, my memory is dying).

The dead, who appear to move through the dry and empty spaces between raindrops, assuming the quality of things observed against the light, the way you sometimes look through the ice of a night.

The dead, who are the conclusive evidence that we can't live only for ourselves and that our lives are interconnected by thousands of invisible threads. And that it is through those fibers that our actions move as causes and the dead return to us as results, as *resolved*; though the dead are never entirely an exact and known quantity, because they never stop adding and subtracting and, calculating, sending us the bill.

The dead, who're not exactly ghosts (ghosts are the invisible sickness, the dead are their tangible symptom of a hereditary, "familial" illness whose "emanations" and "effluvia" are, above all, so recognizable and easy to share).

The dead, who, supposedly, end up being property of the living ("My Dead," we say, in uppercase) when actually they are the ones who possess us, the ones who refer to and orient and direct us as their lowercase "my living."

The dead who are like adoptive adopted children, always demanding, exceedingly ill-bred, making the living stay awake to play with them until they're exhausted, until the living die of weariness.

The known dead and the yet-to-be-known dead and the dead who know all of us.

H

ere they come, they're already here.

Do they arrive like coins clinging to the sides of a singular and unrepeatable whale? Nah . . . Nothing so grand or impressive or honorable. Defeated, the dead pull themselves along, going here and there, sighing in dismay, so weary of being dead, dead of weariness, barely dragging their feet on the longest of marches.

The murmur of all the Confederate and Union dead (all of them now marching under the tongue of a single flag, snapping in the sad wind and stitched with the legend MORS VINCIT OMNIA, filing impeccably by and in tighter formation than when alive, disciplined and uniformed as never before, because Death is uniform and disciplined) and the whisper of all the dead who suddenly found themselves dead and all together, sudden white crosses in the crossfire.

To some and others and all of them (now drifting across blasphemous battlefields transformed into holy cemeteries where so many drowned in their own salty blood), I dedicated a cycle of poems ("reminds you of no poetry you have read," one critic fired off with aim more twisted than wicked) to see if in that way they would leave me in peace and grant me the truce that the living would not.

But it wasn't meant as some kind of anti-war plea (something as useless as, someone will someday think, proposing an anti-glacier novel), but as a sort of peaceful and conciliatory requiem to and for all of them.

And, anonymous and distant, they did me the favor of liberating me, at least for a while, from the spectral voices of my more proximal dead.

Dead acquaintances like my always bellicose and ready-for-battle grandfathers (soldiers of my own blood, the worst of both worlds). One and the other recriminating me for not having enlisted, no matter my already advanced age, my multiple health problems (bad back, sciatica, vertigo, bad eyesight that obliges me to request a special typographic design for my books, not to mention my prophetic visions), and maybe the worthiest of consideration though difficult to consider: my increasingly singular idea of patriotism as something that should transcend the merely national and assume dimensions that transcend all borders. And that the end of war doesn't bring peace but a prolonged period of reprisals and of score-settling and reinventing history (wars are machines for generating warring fictions), where the winners and losers finally reach an agreement that the truth of what happened is too frightening to accept as true. And that in that way, better, the most appropriate thing to do is propose a new revisionist reality that's more tolerable and, above all, more . . . useful for both sides.

Suddenly, everyone is a writer, everyone a rewriter.

And sure: those orations and eulogies that I dedicated to the fallen soldiers and those raised up in glory weren't intoned or recited with great devotion or emotion in my pen's voice (death, by definition, tends to be precisely unjust; what's the sense then of finding just the right imprecise words to give it life in writing?). And I came to all of that through exceedingly personal and egotistical motivations: I began writing poetry (on the sly, thinking that in that way I could stop writing prose) the way someone is cured of a very serious illness by contracting another that they want to imagine less acute and easier to survive.

Poetry, I thought, was a form of failure in itself that wouldn't hurt as much as failing again in a novel. But, oh, being who I am (and knowing that the writing of a powerful book will always demand the selection of a powerful subject), it wasn't long before I set out to write a cathedral of iambic tetrameters in four parts. Another bestial and profound leviathan. And thus my *Clarel: A Poem and a Pilgrimage in the Holy Land*. Really a stowaway novel, setting sail clandestinely between the rigging of verses: perhaps that secret sequel more insinuated than announced in the last line of *The Confidence-Man* (that ambiguous promise of "Something further may follow of this Masquerade") but, in addition, the coded culmination of all my previous books. Not a way to decipher them but an instruction manual to make them even more obscure and only worthy of those initiated in their secrets.

Thus, there, also, another book both dead and immortal at the same time. Another of my past-tense books for the future that might only interest the dead that haven't yet been born. Almost eighteen thousand verses inspired by my pilgrimage of fifteen thousand miles to the biblical homeland that (as I anticipated) almost nobody understood and to which one reviewer dedicated what was possibly the most painful critique: "It should have been written it in prose," he said. Other critics, possibly more ferociously merciful and clumsier at the easy art of the insult, said things like

"I got lost in the overwhelming tide of mediocrity," or that it was "a vast work ... destitute of interest or metrical skill" with "not six lines of genuine poetry in its one hundred and fifty cantos."

What was I looking for there? What did I hope to encounter? What did I fantasize I would find in that ancient terra firma? Something I hadn't found in those still more ancient yet ever-shifting and constantly renewed waters of the seas; in those deserts that once, millions of years ago, were oceans and in whose dry beds, every so often, prehistoric harpoons are disinterred? God? A less absent and more interventionist God?

I remember how I once told Nat H. my idea of a heaven for writers: he and I, together, in a cool shaded corner, drinking champagne (I refuse to believe in the possibility of an abstemious Eden), with our celestial legs crossed and sitting on celestial grasses and recalling our past lives and composing comical and celestial songs with titles like "Oh, When I lived in that Queer Little Hole Called the World" singing from the greatest heights to that minute and strange hole in which we'd once lived and died and, between one point and the other, written our work as if our lives and deaths depended on it.

Nat H., as usual, perceived then the permanent anxiety beneath my occasional jokes and (with that genius for synthesis that always set him apart) reduced me to someone who "Can neither believe, nor be comfortable in his unbelief."

And, of course, he was right. Thus, I always felt like a man who cast doubt on all earthly things to intuit something divine. Someone in Purgatory whose nostalgic ballads were sung more to Hell than to Heaven, just as, during the Flood, the whale spurned Noah's Ark, knowing himself better able to survive on his own and with no promise of company, in exchange for reclusion and being one among so many.

As in my life, so in my work.

I suppose that what I needed was to believe in something to, later, stop believing. To discover in the divine a reflection of my own mortal journey in the eyes of others. Knowing this to be impossible, I was somewhat more merciful with the hero of my verses, offering him the closest possible thing to a happy ending: at the end of his long journey, after nights of agitated dreams and erotic fantasies, Clarel (the traveling protagonist of my poem) receives the visitation of multiple specters, the ghosts of people he met on his adventure, and begins his return home, crossing the sea, to reunite with his people, his living and his dead, in a country that hadn't yet been able to bury all those who won and lost in the war, but where they suddenly found themselves all equal (unvanquished vanquished) and in a place from which it's impossible to launch an attack or beat a retreat.

That's how I feel.

In any case, that avalanche of strange and uniform uniformed dead. Those thousands of subjects kneeling before their Unmaker, before Death whom I've named The King of Terrors, but who no longer frightens me and who, sometimes, feels more like The Queen of Love, because, if you've got to believe, why not think of this life as the infancy of immortality. A multitude that helps me distract myself a little as I struggle to identify all my dead relatives. But that consolation is short lived; because those ever-proximal dead (waiting or on the waiting list) are the ones who never return (who never return as living) but who never stop coming back (coming back as dead).

Yes: I've reached an age at which the cemetery becomes a second home. A place you keep visiting so you'll be visited. Warning: if you don't go there, it's even worse, and you start to feel as if gravestones were popping up and spreading in the garden or basement of your home.

All of those loved-ones living there, underground, emitting bright and telegraphic dots and beams from their decomposing bodies (like the ones that gleamed atop masts during storms, *corposanto* and *capra saltante*, in the name of Saint Elmo) like words in a new yet ancient and universal language: The Frozen International Language of the Dead. All together and rambling and boasting in that home, bitter home. All of them as if piling up on the shelves of a place that's something like a beloved library (arranged by name and dates of arrival and departure) where you once knew how to swim and that now you stare out at from back on the beach. And you do so carefully, barely getting your feet wet, for fear that a treacherous current will electrocute you and drag you out to sea.

All those dead people like dead letters with no clear sender or recipient, piling up and waiting to be reclaimed and read. And no: my few experiments with those intermediaries who call themselves *spiritualists* (so sought after and in vogue these days, their thing like a parlor trick for bored widows) never bore fruit. Nobody knocked three times or spoke to me through someone else's mouth. The only trance I ever fell into was one of annoyance. Why did people go looking for something that was or should already be in their memory? I wondered. Didn't they remember the advice those same loved ones had given them when they were alive and now that they were dead needed to be remembered? What interest could the Beyond (if you believed in it) hold, when (if it existed) sooner or later you would end up going there? On the other hand, didn't they find it a little odd (and in clear conflict with the dictates of their faith) that God or the Devil would allow guests to send and receive calls and messages as if they were at the reception desk of a grand hotel?

Thus, it didn't take me long to realize something that, actually, turned out to be quite obvious: it should be the dead who contact the living; because only the dead have the knowledge about where they come from and where they've arrived to and about how to cross back over that seminal and ectoplasmic membrane that they've already crossed. That *nekyia* like a Rubicon.

I always ventured (and now I am beyond certain of it) that we've been living in grievous error when it comes to the matter of life and death.

It strikes me that what many of my relatives and critics understand as my shadow, here on Earth, is actually my true substance. And that (as I already said) the shadow that animates our bodies is nothing but the soul. And that the soul is the shadow that is projected into the body, that travels with us, that takes and carries us from one place to another and from this age to that age, understood as successive and increasingly distant ports that we never return to and never repeat throughout our voyage. That icy shadow that is the soul dissolved in all that water that constitutes most of what we are: that miniscule yet vast ocean that we don't sail but that sails us and uses us and contains us like a container, like a vessel not on but around the waters, to move from here to there, to there and back again. Thus, we're our own ship that, every so often, more often all the time, as we traverse the compass-less map of our lives, is plagued by mutinies and storms. Until, weary of traveling, we go under.

Understanding then and thenceforth that the true challenge doesn't pass through attaining a placid and fluffy cloud atop which to sit motionless and vegetate in the Garden of Eden (and I always wondered why Paradise doesn't, like the Inferno, have classificatory circles; because benevolence, I think, also has its various gradations and intensities and is not uniform or compact, much less innocent or disinterested) but through setting sail aboard that ever restless and entangled and uprooted shadow.

Accepting that the greatest discovery will be that our soul survives us and our bodies by being incarnated in what we are able to create in our lives.

And that, in that way, our work outlives our lives.

Wilder and lusher; more earthly forest than celestial orchard. It strikes me that when looking at spiritual things we're like little fish looking up at the sun through the water and, confused because they know nothing else, think that the heavy water is the lightest air. I, on the other hand, think that my body is nothing but the remnants of my higher being. In fact, take my body, anyone who wants it, take it, I say and insist, use it to whatever ends seem most useful and necessary and beneficial—*that* is not me.

And, of course, as I already warned: the distraction (I shoot off these thoughts like fireworks) is brief; and my relief at not recognizing my dead in the crowd is short-lived, because (hearing here my not-entirely involuntary invocations) locating me is no trouble at all for them.

Thus, they don't delay in lining up before me, possibly drawn by the offer of my body, but more interested in the liquidation of my mind.

Then, the landscape (the *sensation*) is so similar to the one through which the ships of my youth drifted when they ran into a bank of windless fog and ended up spending days and weeks floating as if in a viscous liquor into which (like sacrifices to the unquenchable Poseidon) anything from horses to books might be thrown, lighten the vessel and aid in its resurrection.

The *dead calm* produced by reading too many *dead letters* that, yes, cannot be returned to sender, because the sender is the message.

The first to return and visit me is my poor mother, who suffered greatly and tolerated her state of "kept relative" for having "married badly" with integrity.

My mother, saddled with my father's name (corrected and appended, but never entirely cleansed or redeemed), like one of those ball-and-chains that restrict the free movement of prisoners.

My mother who always thought of me more as my father's son (and she feared that something of him *must* have infected me during his decidedly vital death throes) and who, even in my fleeting moment of sales' success, never approved of my adventures or of my books, which she always considered fantasies as improbable as the fantasies of the man she'd married and, along with that and with him, the contagion of all his grievous maladies and their even more acute side-effects.

And my mother doesn't come alone, she's accompanied by all her sons and daughters. My sisters and brothers (among them Gansevoort, my mother's favorite; but better not to think too much about them, because the truth is that, though I loved them, I never felt close to them) who died, if not young, then at least before I did, becoming names in stone to be uttered, every so often, in voice and in word, but not in my voice, not in my words.

And in her and their wake comes the still greater pain of my own dead children.

And I don't like people who talk about their children (living or dead, but especially when they're young), because they always strike me as somewhat perverse or, even worse, hypocritical: trying to coat in honey and sugar that indigestible and bitter terror that has entered their lives never to leave and that they dare not acknowledge every time they peer over the edge of the abyss of a cradle.

I no longer speak of them, but I do speak to them: in the present tense, as if they still had a future and weren't an increasingly intense and painful past.

And there's only one thing worse than the pain of a dead child: the pain of two dead children.

Something that razes everything to the ground and then, almost mysteriously, is followed by the relief of a great liberation. Could that be what those sailors from the East were talking about, the ones I once spoke to in the middle of a tsunami? That supposedly vivifying Nirvana or Bushidō of feeling already dead? The Manna of the Māori? Who knows . . .

But I don't really believe that, I can't believe that something like that is entirely possible and, as such, deserving of a name and being part of a religion. Because often something that might turn out to be a surprising and effective way to make events accelerate in a novel (and in itself any dogma will always be novelesque) ends up becoming (becoming bad, becoming something very bad) the most desperate and paralyzing of aberrations on this side of fiction.

Something that drags itself and drags us through the slowest of hells. Because (what name can you give that state in which the most terrible thing that could happen to you has already happened, so that now, at the same time, in a way, it never stops happening and happening to you?) you'll never feel anything worse than that. Because there can be no greater defeat in life than having your children set off ahead of you down the road that leads to death and to reach it before you do. Because there could be no greater failure than failing to keep your promise (the promise that nothing would ever happen to them) to those who had once been little babes whose small and fragile heads, fontanels open like dolphins' spiracles, you held in the palm of your hand, thinking (though only for a few minutes or every so often) that you would give your life for theirs, because, at the same time, you were then capable of ending their lives. (I don't want—nor can I, nor should I—to imagine what the experience would be like when the children die very young. Could it be something like—the complementary flipside—losing a parent as a young child? If that's the case, then I've embarked on both expeditions—I've gone and come back—and survived them only to be left shipwrecked and stranded without possibility of rescue or return; understanding that if the death of a parent is like the disappearance of a theretofore omnipresent planet, then the death of a child is like the dying of an entire universe that will never be there again, leaving you alone and flung out of orbit and with no sun to light your way or give you some refreshing warmth or pleasant shade.)

Whatever the case may be, the truth is that after such a catastrophe, you gain access to the inescapable flipside of that right: a peace that's alien to that alienated world. (A lawyer once confided in me that his favorite clients were murderers; because having removed from the world the people who upset it and upset them, they were the most docile and obedient and respectful. And maybe it's on the basis of that comment that I've erected the gallows of my own imagination, so that there, on the deck of the *Indomitable* or of the *HMS Bellipotent*—I'm still unsure of its name—hangs my immaculate and accidental and incomplete seafaring homicide. In its own way, the last of my children. In those loose pages that I'm not all that interested in stringing together because that would be like losing him too, like losing Billy Budd. And that's also why I can't help but wonder if—a different spectrum of the same color—the peace of victimizers might not be the same as that of victims.) Maybe that's where the shadowy light in the eyes of survivors comes from, like dusk wishing it were dawn. A harmony and a stillness that are not exactly configurations of pleasure, but not exactly of suffering either. And, yes, one of the most enduring forms of love is the perseverance of remorse. Nothing impassions and pacifies quite like shame. Now, in my case, the afflicted love is imposed over and above all taste or preference. Always there, everywhere. Because it doesn't take long to discover that the dead take up far more space than the living. Because their not-being-there is like being everywhere. Because almost right away you think you see and even hear someone who is no longer anywhere everywhere, not as if by the art of magic but by a trick-less illusionism, by the truest and most bewitching of illusions.

Presto! And soon but thenceforth forevermore, you experience the full view of an impossible-to-refill void; but, oh, lucky too are those who at some point have enjoyed the void that those absences leave: because what also dwells there is the uncommon privilege of a void overflowing with their presence. Thus, therefore, the surface of that deep void must be protected, as if it were the fullest of spaces wherein to float with the saddest kind of smile but a smile all the same (and I always remember that distant proverb that reveals that time spent smiling is time spent in the company of the gods; though the proverb neither clarifies nor adds, perhaps because there's no need to, that only the gods are allowed to really laugh and that, most of the time, what makes them laugh hardest are mortals' sad smiles, smiles like mine). A smile unforgettable in its sadness. That kind of sadness that, on more than one occasion, tends to travel, inseparable, in the company of a fury always on the brink of being unleashed, like one of those storms that seem to rise in a matter of seconds. The smile of someone granted the anguished honor and painful pleasure of having so much to remember and so much to never forget.

Thus, then, it is the survivor who truly rests in peace.

And once you reach that point (not of an ellipsis, not of a new paragraph, but the endpoint of a final period), you discover that nothing matters anymore and (joy, joy) literature doesn't matter either. Literature, which I said goodbye to perhaps because I was never able to say goodbye to my children.

First the eldest, the first to depart. Malcolm, who at eighteen enjoyed strolling around in his army uniform and for whom happiness was a warm gun, and whom I argued with the fatal night of September 10th, 1867, and who left the house shouting and got home late and drunk and never came down for breakfast. And when his mother went up to wake him, she found him in his bed with his head blown apart by a pistol shot. Was it suicide or was it (as we finally managed to get the medical examiner to state, in order to give Malcolm a dignified burial) a sad and stupid accident, the result of sleeping with a loaded revolver under his pillow? Does it matter given the fait accompli? Does it matter if one is only a suicide in the brief yet immense act of suiciding, just as one only dies, verb and not subject, in a matter of seconds? (A man dead by "natural causes," as you know, is for the use and misuse of those who survive him and, forthwith, resuscitate him, often with incorrect corrections. A man dead by suicide, on the other hand, will forevermore be, for them, the far more painful of open endings.) Or does it matter more that, from the day he was born, I'd loved him and wanted him to be a prodigy and even joked in all seriousness about naming him Barbarossa Adolphus Ferdinand Grandissimo Hercules Sanson? But Malcolm ended up known more and better by the far less epic nicknames Barny or Macky or Mackey. Now all that remains of all of that and all of him is his terrible smile from the Other Side.

A smile that's the same smile as the smile of my other dead son, Stanwix, Stannie (mea culpa: maybe it was I who condemned him to defeat by christening him with the name of an insuperable ancestral victory). His is a smile full of teeth that seem to glow in the dark, the smile that, I suppose, those who have inherited the vampiric and possessive familial gene of failure smile at their forebearers through the storm. They offer it up to the most immediately responsible party, who, in turn, inherited it too and, oh, failure like an infernal yet affectionate hound that never stops nipping at your heels and wrapping around your legs, rolling on the ground and rubbing against you until it reaches an ecstasy of howls so like the moans of men in similar circumstances.

Stannie, who was born weak and suffered a variety of maladies throughout his brief life, and who tried everything, even (perhaps hoping to win me over) traveling far away, all the way to China, passing through Cuba and Costa Rica and Nicaragua and the southern states only to, in 1886, already deaf and with nobody to treat his ailments, fall still more ill in the abyss of a Dakota coal mine and die with ruined lungs in San Francisco, breathing in ocean air redolent with the scent of lead and gun powder, its quaking and vertiginous streets overrun by pioneers competing to see who had the highest caliber.

And I can't keep thinking about all of this, because all of this is almost everything and, if I were to continue thinking about it, I would drown in nothing. A nothing that even includes the near impossibility (because of the fear it produces in us) of imagining our own children grown old, like wizened infants we can no longer console when they wake in the middle of the night, crying, calling out to us, having forgotten that we're no longer here. And so (and I remember how any death taking place aboard a ship, generally someone falling from high on a mast, forced the crew to pay it little mind or anguish beyond the farewell ceremony and surrendering the body to the maw of the open sea) I read and walk and eat and speak as if nothing had happened; as if I didn't know that death is The King of Terrors when he bursts in like that and breaks a father's heart. I convince myself that I'm at sea, that I'm far away; but I also know that it'll be hard, that it'll be impossible, for my heart to be cleansed of misfortune the way spilled blood is washed off the deck of a ship.

Mackie and Stannie.

One beside the other.

Underground and overhead the sky.

Stretched out and inert, like parentheses, with a vacancy between them and their tombs, waiting.

I don't visit often, but before long, when I die, I'll go there to live with them.

Without warning, a welcome interference: the dazzling shadow of a man not of my blood but of my ink. I like to think that he and I were brothers and sons of the same demanding mother called literature. Nat H. for me, the immortal Nathaniel Hawthorne for all other mortals. The greatest mind for once in perfect synchrony with the greatest heart. That heart that I felt beating beneath my own ribs, because I liked to think that mine beat under his. The only being who (with his idea of the past as something that doesn't pass, with his bewitched witches, with his mad and maddening communities, with his faults and sins, with his cursed lineages and his blessed myths, with his tales twice told) inspired me to reach for the highest heights. Nat H. who understood me like nobody else, and with whom I spoke at length about time and eternity, about the ways of this world and the next, about authors and editors, and about all matters possible and impossible.

Someone interpreted my ardor for him as a longing for that forbidden love between men and deemed it "more than obvious and unquestionable" in the "sexual exaltation" of some of my letters to Nat H. Letters where I wrote things like "You are the bearer of the divine magnet and my magnet answers it. Which is greater? A silly question: they are One"; letters in which I invited him to visit me on my farm and if he so wished he could "spend his whole stay in bed" receiving and enjoying my attentions.

To all of them I say here and now that, at least for me, what I felt and still feel for him was and is something far more profound and unfathomable than everything they accuse me of and condemn me for. It was something far more powerful and permanent than an always fleeting and amorous mood or than a seismic replica of the ruined Sodom and Gomorra or than a vulgar bodily hunger transferred or hallucinated by my father (insecurely and angrily I protest here, though I know that it is and will be in vain, against all vulgar and automatic and crude reflexes that seek to link the uncertain Nico C. to my true Nat H.).

I (who always loved without remorse or shame) am not like my father. My father might have opted to deny it all or hide behind the alibi of a spell he fell victim to in his youth and was never able to entirely break free from; thus, I think, his Puritan guilt and predisposition for the abyss. I can imagine it: my father dragging himself through the streets of Albany, stoned by the looks of his relatives and acquaintances, an invisible yet in-plain-sight scarlet letter embroidered on his jacket over his broken heart.

I didn't understand back then, with a big pencil in my little hand, at the foot of his bed, but I do now: the fluid and changeable meaning of the term *possessed* and, yes, I might be getting a little ahead of the ideas of my time, availing myself of the revision of old customs, like in my unfortunate *Pierre; or, The Ambiguities.*

Or, maybe, again, it (the thing about my father and his persecutory relationship with that strange and more or less mythical creature, his hallucinations, his senselessness) was all real. And it was from his "incident" that I inherited (a kind of profane transfusion of ice?) that strange ability to project myself into multiple times at the same time, influencing for the worse now but for the better later how I have written my books, advanced for me and behind for my readers. (If this is true, then maybe the world is a far more interesting place and, surprisingly, full of infinite possibilities.)

In any case, I was not and am not like him.

And, sure, once more: it's possible that I've gone overboard in my enthusiasm and that Nat H. (as I found out that he told someone else) had, in the end, experienced my, in his words, "maniacal intensity" as somewhat exhausting. And I wonder if, when Nat H. wrote that thing about "amid the fluctuating waves of our social lives, somebody is always at the drowning-point," he was thinking of me, as if, from the sharpened tip of his steady pen and from his well-built seawall, he were watching me being pulled out to sea by a whirlpool of salt and foam with no possibility of return.

So it was that I drifted away.

So it was that we grew apart.

Then Nat H. accepted that consulate position in Liverpool. And we didn't see each other again (I was surprised by the way the time had passed on his once-seraphic and now-ravaged face, like the face of one of those future saints, perched forevermore atop a column in the sun) until I visited him there, returning from my last great journey. When I gave him the manuscript of my latest novel, my only luggage apart from a toothbrush and a nightshirt. I travel light and fast. My novel is heavy and slow. I already mentioned it. *The Confidence-Man: His Masquerade* à la Chaucer in *The Canterbury Tales* with a conman hoodwinking all the passengers on a steamboat bound for New Orleans (taking place on the first of April of 1857 and soon to be published on that exact day, an idea that my somewhat naïve publisher thought to have some marketing or commercial appeal). I gave it to Nat H., warning him without any drama and almost as if referring to some banal atmospheric phenomenon, that it was my "farewell to prose" (warning him that, once again, it throbbed with my disheartening and dispiriting damnation of the temptation to try to conform to the demands of the "diabolical dollar"; knowing in advance that what I was most interested in writing was off limits because it wasn't considered commercially viable; being aware then that I couldn't write "the *other* way" either; and that for that reason, everything that bore my name and signature would always be doomed to end up like a confusing, failed specimen, impossible to domesticate and combining parts of different animals, like in those medieval bestiaries). And I added that it probably (and so it was) wouldn't take long for it to be deemed incomprehensible by practically all of the only followers I had at the time, the ones who were following me in the worst possible way: as critics who seemed to understand a condemnation of Melville as a kind of obligatory rung on the ladder and mandatory exercise in their professional trajectories. Critics of the kind who tend to be offended by anything that displays any talent, because that talent is something they'll never have and never be able to acquire, and that's why they end up scorning all talent in others: because *that* is their only talent.

Later, Nat H. and I go out on the balcony to smoke cigars and sip cognac, staring out at the River Mersey, and then we go walking through Southport, out in the dunes and wind. Me, the most depressing of Falstaffs and Nat H., the most sorrowfully uneasy of Henrys, with no desire or need to evoke our past. And, of course, to break the ice (breaking the ice!, a fixed expression for many but one that unfixes me), I couldn't help but return to my own obsessions and, oh, few things stimulate my loquacity more than great masses of moving water. Thus, I began to speak (with the circular phrasing and sentences characteristic of my youth and that, with a combination of wonder and horror, I already believed sunken and gone forever) about having lost the compass and the beat and the rhythm that aided me in identifying what people call happiness. That thing whose sign is a laugh, or a smile, or that silent serenity on the lips that precedes and survives a laugh or a smile. That thing that, on more than one occasion, might be the unhappiness of everyone else.

I told Nat H. that I could remember, with a bit of effort, times when (it seemed to me now) I *could* have been happy; but that those times were no longer in my conscious memory. Which was why, to access them, I had to do something very similar to imagining them first and writing them later and that, of course, *that* cost me more and more effort all the time and brought me less fulfillment and satisfaction; as if it were a kind of drug that, from having abused it too much, had almost no effect on me anymore, now more placebo than pleasure. Nor was it, I told him, that I *really* yearned for all of that; because at that point, my spirit was seeking a different kind of nourishment than what happiness offered. I told him that what I most longed for was peace; that I prayed for it and in its name; and that I understood it as a form of immobility, like the stillness of the trees: absorbing life without going out looking for it, and existing not in a single sensation but in a plurality of sensations. Wooded and wild, interweaving branches and roots, leaves (and pages) never blank and evergreen and with no doubt that they would always return after the autumn and winter had passed. In, I insisted, the most popular of sentiments, but born of the communion with what could only be a divine mechanics. That thing that I'd discerned as a characteristic feature of America, not reduced, but, yes, hubristically and modestly, granted to that one American that was me. And, once aware of it, I explained to my comrade, I could once again become part of something, the way I'd once felt I was part of the crew of a ship, a ship built with the wood of fir and chestnut and teak trees.

I told Nat H. that I'd become convinced that there could be no perfect peace in individuality and that, as such, I hoped one day to feel absorbed by the penetrating spirit that animates all things and to cease to be an exile in the drift of the world of men.

And, seeing that Nat H. didn't seem to react, I raised my voice even higher and redoubled my effort. And then I expressed my desire to be "annihilated." What he understood (because that's the way he wanted it, perhaps because it struck him as more comfortable and less unsettling, and that's how he described it in his notebooks and even in one letter not to me but to someone else) as my "morbid state of mind" caused by "too constant literary occupation, pursued without much success, latterly."

Ah, my beloved Nat H., who found me "a little paler, and perhaps a little sadder, in a rough outside coat" (again and while I'm at it, now with more vehemence and less piety, I'll say that he didn't look especially healthy *either*, and that he'd lost the aspect of romantic landowning gallant that he had when we first met) listening to me with one of his inimitable smiles.

And then, in Liverpool, I experienced again something that'd always intrigued me about him: a certain lack and a *roundness* to his persona and personality. A categorical and robust *sphericity* (all of him continuous and slippery curves, no protrusion to cling to) and, at the same time, an absolute absence of all the angles and angularities clearly discernible in his writings. In the immense power of darkness in his luminous stories that (he told me once) he composed out loud, strolling along the solitary beaches of Salem, to only thereafter return to his desk in the attic and transcribe them as if they were being dictated to him by a higher being that was none other than himself. Again: there was an unsolved mystery in him and an unrevealed secret that, probably, if it were known, would end up disappointing. Which is why I didn't try to solve it, to avoid that disappointment. If things go well, if the man and his body of work are truly great, the question always turns out to be more thrilling than the answer.

Likewise, Nat H. was never interested in the absolute and possibly annihilating illumination of any mystery but, rather, in its enticing and safer contemplation. And so (he told me this himself) he was never that drawn to attending mass; but he was always fascinated by spying (all together, amid whispers, communing in that almost miraculous moment of believing they believed) on all the praying faithful from outside and through the windows of the church.

That was, I think, with a combination of intrigue and pity but keeping my distance, how Nat H. always looked at and contemplated and spied on me.

So, was I bothered by his affected compassion?

Clearly I was.

Did I think that I deserved and was worthy of it?

Of course I did.

His sudden death was a harsh blow.

A blow that I felt with even greater harshness when I read his exceedingly vital obituaries (obituaries are public machines for making private memory and uttering personal prayers for the dead; obituaries make anyone feel that they could be a writer, because, after all, they will always be, even the most faithful, an ever-blossoming though sometimes—better not to cling to it too tightly—also very weak branch of the tree of fiction). I saw in those obituaries how they raised Nat H. up onto the altars of

"Great American Tradition" (along with James Fenimore Cooper and Washington Irving; the most audacious dared to add Edgar Allan Poe, whose visions and vices, it seemed, were considered more respectable than my own, and with him, I suppose, they deemed occupied the only available spot for family-lunatic and creator of a sailor alienated by symbolic whiteness in Antarctic expanses whose name I can't remember, though it was one that seemed somewhat absurd and more Dickensian than, forgive me the adjective, Melvillesque . . . Ah, yes: Gordon Pym). And how, also, in the ample space dedicated to his elegies in the pages of newspapers, I wasn't even mentioned among his grieving colleagues, except as an accessory and only as the writer of some laudatory critical piece on his *Mosses from an Old Manse* without, again, any reference to *my* body of work. And the truth is that I would've been pleased had one of his glossators at least rescued from drowning the detail that I dedicated—"in token of my admiration for his genius"—my *Moby-Dick* to him, and mentioned that, without his influence and example, I would've never written or dared write something *like that* and no no no: my leviathan to be pursued and never caught and vanquished is *not* a symbol of his figure, but, with that book, I *did* aspire to be at the level of his talent and friendship.

In any case (and saying what they say and not saying what they don't), his fugitive Wakefield and my prisoner Bartleby, I think, go and will always go hand-in-hand, inseparable. Wakefield & Bartleby: their names like a wind-rattled sign announcing the most spectral and anticipatory of partnerships, not necessarily commercial, not necessarily appreciated in their time, but definitively influential when it comes to future transactions, preferring not to do conservative business now but to wait for the most intrepid markets of the future: the two of them and the two of us, I believe, I'm completely certain of it, invented *something* there. There, in their names, the diffuse yet exceedingly novel figure of the non-hero, of the one who is not, of the one who does nothing and has nothing to do, of the one who prefers not to and not to be.

In the winter of 1865, I visited Nat H.'s tomb and there, I composed a poem, a funereal song, and I titled it "Monody," and its opening verses are "To have known him, to have loved him / After loneness long; / And then to be estranged in life, / And neither in the wrong; / And now for death to set his seal— / Ease me, a little ease, my song!"

And I remembered then that Nat H.'s father had been a ship captain who died of yellow fever in the Dutch colony of Surinam. And that I'd once thought that this was an unmistakable sign that I might well have been his (his father's) lost spiritual son; and I also thought about how my own father, bourgeois and sinful, was far closer to my friend's literary preoccupations. And in that way, standing before his tomb (fantasizing that, in error, we'd traded fathers in the same way that children are traded in melodramas), feeling even more bonded to Nat H. than I'd felt before: his heart stilled and distant and sealed away and underground, without that preventing me from hearing the benevolent song of its beating, everywhere and all the time, giving me some semblance of peace.

Now, Nat H., beyond all the things of this world, sends me signs and asks me to draw near, as if wanting to tell me something of great importance. But, when I take even a few steps in his direction, his figure trembles like an unreachable mirage and, again, slips away and leaves me so alone.

And, contrary to what so many illusionists sell to so many delusional audiences, there is no magnetism sufficiently powerful to reunite the living dead with the dead living.

And so Nat H. and I say hello and say goodbye, like two ships passing in the night, saluting each other with flags that (nothing could make me happier than to discover this) are and will ever be the same flag, though we're traveling in opposite directions.

Then, next, comes a tumult of old Melvills and Gansevoorts who seem, at the same time, to ignore me or demand my attention.

One of them (my grandmother?, my older brother?) shouts at me that they never understood me, that I never knew how to make myself understood. I shout at them to never forget that they were the ones who, at family gatherings—upon my return from my early voyages, perhaps tired of listening to me boast with a mouth full of salacious and spicy anecdotes at lunches and dinners—suggested, "why don't you put all of that in writing" to "see if you can get something out of it." (Even though I know that I don't have anyone to blame or take responsibility for everything I've written, not even myself. I know that the alacrity and impulse to tell and swap stories, as if they were the most valuable of properties to be shared so that others can improve upon them and make them their own, is something far more mysterious and probably comes from the deep past and walks and seeks alongside that other mystery that is the religious vocation and the alacrity of a Higher Power. I know it to be something carved into the mainmast of human nature, stuck there like an eight-escudo equatorial doubloon. And that is, no doubt, what distinguishes us from all other earthly organisms: that thing that causes a monster from the Old Testament that everyone believes in to be translated into a private monster that only I believe in. And, oh, the irrefutable proof of all the foregoing is that I haven't even finished thinking it before another possible new version of the already old story occurs to me. But this time told by the great white whale, from her own mouth, in a few limited pages, alone and without any documentary support, sung in her own voice, in a thick and liquid prose, telling the auditorium of the seas and balconies of the waves that she's so sick and tired of that madman with a pegleg and steel and wood harpoon pursuing her incessantly. And there, she, saying that she's very sorry but that, *yes yes yes: You can call me Moby-Dick*, the time has come to *prefer to* and to put an end to the whole thing. And to only pardon the life of one sailor and leaving him adrift but, at the same time, taking possession of him, elevating him to captain and decorating him with the honor and condemning him with the responsibility of telling the story and . . .)

And, again, a sudden and blindingly white glow from who knows where.

And when is it (in what epoch could it be) that now, alongside my dead relatives, I see colossal figures emerging from a beam of light and bursting into color across a white screen? And there I see a tale of righteous guardians, wearing colorful outfits that cling to their muscles like second skins (like the suit that, according to my father, his cosmic and magnificent Venetian host wore?). All of them leaping, without any explanation as to how, from nation to nation in a matter of seconds (making my greatest fantasies come true). And, in addition, appearing to enjoy the oddest of metabolisms: because, my curiosity gets the best of me, in the beginning we meet them as all-powerful children, but once they reach what appears to be more or less their third decade of life, they cease to grow and remain forever in the plenitude of those years. And with a combination of awe and terror I see that one of them (sporting a cape and clad in blue and red and yellow and with an irrepressible curl on his forehead that reminds me of my father's in that portrait, and could this be my way of sublimating him, granting him a future heroism that he never had?) battles a creature that's called "A Super Moby-Dick from Outer Space" and that he grabs it by the tail and hurls it beyond the stars, perhaps transforming it into a new constellation and . . .

And then, without warning, the beam of light blinks out and my dead all fall silent and part like the dead waves of the dead Red Sea to make way for the main attraction.

Here comes Allan Melvill, my father.

Enter Ghost.

Do the dead stop aging in the moment that they die, even though, as the story goes, their nails and hair keep growing?

Or is it possible that they're allowed to choose the age they'll remain for all eternity?

Might this be a gift given among the clouds or the flames, distinguishing those who are no longer here from those who remain and who, desperate, often, feel far younger than they really are?

Though now my face doesn't have the age of my thoughts; nothing in me, nothing in the features of this wrecked being, recalls the man I once was on the high seas. No trace remains on my skull of the skin once bronzed by the Pacific and now furrowed by warring lightning bolts. Thus (knowing the answer perfectly, because it's already there in the question) I wonder who that increasingly diffuse and now almost-invisible stranger who appears to recognize me from the other side of the mirror every morning is. Someone who mimics each and every one of my movements beneath a mask with a beard and wrinkles (in England, there's a popular superstition that holds that we won't know we've died until we no longer see ourselves reflected in the mirror: I barely see the mirror anymore) that's nothing but a mask of myself.

My father who will never have a face as old as mine.

My father, frozen in his death and forever young and younger than I in his immortality, like those antediluvian creatures preserved in the ice.

My father who could be my son.

My father (the rules that govern the spirit world being what they are) appears to have chosen the age and appearance that he had in the days when his first portrait was painted.

Nine years before my birth, but an eternity in relation to his ascent and fall.

Then, again, my father: the first of my dead, the first to die before my eyes. That dying (verb) that doesn't take more than a second and that death (noun) that, immortal, will be projected out across the years. Then and thenceforth, me, living his death and giving him, the man who gave me life, his death. The death of his life that was snuffed out right in front of me, like a lamp that runs out of oil and, suddenly, his bound body was free. His body not dark but yes extinguished, empty, silent; yet so eloquent, so *narratable* from that last damned second of his life and first second of his death.

Now, returned, my father appears splendid but remains bound hand-and-foot to his bed, asking me during a lull in his fever to, please, turn around those portraits of him that now are his only horizon. Especially the first one. So small and humble in its intentions, but my father can't stop staring at it with the same wide eyes and dilated and telescopic and microscopic pupils of people who lose themselves in the immensities of the Sistine Chapel's magnificent skies or in the overpopulated infernal miniatures of Hieronymus Bosch.

"I don't want to see it anymore . . . That one on the left . . . The oldest and truest one, the one that your mother likes least, because, she believes, she says, that it's the portrait of a man in love but not with her and . . . oh . . . in a way she's right, poor Maria, but at the same time so very wrong . . ." he says to me.

And I turn it around and almost expect to see, on the flipside, a painting of my father's back and the back of the chair he's sitting in. But no, there's nothing there; nothing but the inscription "Commissioned and paid for by . . ."; and then, illegible, a name crossed out with the same force with which one tries, in vain, to forget something.

Then my father calls me and asks me to untie him.

And, like a good son, I go to him and, again, I obey.

And, now, at long last, blessed be this moment when I finally, as I didn't do back then, carry out (in writing and so many year later) his last wish.

Thus (then but now, *see* him and *read* him) Allan Melvill fleeing for the last time from Manhattan, but this time he's not alone.

I accompany him.

I go looking for him and I find him, and I don't erase his flaws but do wash away some of his guilt and modify him according to his wishes, which, clearly considered, are not bad for anyone and are rather modest in what they request.

I am again who I once was.

I am again the disappointed boy (and there's no better or worse misanthrope in old age than a boy disappointed in childhood) who will do whatever he must to overcome his disappointment.

I am a boy again, but a boy who already knows what he will and won't be when he grows up, a boy who already knows how the story will end.

I am an aged boy who rereads so he can rewrite, so he can be rewritten. I am a new old man (one can only launch the reconquest of the past with weapons held aloft in the present) who, first, must retell and write down everything that led my father to this moment in which he asks me to recount everything that's already been discounted, like another version of the same legend.

I am the past witness and present rhapsodist that my father needs to document and sing what he deems his moment of glory, his triumphant farewell, his long-delayed bow and his *exit ghost*.

Does my father whisper then the idea that he's the little ghost crying out for revenge and that I am the great son who, with impassioned spirit, will go out to get it? Does he joke that he stages and performs a kind of leading-man Perceval (before Galahad would rob his starring role in subsequent versions of the myth) so that I will walk at his side as his devoted and valiant squire?

I think not.

That wasn't his style.

It wasn't his way to draw on the few things he'd read in order to read himself better.

And the truth is that our sad figures are closer to those of the exalted Quixote and his resigned Sancho.

Thus, again, but as if it were the first time, we arrive to the dock and the waiting ship, no longer the *Swiftsure* (though I'm relying on many details captured that night for this rewrite) but the *Constellation*: a name perhaps less swift and sure than the first but, also, more befitting; taking into account that my father and I now appear to be moving through spatial frontiers of an unexplored and dark territory, full of unforeseen possibilities whose points of light must converge so that the darkness can assume a more or less coherent shape and help divine the nature of the body that projects it.

And so it is and so it goes: the *Constellation* sails up the Hudson to Poughkeepsie and can go no farther: the river has frozen. Long before in any other year. Nobody understands why or what caused it, except for my father, who can't help but see it as another ominous sign, meant for him and him alone—even the forces of nature are arrayed against him.

"But not even this will be able to stop us, Herman," he says in a voice of exaggerated enthusiasm, like a traveling theater-actor on an unmoving stage, preoccupied with being heard and adored even in the most distant and cheapest seats.

And he says it almost hoping that I agree.

And I agree.

And, of course, there's nothing more dangerous and thrilling for a broken man than convincing himself he's a hero.

So we strike out on land, renting a horse-drawn sleigh and make it to Rhinebeck, where we spend the night. My father talks in his sleep and when awake, it's all the same. He recites numbers and erects tall columns of everything he *owes* and builds small tombs of everything he *owns*.

The next morning we procure another sleigh, uncovered (and snow and the cold cut like pages turned too quickly), and we make it to the streets of a town with the uninspired name of Hudson. And we spend another night there (more numbers in the dark in my father's voice, which, now, reminds me more and more of the frightened whispers of the sinners at mass enumerating verses) waiting for the storm to abate.

A day later, another sleigh (covered this time) and (according to my father's journal) "at 1/4 to 5" we cross the border of Greenbush, on the opposite bank from Albany.

From there, on the far shore of a river of ice, we look out at the lights of our city, which, suddenly, feels more ours than the Manhattan from which we'd been expelled. And among those lights (brighter than all the others, like one of the constant and essential stars by which even the most confused captains manage to orient themselves) we think we can see the one shining in our house. Then (night falls without warning, like one of those elliptical music-hall backdrops that, with a harsh and descending sound, suddenly, transport the actors from a forest to a temple collapsing into ruins atop its parishioners or to the most angelic of heavens) my father looks at me in silence and says nothing but communicates that nothing in the eloquent and mute language of desperation and euphoria. My father shrugs and arcs an eyebrow and, with something resembling the softest of slaps, tosses back that curl from his portrait (that portrait that, I realize, is not a portrait *of* him but a portrait *on* him; not *his* but *about him*) as if he'd painted himself so long ago and were now retouching a small yet decisive detail, fantasizing that it would change everything without altering his face. But, a second later, the curl is back where it always was.

And my father smiles.

And I smile.

And no words are needed to know that we've both made the decision; and that we've made it all the way, fully and completely.

Thus, we decide to walk across the frozen waters of the Hudson River, there, before us, motionless, as if time had stopped. It's not a great distance, nobody would consider it an epic odyssey to be sung over and over across millennia. Neither my father nor I are wandering men of great cunning or worthy of the singing of the muses.

It's no admirable adventure, though the distance is considerable in the cold and the dark and the wind (the wind, which has the shape of everything that it moves and through which it blows: pine boughs, owl feathers, and how many years has that hat been there, suspended in the air?). But it's clear that, for the purposes of the story of our story, that distance is equal to the one across which, almost infinite, the loving forces separating the sun from the other stars stretch out.

Before walking across the water, my father writes something down in his diary (on a page where his handwriting cuts off so that mine can begin) and, I can't let him write something as banal and material as the sums of money spent on our trip.

So I write that my father writes something else.

And I write that what he writes is "Find yourself wherever you find yourself, near or far, if you can read what I now write, please, remember, remember me, remember us like this."

And then my father squats down beside me and puts his hands on my shoulders and looks me in the eyes with his eyes full of tears (really it's his tears that are full of his eyes). And (again: it would seem the privilege and the punishment and, finally, the responsibility of children to put right the actions of their irresponsible parents) he tells me something he never told me before, something all parents should, always, tell their children. Magic words that break any evil spell and invite the most benevolent of fantasies to be cast in its place.

My father, just then and without warning, speaking like an ambassador of his past, awarding me the letter of safe-passage for my future. And I, upon hearing those words, transcribing them here and now in a voice (could the sound of that voice be another of those dispatches from the future?) like the voice of a writer who is not me. A writer who will come after me, a writer who is already coming, but not yet with these words, in one of his books that hasn't yet come into being. A writer with the word *Portrait* in the title of one of his books, a book I read and in which I admired (especially the almost-spectral-yet-living figure of the incurably ill man only concerned with alleviating the woes of the protagonist) the possibility that feelings could also be symbolic of extreme forces incomprehensible to ladies and gentlemen. A writer who might not yet have acknowledged me (he has acknowledged Nat H.), but whom

I already acknowledge as sailing alongside me: another writer who will risk everything to be more and better and who won't end up being understood by his soon-departed contemporaries but will be admired by yet-to-come strangers.

One of my kind, he and I all one, yes: two self-exiles.

But none of this matters anymore.

What matters, yes, are my father's words (in the darkness, standing on the bank, soon to cross that petrified river for the last time in that last fading twilight) falling on my ears like the snow that falls now, again, and keeps falling across the universe and the living and the dead and the survivors, who are far lonelier than the dead and the living.

He never spoke like this, but my father speaks like this now and forever, from so long ago, trapped among the twisted stars, the traced lines, the flawed map that, at last, brings him to this magic moment of loss to be regained. Thus my father continues along the path that brings him closer to my hope, without guile or deceptive devices, beyond my need to believe in him, to make him someone to believe in, to finally find a way to make him believe in himself again.

He speaks to me like this:

"Live all you can, Herman. It's a mistake to prefer not to. It doesn't matter so much what you do in particular as long as you live. Because, if you haven't done that, what have, or will you have, done? . . . I didn't live enough. I didn't live all I could. And now, I'm too old; or, nearly fifty, too elderly . . . This place and the impressions of these last days together, as demented as they might seem to you, have offered me the most convincing of messages and have ended up convincing this broken man that I am. A man you won't ever have to be like, because this is, probably, the greatest thing I have to teach you: to not be like me. I won't be a good example, but I will be exemplary when it comes to all the wrong you might do or all the wrong that might befall you. This is my use to you, the lesson to impart before my departure. Thus, in a way, I will always protect you from injustices and deceptions, rising above the oceanic gravitational currents . . . From familiarity with the illness, with patience and silence, will rise the knowledge of the cure and the ability to find the dawn in the dusk . . . Dear Herman: memorize and learn me by heart, but never put the theory of my nonexistent existence into practice. Listen, listen well: what's lost is lost. And you never get it back. Don't be like me . . . Never surrender or yield the dream of freedom to your enemy. Because then you'll be nothing but the sad master of a truce-less defeat, where you won't even have the memory of that dream to cling to, though you float at high sea like the lone survivor. Keep in mind, always, that the truest and best stories only happen to those who know how to tell them as they should be told . . . And, oh, I always thought mine was a good story, but the fact that it happened to me in the first place left me too frightened and ashamed to ever tell it . . . What was it that happened to me? Who knows . . . I suppose that, in the right moment, I was too stupidly wise or too wisely stupid to understand what that dream was. And I let it slip away. I freed it, yes, but in so doing I condemned myself. And, thus, all I am now is someone who reacts to my own successive mistakes. Herman, here's my message in a bottle: do whatever you want to do so long as you do not make the error I made of convincing myself that I wanted something I didn't really want and that I didn't want what I really wanted. Because it was an error, the most insurmountable error . . . Live! . . . And don't settle for being the mere ambassador of your story, a stranger in the borrowed land that will never recognize you as part of it. I invite you to travel to a land that, if all goes well and you're worthy, will closely resemble you. I hope that, without borders, the whole world ends and begins again for you, but that all of it is your homeland . . . I won't be able to find you there; but I hope that, in your memory of tonight, you find me as I find my roots in you. It waits for you there. I wait for you there. There you go. There you'll go . . . Be a captain. Even if you're a mad captain. Better that than remaining on land. Or at least be a sailor when you feel that irresistible impulse to see the liquid part of the world, to dissipate the melancholy of your ideas and regulate the circulation of your heartbeats. What's important is to be in command of your fantasies and to make them real. Enter and exit and go and see and come back home. And so I say it again and I pray for it: let your life be your world. And let that world have neither limits nor limitations. And, every so often, let yourself remember tonight and these words that I say to you now. And let them be words worthy of putting in writing and speaking aloud. Never fall silent. Speak with the best writing, Herman! And let them hear you reading you and reading you hear you! And, every so often, when the sun sets or the moon rises, on land or on water or on that combination of the two that is the ice, like this ice that we'll walk across together now, let my name be worthy of being one of the words that you live and write and speak."

Yes: now and then, my father said everything that a parent should say to a child, everything he'd never said to me.

My father embraces me (an embrace is a ghost because it only belongs to itself, someone will say and write) and doesn't kiss me (because if an embrace is a ghost that actually only embraces itself, then a kiss is a vampire, and a vampire is always searching for the other).

And am I weeping then, or do I weep now? Do I weep for him or weep for myself? Do I weep for the century that's ending where

I never found my place or for the century that will soon begin and where maybe, who knows . . . ?

One thing I do know for sure: very few are the stories (among them the many that you carry inside you like identifying documents to be shown to and required by customs authorities, like a clinical report that shapes or gives shape to a physiology and a personality) whose telling is so decisive that, in the end, they are precisely formulated and worthy of being written.

Maybe this is so because the heart rarely tells the brain what it needs or because the needs that arise in the brain lack the flames of a voice that can light a fire in our hearts.

I want (I need, I long) to think that this last story that I have told transcends those limits and limitations and finds a way, for once and at last, to make everything flow, as the water flows beneath this heavy sheet of ice that stretches out at our feet and, oh, then and now, the rare and eternally childish pride of feeling myself the owner of the first footprints pressed into new snow. Snow that was maybe invented just so that we would know that someone came and someone went.

Then (having said everything that he never said before but says now) my father rises and embraces me again and takes my hand and asks if I'm ready.

And I say yes.

My father removes his whale-tooth comb from his jacket pocket and tries again to discipline that mutinous curl on his forehead and, as with so many other things in his life, fails to do so: not even his own hair obeys his orders.

And he gives up and, nonetheless victorious (because, so near to death, it is I who prevents that last correction to the best errata; of that small whorl atop his forehead that, like a biblical mark, aside from punishing him, perhaps ennobles and explains and redeems and eternalizes him and makes him more powerful than any possible or impossible creature of legend), Allan Melvill smiles the saddest smile in the universe.

The smile of a father and not the smile of a child.

A smile that is the best shelter against the cold of my already ancient childhood that I'm now redacting and that directly borders the cold of this brand-new old age that doesn't allow for any change or correction: the regained cold that we felt when we were children, but with the difference that now it is a cold that doesn't anticipate any warmth to come and thus, for that reason, we attempt to distract ourselves and to distract it with the lukewarm lie of an "Oh, the truth is that it was so much colder when we were little than it is now."

A smile to be watched over by enduring pigments and prophetic verses in the refuge of art. Or at least that's how I want to see it and feel it and put it down in writing to be read aloud here and heard as I now hear it and I hear him, its cautious bearer and generous messenger.

And, smiling, my father says first one foot, and, seeing and making sure that the ice won't break, only then the other.

And then, already out on the ice, balancing and taking cautious steps; the way one enters an unknown house or leaves a known house to venture out into an unknown world. Because, of course, the feeling is at once very foreign and familiar: suddenly we're somewhere we've never been though we've been there so many times or somewhere we dreamed of going (and in that way went) so many times.

But never *like this*.

The feeling of writing or saying something that was never said or written, though you never stopped thinking about it in the same language and same words as always.

Walking is the known.

The ice is the unknown.

Walking across the ice then.

Thus, again, first one foot and then the other.

And (write it and celebrate it as if it were a historical event or one that, at least, will change my story) it's the night of December 10th of 1831 and Allan Melvill and his son Herman cross the frozen Hudson River on foot.

There we go, here we come.

Singing like sailors singing to the sacred and holy hour of weighing anchor.

What comes next is what remains.

The cold that won't relent.

The ice that will never melt.

The unforgettable memory.

What never came to pass but soon will come to pass.

What never happened but what from now on will always happen and, please, let it be so.

And it's no cathedral nor does it want to be.

Just a small altar in one of those side chapels.

Or not even that and better yet: a small confessional where someone speaks and someone listens.

That (my father and I crossing the frozen Hudson River) is the last thing I write, pages that will never be discovered by any academic.

And, for the first and last time throughout all of my work, it's the story of a victory and not of a defeat that I now burn in the fireplace of my study: because flames are the final destiny of the most authentic and ancient titans.

But, like all victories, the one I narrate there is brief: when we arrive home, my father and I are welcomed like heroes.

And, then, once again, it all becomes how it was.

I could, also, not stop there and keep going for a while, I think, I imagine, I venture.

And, perhaps, starting to invent and reinvent what could happen based on what could end up happening later, beyond the definitive fever and terminal delirium. What do I think that I thought then? I thought about doing what I think I'm doing now. I thought: "When I grow up, I'll save my father."

Describing then the way in which I untie my father (as if I *did* it, earthbound knots far simpler than the ones I would later learn at high sea; but it was already too late: I untied my father to free him from this life so that, just a few minutes later, he could die in bed but in freedom).

I untie him and imagine that I help him ("Boy now got a 'ittle Pa") get dressed in his best finery, and I lead him down the stairs, and I sneak him out of the house.

And we arrive to the bank of the Hudson.

And I build a raft and we break the ice by smashing it with an oar.

And (his fever and delirium are left behind, forever; and somehow I make it so that the Hudson flows into the Mississippi) we flee downriver and have a series of great and exciting adventures until we reach Samoa or Florence or, at least, New Wye.

Or maybe I propose a far less spectacular and more domestic possibility: I go door to door in Albany and spark the Christmas miracle of neighbors entering our ruined home en masse to save us from penury and jail. All of them contributing stacks of banknotes to a basket that appears bottomless (like in that "projection" that my father said he saw dancing like a watery reflection across the walls of a Venetian *palazzo*), because they always considered my father the best man in the city, the most marvelous of all for the simple fact of having lived and existed.

But soon, I find, I have nothing left to discover or to tell, I lack the strength.

Far away, long ago, what I felt in the rainy Novembers of my youthful soul, when I passed by funeral parlors and stopped to look at the coffins piled up like the random and disordered volumes of an encyclopedia awaiting new entries among those that come out. And then that bitter and wrathful taste flooding my mouth. And I had to stop myself from knocking the hats off the heads of strangers who told me that yes, that now it was time, that, once again, the time had come: that the best thing to do to keep from going mad was to make for the *mare firma* and cast off from the shifting earth. And that sailing first was what preceded writing later, that going out to sea was just the obvious metaphor for shutting myself in to create.

No: my powers are not as powerful as they once were.

And, even if they were, I've learned that they shouldn't be abused. It's not prudent or wise to contribute to confusing the navigation routes that people travel with the ones that characters frequent (though it's also true that no person attains the noblest and most invulnerable posterity until he's elevated by his peers to the seat of honor of a character).

The vast geographical distances I once sailed to arrive to the farthest reaches of the world (the same power that once transported me from the domestic transparency of the ice to the epic whiteness of a whale) now piss themselves and sink into the short mental distance that takes me, from one room to another, to confinement in my house after my strolls across this island that's not a desert island but one where I feel like an isolated and singular deserter.

Yes: the imagination (that supreme delight, as someone would one day say, of the immortal and the immature) should have limits.

I didn't know it at the time and hence my disgrace, my other form of ruin, for having squandered my gifts and my "dream of freedom" on beings incapable (but I don't blame them for it, I cannot demand that anybody sign up under my command to pursue the unattainable) of appreciating it fairly and even admiringly during its reading. Those who understood my early books, assumed to be autobiographical, as the hyperbole of a fabulist, and my subsequent ones as the true and irrefutable proof of my madness. But it wasn't that I lied to them: it was that they believed me.

It's funny: in books, people tend to praise the invented when it finds a way to resemble something real and the real when it finds a way to resemble something invented; and damn you, common readers of normal novels; and bon voyage to all.

Now I (having deciphered and celebrated my father and master and commander with the most hubristic of anguish and the humblest of solace) sail on alone.

Now, every night, I just venture out alone to cross my own frozen Hudson River.

I already gave this warning, already wrote it, already said that my ambiguous Pierre says and said it (and here comes one of my typical tirades; I'll excuse myself by promising that it may be the last—almost-last—one you have to hurl a harpoon at and pin firmly down so it doesn't end up sweeping away everyone and everything): if it's true that, when the mind wanders errant through the early, elastic regions of the most evanescent inventions, it ends up giving a concrete form or characteristic to the multiple masses it is molding out of the ceaseless dissolution of its previous creations submitted to the symmetry of the form; if, I repeat, that is our mind's process, it's also true that the symmetry of the form, attainable in pure fiction, is not easily attained in a narration that, in essence, has less to do with fable than with reality. Truth told in an inflexible way will always have its dark corners. Thus the conclusion of such a storyline is, in the end, far less complete than that of one of those architectural finials in the form of an artificial and artful and never-to-wither flower, crowning rooflines sustained by a masterful though never flawless girder.

Thus, I have chosen to truly end inventing.

I have preferred to fail with originality than to succeed as an imitator.

I've tried everything; I've done all I could.

But I'm not seeking forgiveness, not hoping to be forgiven.

I don't believe anybody can understand me just as nobody has understood my attempt to write a deliberately inexplicable text, a text that would be a comprehensive symbol of this also inexplicable world.

I don't seek pity or comfort; I just ask that everyone let me be, that they leave me alone, to keep myself company and be unkept by everyone else, in the most eloquent of silences.

That all of you hear in my silence the silence that, for me, is like a cataclysmic orchestral crescendo (a day in the life and having read the book and wanting to turn you on and excite you and roll all of you up like a painting leaving its frame), like the sound of the end of the world.

That white and empty silence (opposite but complementary to the overflowing and frozen and azure and transparent and snowy delirium of my father) that will end up filling all things the way I, years ago, filled that notebook with my childish handwriting and adult voice. With calligraphy more twisted than curving, loose and wild words, orthographical errors sometimes devolving into metaphorical truths. Half-thought ideas from which I now reconstruct my father's words; adding the rooms of my theories and practices to the mansion of his dying; giving life and opening the doors to a vocation that I lock now forever and hurl the key into the waters of my silence.

That silence that begins here and that won't leave anything standing but the path of the lotus-eater, so that all is forgotten and engulfed by the Lethe River or evoked and surfaced by the Mnemosyne River: both of them glacial in their coursing, so easy to confuse and so difficult to cross without them crossing through you, freezing the memory in your mind and in your heart.

That silence that once you hear it you have to keep it (and I wonder what that place is where only silence can be kept).

That silence that's fast approaching and that will be heard from here onward will be a bewildering silence that knows that everything left unsaid is said forever.

Yes: everything that I had to say has already been said.

This is my last dive into the depths where the monsters dwell. Never again will I submerge myself in the stagnant sea of literature. From here onward, I'll memorize verses that I'll never even put in writing and much less try to publish. And (again, I insist, my exact situation won't appear on any map, because real places never do and so I, in myself, will be a true location and with only room enough for one) I'll stay down there: holding my breath (holding my inspiration) until my last exhalation (my last expiration) and without any expectation of being saved by some benevolent vessel.

All I ask, as my last will, is one final letter.

To the man or the woman who, from the impossible reading of this account (which nothing and nobody stops me from dreaming of as a book, for me ungraspable yet grasped by your hands and eyes), invents a way to print that letter *e* (that letter *e*, that *e* between parentheses, that in a way is me, and that separates me from my father only to bring us back together, to reunite me with him) in an almost translucent way, as if it were the most alive of ghosts . . . And I make a last request, almost a plea of that *e* appended to my father's name that becomes my name: understand him and me as separate parts (invented and dreamed and remembered) of a whole. Both living forever, over and over, the paradox of feeling terrified by the possibility of being heroes, even if just for one night: possessing and having that fear that is only known and attained on that bank opposite of absolute valor. And know that, if you can do that (oh, thank you, thank you, thank you), you will help us find ourselves, at last, in the ocean of our consciousnesses.

Meanwhile and in the meantime (as if he were a parrot on my shoulder, speaking to me ceaselessly, throughout my wanderings along the banks and cliffs of the avenues of Manhattan, like a submerged animal, the harpoons of skyscrapers protruding from its back) I take the memory of my father on a walk.

The memory of me and my father sitting below deck on the *Swiftsure*; and me inventing now that he, to ease the fear and the shame, distracts me with the idea that the most valiant and proud Achaeans must have felt "exactly like this" waiting inside the belly of a wooden horse at the gates to a besieged Troy.

The memory of my father walking across a glacial river to meet me, wishing I were there with him, not thinking that it wasn't the right place or time for someone my age to be; but what does it matter, my father says, because over the years, all of this will be transformed into an unforgettable and great story, another memory to remember.

The memory of my tormented father bound hand and foot to his bed the way others are bound to the helm in a storm to keep them from being thrown overboard or willfully throwing themselves overboard, seduced by Aglaope (Of the Beautiful Face) or Thelxepeia (Of the Soothing Words) or Thelxinoë (Of the Heart's Delight) or Pisinoe (The Great Persuader) or Parthenope (Of the Scent of a Maiden) or Ligeia (Of the Stolen Name) or Afti (The Swimming Pool Swimmer) or Leucosia (The Pure) or Molpe (The Inspiring) or Raidne (The Improver) or Teles (The Always Perfect).

The memory of my father looking at those memories that were the portraits of my father.

And the memory of my father (which is now my memory and, yes, I miss him and feel him and touch him) wanting to remember crossing the ice of the Hudson River not alone but with me.

And me beside him, listening to him remember, always and forever, taking notes. Me being infected and intoxicated (from there, from him, the feverishly long and winding and submarine sentences of my style) by the voice of his drowning reason. His voice that'll be the irresistible voice of my vocation, my calling, first calling me to flee and *give myself* to the sea (and I love the idea that one, so young, can *give himself*, surrender and offer himself up, to such immensity) and only later the less authoritative voice of a longing to reach a safe harbor.

And to do it all in my own calm voice, but in his name, in the tempest of his name.

Rest in peace (the peace that should never be the peace of oblivion), unforgettable Allan Melvill. Goodnight sweet dethroned and exiled prince whom I bring back home: birds atwitter above your still yawning abyss to be covered by the great shroud that stretches out without limit; because how do you put limits on something that's no longer here but that I keep seeing and thinking in writing as if it were.

Me clinging to my desk like a sailor to a carved and tattooed and floating coffin.

Me clinging to the dead, who live on in the living, in the living who end up telling their tale.

Me being sucked in by the vortex, spinning like Ixion in Tartarus, only consoled by the song of Orpheus.

Me with pupils like black bubbles always about to burst but not yet, not yet . . .

I don't know what awaits me when I leave this limbo, like a sea without winds or tides encircling a Caribbean island where all the days are the same and love is eternal but never requited.

I don't know what will happen when I cross over to the Other Side.

But whatever it is and whatever comes, I'll go with a smile. One more smile. One last smile. That smile that, in life, is the ship on which all ambiguities sign up and sail and sink, but that (soon, I can almost feel it casting off from the corners of my mouth) ends up becoming something true and sincere.

After all but in the first place, I was always someone wrecked by a confessed and eternal longing for all the faraway things of the world that I left and will leave behind: I'm not convinced that there's a life after death, but I am convinced that there's a dead-life before death. I say it with the uncertain certainty of someone who has consciously studied and practiced his mortality and knows that soon he will melt into everything that will exist after his death but that doesn't yet contain him. Oh, a solitary death, after a solitary life! Now I feel my greatest glory is in my greatest suffering! Coming from the farthest reaches, audacious waves of my whole my past life! Let them now take the shape of the immense and singular wave of my death! Then my memory will disappear to remain (fragmented, imprecise, reduced) in the memories of those who knew and survive me. Then they will die, at which point the only trace of me, like the naked footprints in the sand of a beach thought deserted, will be the one left in my books and the one of my voyages (remembered or imagined) in those books. And, sooner or later, all of those pages will melt into oblivion too.

And everything once solid will be liquid again.

Which is why I loved sailing forbidden seas and proving over and over that it wasn't dust whence we came but water. I knew then that the human race is divided into three big groups: those who long to see it all and those who prefer to always stay at home. And, of course, between the ones and the others, an indecisive majority fantasizing in one direction or the other.

I barely hesitated.

It took me no time to understand which side I belonged to. And, once I knew, I docked on the most barbaric shores, convinced that I could even blot out the sun if I felt insulted by its light.

And, there and from there, I was able to learn everything, everything else. Without fear of what might happen to me or what I might happen to think, on the wood of the ship deck or the wood of the desk (and it is that fortitude and daring that I invoke now, before my final departure), because I always considered ignorance the mother of fear.

Another writer will come in my wake and say something in his writings (after adding a *u* to his surname and saying he envied and admired my writing) about how his mother is a fish.

My father is a whale.

And I am his Jonah.

If there were justice and if I had time (there isn't and I don't), I would congratulate myself for having exercised the ultimate power of rewriting what happened by chasing down and hunting the fiction of my father.

Declaring him innocent in his guilt.

Exculpating him of all debt to me so that, when all was said and done, he would bring me back and spit me out (already hopeless and nearly drowned) onto the disenchanted shores of my solace.

And once there, broken from the breakwater, harpoon him with a new and better version of what happened, what should have happened; because contrary to what you think in the beginning, in the end it's not the parents who write their children but the children who rewrite their parents: there and then, he and I, together and whole, crossing the frozen Hudson River. The river that crosses through us and into which all things of this world end up melting. The river flowing beneath the frozen foundations of time and climate, where everything has already been and hopes to be again, for the chosen few, we travelers, for us then, at least for the few blessed minutes that it takes us to reach the far shore, understood as the next and closest and most-loving of lines, at the turn of a page, back home.

Feet firmly on the ground, arms aloft, thumbs down.

Such is life, such is happiness.

And (no, again, because 'twas never thus, because had it been, it would only be so now) both of us arriving home. And, as a reward, my future fortune and that of my family changing for the good, changing for the better, until it came to the happiest of endings.

If he died believing it, then I should well be able to live whatever life I have left believing him, believing in him.

But that's not possible and, better, with humility, to go no further than the crossing of a frozen river.

Like I said: I won't fall back into the excesses of imagination of the young man that I no longer am.

I prefer not to.

Reality (and that mysterious part of reality that is the irreal yet true faith in something, even if that something is not part of reality) doesn't work like that.

I aspired (and will continue doing so until I expire) only to a Supreme Reality, always sailing alongside an Absolute Fiction: two galleons assumed to be rivals but actually moved by the most complementary and piratical of ambitions.

A reality far better and realer than reality and a fiction breaking the confining fluvial ice beneath our feet, setting off aboard abstraction and change in the name of the pleasure and the genius of the limitless sea. That sea that isn't a mask but a mirror and, in it, a face: the shared face of all humankind. One and the other, Supreme Reality and Absolute Fiction, obeying orders just to experience the almost-immediate ecstasy of a mutiny in the middle of that ocean that is my father and the father of my father and the father of his father and that father that I am now. Once children all. Altogether, in alliance, aboard this Ark (the Ark of the mind that will sink and be extinguished or that will float and fuel the fire of books) still moored to the dock haunted by the bleeding chains of the at once generous and vengeful spirit of all those yet to come: because they will be the ones (the ones invoked in the name of love or the continuity of the species) who will recall them and cast light on their shadows.

Thus, on the far side of the Flood, dragged by the deluge of what was, all I have left is enough strength and space (like five thousand years ago; without overreaching and on the way out and without going into detail; *and I only am escaped alone to tell thee*) to reach my conclusion by concluding that, yes, everything begins with parents and children and that everything ends with children and parents.

And that (*Glaciology Melvillogy Gelum Mellvillum*) everything that opens and closes with the ice of the parents will melt into the water of the children, who, in turn, will be ice so that their children can be water; and on like that until the last freeze and the last thaw of that last season that is parenthood and to which you only descend by climbing aboard that ship crewed by immensely small and loving and despotic captains.

And that there's nothing but the ones as the story of the others and the others telling the story of the ones (one's own books and the books of others will *also* and *also not* and *never* and *forever* be children and parents). And all of them there, trying to mutually perpetuate and describe and, reading and writing each other, immortalize themselves, as if in so doing life was lost and death was won.

And that from there, from that dynamic friction, came the electric ghost of the ones howling in the bones of the others' faces.

And that it is good that it is so.

And that it came to an end.

Here comes to an end everything this shipless sailor—orphan in reverse and in advance—had to find and to tell. Cut off and deficient, interrupted and deprived and never justified or justifying himself through the ways of this world that we believe ours and forsaken by its True Creator, who (another father-son story, never forget it, how could it be forgotten) also knew to abandon the Messiah to his fate so that His Will could be done and everything could come to fruition.

He whose cruelty or disinterest are difficult to explain. Though, perhaps, the reasons for His often-irrational behavior are far simpler and more comprehensible: maybe it's all due, simply, to the fact that God is really old, His behavior already somewhat erratic, His concentration on this or that no longer what it once was. And thus, His incomprehensible pronouncements and rants that were translated into catastrophes public and private, collective and individual, end up somewhat difficult to justify and, very often, to forgive.

He in whom I never entirely believed (I have nothing left to lose; it's far easier to believe in God, in that forever external and absent *Our Father*, when you no longer believe in anything; so it can be what He wants or doesn't want, knowing as I do that a faith that cannot tolerate the truth is not worthy of calling itself faith and that it cannot be denied that, over and over, I have been confronted with truths that only lead to the quicksands of uncertainty); but, also, believe in Him or not, you cannot help but believe you believe in Him when you pray to Him and grovel before Him with the most hopeful of hopelessness.

He in Whose Image and Semblance I don't wish to be made (resembling a god without being one might be the most simultaneously divine and profane of punishments); but unto whom, nevertheless, I now commend myself, asking Him to help me in the composition of these final sentences that I want to sound like a prayer.

He for whom so many wait so that it's He who, in the most Final of yet-to-come Judgments (but not for that reason sound or conclusive or unquestionable when it comes to the mercilessness of its verdict), reveals what the Last Word will be.

That Last Word spoken first as a test to hear how it sounds (the Bible doesn't specify which of them, but you intuit or, at least, I intuit which one it is; because my craft was always that of intuiting things relative to the digression as dramatic gesture) on the supposedly restful and dull seventh day of Genesis. Though there and then, when all the Creator's creations think He's resting, really, like the maddest of mad captains, He's already planning how it'll all be when all of it ceases to be, and what course to set upon ordering the anchor drawn up and the windy sails of his Discreation unfurled.

That Last Word that, during the debut of that singular and long and revelating day and the Great Tribulation of the Apocalypse (not to be marked with a small white or black stone but with a giant and frozen and transparent rock) will be uttered one final time.

And that Last Word will be His Name.

And in His Name (*Call Him* . . .) will be enunciated and announced that Last Word.

With each and every one of its letters but without a final period.

And upon hearing it (in the nebulous astral ocean where the constellations sail with fixed direction but uncertain fate) the crews of stars, dressed in striped sailor cloth and all blending together, will be extinguished as if they were drowning. One by one, in alphabetical order, from lowest to highest rank and myth, from the surface of space to the bottom of the sky.

Thus, until there's nothing left to read there above; because, lost children and missing parents, no light will shine in the firmament (His Name) nor lighthouse on this earth, just one page among millions (His Work) to be torn out to illuminate and guide and rescue and free us to tell the tale right here.

Here, out on the unbounded oceans, where there's no one left to help us live to tell it and, when there's nothing left to hear, to write and read it or to read and write it.

And then, at last and in the end and in His Name, we'll hear His Voice, and we'll see His Last Word.

And that Last Word will be *Sea*

YOUR NAMES;
OR,
THE ACKNOWLEDGEMENTS

Allan Melvill (1810), John Rubens Smith

Watercolor, gouache, and graphite on smooth off-white wove paper

8 ⅞ x 6 ¾ in. (22.5 x 17.1 cm)

The Metropolitan Museum of Art, New York

On pages 109-110 of the English version of my 2019 novel, *La parte recordada* (published in English as *The Remembered Part, 2022*) (and in a context where the narrator is criticizing the proliferation of fictions about the lives and work of real writers), it says the following:

> And, yes, he'd once fantasized about writing a novella about Herman Melville's father: a beautiful loser, walking across the frozen Hudson River to return to his family and die among them amid deliriums and with his young son seeing it all and taking notes and thinking of the whiteness of the snow and the ice that'd struck down the author of his days and who'd once described him as "very backward in speech and somewhat slow in comprehension" and yet with a gift for understanding "men and things both solid and profound."

This—with all the salvos and excuses in this case—is neither more nor less this book,* which, I hope, distinguishes and distances itself at least a little from the generalities of the (out) law of a trend that hasn't passed but strikes me as increasingly superficial† and is so criticized by the "hero" of my previous novel in rants intended to be both fierce and solemn, taking on not only the "owners" of the business but also their "clients," who . . .

. . . wanted to be told little stories so they could retell them later. They weren't interested in literature but in being able to say they were interested in literature and—like proof, like someone repeating an alibi—having a couple anecdotes to regale people with at parties. Better than reading James Joyce was to know the story of James Joyce's crazy daughter. Or the tale of the one exceedingly-interesting-for-how-uninteresting-it-was *en sociéte* encounters between James Joyce and Marcel Proust, which was better than reading Proust.

And so everything, for them, had to have a reason to be real. A reason that was figurative and never abstract or open to multiple interpretations. They needed the

---

* The casting off of this idea in the shipyards of my memory struck out upriver long before I started writing my triptych, when in 2005, I read Andrew Delbanco's *Melville: His World and Work*. Since then (as several of my closest friends could attest), I couldn't stop thinking about a couple of lines in that book that give the clearest account of the story of Allen Melvill crossing the frozen Hudson River. And I told myself over and over—like the re-writer that every writer really is—that it'd been a shame that he didn't make that crossing with his young son Herman (and future Melville). And that from that episode arose then his so profound and leviathanic obsession/fascination with the whiteness of all white.

† For the moment, *Melvill* alters and inverts the typical device of this species: it's not interested in inserting the figure of someone more or less irreal (or about whom little is known) into a landscape frequented by an illustrious person or character, rather, to the contrary, in having a very celebrated individual strive to *realize* someone about whom little or nothing is known.

official and verified version of all things and even better if it was about or bound up in a story "of overcoming." And so too they convinced themselves that the bastard nonfiction was working for them while, reading pure fiction, they felt that, in a way, they were doing the work for the writer. That it condemned them to doing forced labor for others. For beings they could never fully trust who, sometimes, gave them the feeling that they were lying to them or trying to confuse them with flourishes of style that they perceived as expressions of mockery. Nonfiction, on the other hand, *normalized* the figure of the writer. And made it more exact and more honest. Nonfiction turned the writer into a kind of didactic informer/summarizer, into someone *real* but, at the same time, someone with a certain air of shamanic guide. And the symptom became, for him, even more toxic when a writer started writing about other writers and what those writers had written. Because, of course, it was far more useful and convenient to write about what you hadn't written and about what others had written. It was something *true* and you could present it as your own just by virtue of repeating it and elevating yourself as a kind of manager/master of ceremonies of somebody else's work: literature of the unrealizable I-want-to-be-like-that succumbing—almost right away and desperately and pathologically—to the irreality of the I-think-I-am-like-that.*

---

* In one of the inserts in future editions/translations of *The Remembered Part*, the protagonist goes even further: "He begged them, though he wasn't without guilt here, to not give birth to novels narrated by historical characters and no no no: there was nobody out there waiting for the interior monologue of the unborn and knifed baby of Sharon Tate or the rant of the ice axe buried in the skull of Leo Trotsky, right?"

A territory and aesthetic that—let's just say it and admit it— I'd already explored in another of my novels, *Kensington Gardens*,* as well as in numerous stories and fragments in other books of mine.

Which is why—again, it's never superfluous to insist on it, whatever everyone else says—I am NOT the distorted and distorting protagonist of my three *Parts*.

Likewise and in the same ways—in *Melvill*—a good number of the names and places and people and dates are real, but many of their actions and thoughts are NOT. YES it is rigorously true that Melvill did go on the then traditional Grand Tour in his youth (there is not, however, any evidence that he visited Venice); that, for some never entirely clarified reason (though perhaps it wasn't that uncommon at the time), he did cross the Pyrenees on horseback; that he was not, to put it kindly, well-suited to business dealings; that on the night of Saturday, December 10th of 1831, Allan Melvill did walk across the frozen Hudson River; and that within a matter of days, he died amid hallucinations after having been terminally diagnosed as "A Maniac!"

It's also assumed to be true (an assumption I didn't hesitate to legitimize) that the true reason why the widow added an *e* to her married name and that of her sons and daughters was the one mentioned here.†

Melvill is, moreover, the direct product of an, I hope, understandable need: after having spent ten years in the expansive and all-terrain writing of *The Invented Part*, *The Dreamed Part*, and *The*

---

* By the way: it's true and well-documented that Herman Melville's Ahab was the direct inspiration (to the point of borrowing and rewriting several of his speeches) for J. M. Barrie's Hook in *Peter Pan*.

† While I'm at it: the book highly regarded by Melville *The Whale and His Captors; or, The Whaleman's Adventures, and the Whale's Biography, As Gathered on the Homeward Cruise of the "Commodore Preble"* is real and was published in 1849 and its author, Reverend Henry Theodore Cheever, lived from 1814 to 1897.

Remembered Part, I needed to search for and find something more focused.* I needed the controlled explosion of a river crossing after the oceanic three-headed and centrifuged and accelerated Big Bang Bang Bang. Something that, as such, would arise from and be suggested by only a couple of moments:† the figure of that man, Allan Melvill, crossing a frozen river to return to the diminishing warmth of a family in ruins and hemmed in by misfortune; and the hallucinated delirium of Allan Melvill and its possible infecting effect on the mind of a boy as innocent as only a blank page can be and what he went on to *write* in it through the years of a life and a body of work.‡

"Since the twelve-year-old Herman had been withdrawn from school the previous October, he was in the house all during the last weeks of his father's life. Whatever horror he and the other children saw and heard during the days before and after Allan Melvill's death was not recorded," Hershel Parker writes in his leviathanic

---

* The idea was that the manuscript wouldn't surpass two hundred pages. And in its first version it was. But the truth is I've never finished a book so far ahead of its publication date, which is why I'm here, now, making excuses for its expansion by saying that Melvill, for once and at the outset, already includes my typical inserts for the bolsillo and translated editions, I believe, I think, who knows.

† I had self-imposed, also, the obligation that the book that came after *The Remembered Part* would not include any writers, but, well, hmmm, you know . . . (Im)pertinent excuse: I would like to think—I want to convince you and convince myself—that here the figure of Herman Melville (a writer who, just to say it, *also* initiated me in the pleasure of and addiction to epigraphs) is kind of the Trojan Horse or, better, the Trojan Whale, inside of which are barely hidden themes transcending the strictly literary.

‡ And while I'm at it, also, finally turning in a delayed and ambiguous vampiric assignment that I've spent decades *studying* for. And a curious/unsettling detail: for my *fanpiro* I first tried to find a name that would sound really Argentinean; and only later did I realize that Nicolás Cueva, translated into English, would be Nick Cave. Right away I thought I should come up with something else (there was no way to *argentinianize* Bob Dylan—Dylan, union of the Welsh *dy* and *lawn*, means Great Tide or Son of the Sea—and the option that occurred to me was Nicolás Limbo; which won't stop all of you, if you prefer it, from being welcome to cross it out and correct it). But in the end (and, I hope, with the consent or at least absolution of Mariana Enriquez) I left it as Nico C. just as it had first occurred and occurred to me. Respect for this kind of coincidence is the closest thing that I have managed to develop in my life to a religious/superstitious thought, for the decades and decades, amen.

and definitive biography of Melville (and the one that offers the most information about Allan Melvill).

And so, for good or ill, *Melvill* aims to be the imagined record of all of that (it's obvious that both Nico C. and everything about the very particular relationship and adventures that Allan Melvill had with him are purely and totally my invention), and I hope that, for the sake of his peaceful rest, it is so.

In any case, *Melvill* was written quickly, interrupting and delaying the progress of four other books that I started around the same time: a kind of Siamese twin to *The Bottom of the Sky* titled *El espacio del mundo* [*The Space of the World*]; *LoveHappyBestSorryEtc.* (which I describe as "My Hugh Grant Novel," given that my novels tend to be rather more Bill Murray); and a diptych about which I prefer not to preview anything.

The whereabouts or fate of this quartet and its order of appearance is now, I fear, somewhat uncertain, but who knows . . .

What I do know is that *Melvill* set sail and went on ahead of all of them and here it is.*

And it's clear that—for obvious and mortal reasons—Allan Melvill was just a fleeting shadow in the life of Herman Melville. And yet, for me, his passage through the opening pages of the following books was as unforgettable as it was inspiring: the one that initiated me in his crossing of the frozen Hudson River *Melville: His World & Work* by Andrew Delbanco; "Bartleby in Manhattan" and *Herman Melville* by Elizabeth Hardwick; the aforementioned *Herman Melville: A Biography, Volume 1 & 2* and *Melville Biography: An Inside Narrative* be Hershel Parker; *Why Read "Moby-Dick"?* by Nathaniel Philbrick; *Melville A to Z* by Carl Rollyson and Lisa

---

* And, above and beyond all the *Melvilleana*, its theme is the same as all my recent books: reading and writing, the mysteries of the literary vocation and the way in which it irradiates the still more mysterious mysteries of parenthood.

Paddock; the essay "Herman Melville's Soft Withdrawal," published in the *New Yorker*, as well as the introduction to the *Complete Shorter Fiction of Herman Melville* by John Updike; and "The All of the If: On the Life of Herman Melville," by James Wood, in the *New Republic*.

A more than pertinent warning: *Melvill* takes advantage and avails itself of much of the information contained in these books and articles, yes; but it does not hesitate to deform it and add to it and resituate it in time and space as best suits it* to recount the past of a man, Allan Melvill, whose life doesn't extend beyond a couple paragraphs or, at most, a handful of opening pages in the lushest biography of Herman Melville,† author from whose books *Melvill* also extracts fragments‡ to rewrite them at will and convenience and, *recomposing them*, even having them uttered in the voices of other people and characters.

And again, just in case, it's never superfluous to keep in mind the infectious ravages of the auto-fictional epidemic: much of what Allan Melvill and Herman Melville§ think and say in *Melvill* is what I want Melvill and Melville to say and think.** The same is

---

* Example: in *Melvill* two European tours are melted into one.

† Again: the one by Hershel Parker, more than two thousand pages long, and hallucinated/anticipated by Melville himself in *Melvill*.

‡ Primarily—more Melvilleanilly *extracts* than quotations—a handful of arborescent paragraphs pulled from the rightly famous chapters devoted to the color white and to cetology in *Moby-Dick*, as well some extravagant reflections characteristic of the always aflame yet somber adolescent Pierre Glendinning Jr.

§ But, just in case, the comparison of buildings with "erections" (as well as multiple other expressions or words that might sound strange or out of place) is rigorously made in Melvilleland. I merely took a stroll through it and heard them on one of its streets from the mouth of the most illustrious writer in that place. And, then, I tried to distill a voice (a *language* for this book, something that always preoccupies me, that each one of my books *speak* in accordance with its needs and plotlines) based on his time and his style (there are winks in *Melvill* to his abundant use of *then* and *thence* and *thenceforth* in my prolific use of *entonces*) that wouldn't be at odds with my style and my time.

** Another example: it was me as a child—not Herman Melville as an adult—who stood in front of a library to try to compose stories from the thread of titles on the spines of the books.

applicable, in some cases, not all (the observations of the critics as well as those of Nathanial Hawthorne are well documented), to what everyone else thought both about the writer and his father.

And beyond all the foregoing (but very close to me, some in a clear and explicit way and others in an allusive and coded way), I cast off here my indebted gratitude to Darío Adanti (and his *Tattooed Whale*), César Aira (for his for me well-founded *Theory of Call Me Ishmael*), Dante Alighieri, Paul Thomas Anderson, Wes Anderson, Blake Bailey (Roth), Francis Ford Coppola's *Apocalypse Now*, James Baldwin's *Giovanni's Room*, Donald Barthelme, Batman, Franco Battiato ("E Ti Vengo a Cercare," "Invito al Viaggio," "La Cura," "Prospettiva Nevski," and "Via Lattea"), The Beatles (and the whiteness of that sonic and retro-anticipatory Moby-Dick that is The Beatles), Peter Benchley, Adolfo Bioy Casares (the ending of *The Invention of Morel*), Ridley Scott's *Blade Runner* and Denis Villeneuve's *Blade Runner 2049*, Harold Bloom, Roberto Bolaño (that for me and in my work recurrent last transmission of his from the planet of the monsters in *Distant Star* here disguised in the sailor garb), Bon Iver ("00000 Million"), Owen Booth, Jorge Luis Borges, David Bowie ("Sordid details following . . ."), Brian Boyd (*On the Origin of Stories: Evolution, Cognition, and Fiction*), Richard Brautigan, Emily Brontë, *The Penguin Book of the Undead* by Scott G. Bruce (ed.), William S. Burroughs, Italo Calvino, Nick Cave (*And No More Shall We Part*), John Cheever, Arthur C. Clarke, *A Natural History of Ghosts* by Roger Clarke, Coen Bros., Leonard Cohen, Lloyd Cole, Joseph Conrad (even though his scornful critique ridiculing *Moby-Dick* and accusing it of not having "one sincere line" in all its pages is one of the stupidest things ever put into writing by a writer of renown), Julio Cortázar (and Paco Porrúa), Elvis Costello, Carlo Collodi (*Le avventure di*

Pinocchio, storia de un burattino), Michael Cunningham, Ray "Big Sky" Davies & The Kinks ("Strangers"), Samuel R. Delany, Philip K. Dick, Bob Dylan (all of his work always, but, here, especially, his voice and phrasing and roaming in "Key West (Philosopher Pirate)",* Geoff Emerick, Roky Erickson ("If you have ghosts . . ."), Camila Fabbri (for "an embrace is a ghost"), Hampton Fancher, William Faulkner (who added a *u* to his surname), Francis Scott Fitzgerald, Penelope Fitzgerald, Gustave Flaubert, Robert Forster, William Gaddis, William H. Gass, William Gibson, Allen Ginsberg, Isaac Goldman, Glenn Gould, *Le voyageur sur la terre* by Julien Green, Garth Greenwell, *The Vampire: A New History* by Nick Groom, Barry Hannah (*Ray*), L. P. Hartley (*The Go-Between*), Nathaniel Hawthorne (*American Notebooks*), Ernest Hemingway, Philip Hoare (*Leviathan, Or The Whale*), Allan Hollinghurst, E. T. A. Hoffmann, Peter Hook(ed), Homer, *Rooms by the Sea* by Edward Hopper, Joris-Karl Huysmans, John Irving, Frank Capra's *It's a Wonderful Life*, Henry James, (who devoted many pages to Hawthorne but next to none to Melville, of all that he devoted to all of us; but here, especially, for that really moving moment with that "Live!" in *The Ambassadors*), Denis Johnson, James Joyce, Franz Kafka, Jack Kerouac, Stephen King (that window of that insomniac childhood bedroom in that house in Salem's Lot), Stanley Kubrick, Jack London (*The Sea-Wolf*), H. P. Lovecraft, Malcolm Lowry, David Lynch, "Long Tailed Bird" and "Women and Wives" by Paul McCartney, Suzy Mckee Charnas (*The Vampire Tapestry*),

---

* And don't forget that a rewrite of Ahab appears in his "Bob Dylan's 115th Dream"; and that he also had the first great renowned pirate-bootleg album titled *Great White Wonder*, and that he referred extensively and gratefully to Melville and *Moby-Dick* in his Nobel Prize acceptance speech, understanding it as that place where "Everything is mixed in. All the myths: the Judeo-Christian bible, Hindu myths, British legends, Saint George, Perseus, Hercules—they're all whalers . . . Ishmael survives. He's in the sea floating on a coffin. And that's about it. That's the whole story. That theme and all that it implies would work its way into more than a few of my songs."

Norman Maclean, Terrence Malick, Richard "Moby" Melville Hall ("Natural Blues"), The Metropolitan Museum of Mordern Art, Steven Millhauser, Haruki Murakami, Walter Murch, Vladimir Nabokov (that paternal/filial dream in *Pnin* that preannounces *Pale Fire*; who said of Melville: "adore him, though quite a strange fellow, would have loved to see him"; and whose *Lolita* can be understood as another obsessive monomaniacal hunt/persuit), Héctor G. Oesterheld, Michael Ondaatje (*The English Patient*, always; and rereading it now I see that it mentions *Pierre*; or, *The Ambiguities* in its pages), Jim Jarmusch's *Only Lovers Left Alive*, "The Little Jew Who Wrote the Bible," Marta Pérez and Enrique Pezzoni (for their translations of *Pierre*; *o, las ambigüedades*, and of *Moby-Dick; o, la ballena*), Tom Petter ("Wake Up Time"), Pink Floyd (*Wish You Were Here*), Edgar A. Poe, Tim Powers, Hugo Pratt, John "Lake Marie" Prine, Marcel Proust, Thomas Pynchon, Quintus Horatius Flaccus, Anne Rice, Lou Reed ("Romeo Had Juliette"), *Recomposed / Vivaldi—The Four Seasons and The Blue Notebooks* by Max Richter, Rainer Maria Rilke, Philip Roth (*The Ghost Writer*), James Malcolm Rymer & Thomas Peckett Prest, William Shakespeare, John Rubens Smith, *Star Trek*, Cat Stevens, Wallace Stevens, Bram Stoker (*Dracula*), *Superman*, "Heaven" and *Remain in Light* and "Dream Operator" by Talking Heads and their twister that never stops, Kurt Vonnegut (for teaching me what Tralfamadoran books are like and how mine should be or how I would like them to be), Edmund White, Jim White ("A Perfect Day to Chase Tornados"), Mary Wollstonecraft Shelley (*Frankenstein*), The Velvet Underground ("Heroin" and "Ocean") . . .

. . . and, last but not least, thanks to Herman Melville (and to his *Collected Works Vols. 1-4* in the Library of America) and my apologies for the extraction and transplanting and rewriting (somewhat playful but, I want/need to believe, always respectful and admiring) of multiple of his fragments . . .

. . . and to Miguel Aguilar (and everyone/so many at Random House Spain: Raquel Abad, Patxi Beascoa, Jaume Bonfill, Carmen Carrión, Silvia Coma, Núria Cabuti, Carlota del Amo, Eva Cuenca, Juan Díaz, Conxita Estuga, Carla Gómez, Lourdes González, Nora Grosse, Victoria Malet, Núria Manent, Carmen Ospina, Irene Pérez, Melca Pérez, Albert Puigdueta, Pilar Reyes, Carme Riera, Cecilia Sarthe, José Serra, Núria Tey, and to all the rest also in Argentina and in Mexico and beyond), Carlos Alberdi, John Banville, Eduardo Becerra, Álex Blanch, Juan Ignacio Boido, Edoardo Brugnatelli (and Mondadori Italy), Martín Caparrós, Mónica Carmona, Jorge Carrión, Rachel Cordasco, Laure De Vaugrigneuse (Seuil), Abel Díaz, Ignacio Echevarría, Gabriela Ellena, Mariana Enriquez, C. E. Feiling, Nelly Fresán, Laura Fernández, Marta Fernández, Silvina Friera, Jeremy Garber, Alfredo Garófano, Daniel Guebel, Leila Guerriero, Isabelle Gugnon, Andreu Juame, Mark Haber, Incoci di Civiltá (Università Ca' Foscari Venezia and Salone Internazionale del Libro di Torino), La Central (Antonio Ramírez, Marta Ramoneda, Neus Botellé, Alberto Martín & Co.), Lata Peinada, Walter Lezcano, Claudio López Lamadrid,* Enrique Lynch, María Lynch (and everyone at Casanovas & Lynch), MacServiceBen (Villarroel 68, 08011 Barcelona / 34-93-1147890 / info@macservicebenbcn.com), Luis Magrinyà, Aurelio Major, Juan Antonio Masoliver Ródenas, Norma Elizabeth Mastrorilli, Fran G. Matute, Valerie Miles, Annie Morvan, J. M. Nadal Suau, María José Navia, Pere Ortín, Alan Pauls, Juan Peregrina Martín, Andrés Perruca, Paula Pico Estrada, Flavia Pittela, Chad W. Post

---

* To whose unforgettable memory I still owe *that* other book.

(and Kaija Straumanis and Anthony Blake and everyone at Open Letter), Patricio Pron, Alessandro Raveggi, Guillermo Saccomanno, Florencia Scarpatti, Javier Serena (*Cuadernos Hispanoamericanos*), Pere Sureda, Florencia Ure, Will Vanderhyden, Glenda Vieites, Enrique Vila-Matas, Silvana Vogt, Villaseñor family, Brian Wood, Giulia Zavagna . . .

. . . and, on the bridge and sturdy at the helm of my days, as always, Daniel Fresán and Ana Isabel Villaseñor.

Greetings and good health, safe travels and safer harbors.

R. F.

Barcelona,
November 2020
February 2021

May 24*th*, *2021*
August 31*st*, *2021*
October 21*st*, *2021*

Venice,
November 4*th*–5*th*–6*th*, *2021*

Rodrigo Fresán is the author of ten works of fiction, including *Kensington Gardens*, *Mantra*, and *The Invented Part*, winner of the 2018 Best Translated Book Award. A self-professed "referential maniac," his works incorporate many elements from science fiction (Philip K. Dick in particular) alongside pop culture and literary references. According to Jonathan Lethem, "he's a kaleidoscopic, open-hearted, shamelessly polymathic storyteller, the kind who brings a blast of oxygen into the room." In 2017, he received the Prix Roger Caillois awarded by PEN Club France every year to both a French and a Latin American writer.

Will Vanderhyden has translated fiction by Carlos Labbé, Rodrigo Fresán, Fernanda García Lao, Andrés Felipe Solano, and Rodolfo Enrique Fogwill, among others. He has received two translation fellowships from the National Endowment for the Arts (2016 and 2023) and a residency fellowship from the Lannan Foundation (2015). His translation of *The Invented Part* by Rodrigo Fresán won the 2018 Best Translated Book Award.